CURIOSITY HOUSE
~THE~
FEARSOME FIREBIRD

Also by
LAUREN OLIVER

FOR YOUNGER READERS
Curiosity House: The Shrunken Head
Curiosity House: The Screaming Statue
Liesl & Po
The Spindlers

FOR OLDER READERS
Before I Fall
Panic
Replica
Vanishing Girls

The Delirium Trilogy
Delirium
Pandemonium
Requiem
Delirium Stories: Hana, Annabel, Raven, & Alex

FOR ADULTS
Rooms

CURIOSITY HOUSE

~THE~
FEARSOME FIREBIRD

LAUREN OLIVER
& H.C. CHESTER

HODDER &
STOUGHTON

First published in the United States in 2017 by HarperCollin's
children's Books, a division of HarperCollins Publishers
First published in Great Britain in 2017 by Hodder & Stoughton
An Hachette UK company

I

A CIP catalogue record for this title is available from the British Library

Hardback ISBN 978 1 444 77726 0
Trade Paperback ISBN 978 1 444 77727 7
eBook ISBN 978 1 444 77728 4

Printed and bound in Great Britain by Clays Ltd, St Ives plc

Hodder & Stoughton policy is to use papers that are natural, renew-
able and recyclable products and made from wood grown in sustain-
able forests. The logging and manufacturing processes are expected to
conform to the environmental regulations of the country of origin.

Hodder & Stoughton Ltd
Carmelite House
50 Victoria Embankment
London EC4Y 0DZ

www.hodder.co.uk

H. C. Chester dedicates this book to his best and most appreciative friend,
Trudy

Lauren Oliver dedicates this book to her father, for all his support,
inspiration, and creative encouragement

"**S**AM!"

Startled by the voice thundering through the narrow attic room, Sam accidentally tightened his grip on the small, scale-model Viking ship he'd been holding, crushing it to splinters.

"Great." Thomas frowned. "Now what are we supposed to use for a Reverser?"

Thomas and Sam were playing DeathTrap, a complex game of Thomas's own invention that used the swirling patterns of the attic rug as its board and various items pilfered from the museum as its pieces. The Viking ship was critically important: by spinning it and seeing which direction its dragon-headed prow was facing, the player might be forced to move back several spaces or even start over.

"Sorry." Sam carefully siphoned the wooden shards from his hands into a neat pile on the carpet. "I didn't mean to."

"SAM!" Goldini the magician popped up behind the series of interlocking bookshelves that dominated the central part of the attic, looking rather like a deranged jack-in-the-box. His cheeks were a vivid red, and the curled tips of his mustache quivered. "I believe this *monster* belongs to you?" As he held up Freckles, the fluffy white cat that had once belonged to the famous sculptor Siegfried Eckleberger, his face twisted in disgust, as though he were clutching an old, extremely smelly sock.

"Oh *no*." Sam scrambled to his feet. The floor briefly shuddered under his weight. Even though Sam was only recently thirteen and skinny as a beanpole, he had that effect: banisters were pulverized to dust in his hand, doors collapsed from their hinges when he pushed them. It was the decided downside of being the strongest boy in the world. "What'd he do this time?"

In the past two months, Freckles the cat—and, by extension, Sam—had at one time or another made an enemy of nearly all of the permanent residents of

Dumfrey's Dime Museum of Freaks, Oddities, and Wonders. He had chewed Betty the bearded lady's favorite brush to smithereens, had shed all over Smalls the giant's bed less than a day after Smalls had declared that he was hopelessly allergic to cat hair, and had clawed to shreds the shawl that the albino twins, Caroline and Quinn, wore slung over their shoulders during their act. He had terrorized Mr. Dumfrey's pet cockatoo, Cornelius. (Cornelius still shrieked "Murder, murder!" whenever Freckles so much as placed a paw in Mr. Dumfrey's office.) Freckles had even relieved himself into Danny's favorite slippers after the dwarf had been overheard loudly discussing the merits of dogs over cats.

"This time," Goldini said, drawing himself up to his full five foot seven, "that *beast* has been terrorizing my bird." He pointed a pale finger to the cage in which a dove was fluttering frantically, eyeing Freckles as though the cat might at any second claw his way out of Sam's arms and lunge. The bird was an important part of Goldini's newest trick, the Incrediballoon, in which Goldini popped a balloon with a long sewing needle, revealing to a delighted audience a live dove.

"I'm sorry, Goldini," Sam said sincerely. He'd never before heard Goldini raise his voice. Usually the magician spoke in a tone somewhere between a murmur and a bad case of laryngitis, even when he was onstage. "I'll make sure it doesn't happen again."

"It better not," Goldini said with an injured sniff. "How can I make a balloon turn into a bird if the *bird* is passing through the digestive system of your cat?"

Carefully, gently—remembering all too vividly the crack of the little wooden Viking ship in his fist—Sam carried Freckles to his usual spot on Sam's bed, navigating the clutter of objects that had, over time, found a permanent home in the attic: wardrobe racks and overturned chests of drawers, three-legged tables and broken armoires, even a darkened refrigerator.

It was a perfect Sunday afternoon in early September. All the windows were open, admitting a breeze that carried smells from nearby streets—hot dogs and roasted nuts, motor oil and exhaust fumes, florist-shop perfume and a whiff of uncollected garbage.

The museum was, for the first time in recent memory, actually prosperous. The matinee performance had been a resounding success. Nearly every patched felt chair in the first floor Odditorium had been full. Goldini had fumbled not a single one of his tricks. Max's knife-throwing act, which she now performed blindfolded, had earned a standing ovation. Philippa had successfully read all the contents of a spectator's

4 ☞

purse, down to the half-empty roll of peppermint Life Savers. After the show, she had been swarmed by a group of single women who pressed quarters in her palm and demanded to know when and where they would meet their future husbands, even after Pippa patiently explained that mind reading and fortune-telling were two distinct disciplines.

On a day like today, it was hard to believe that less than eight weeks earlier the museum had been on the verge of shutting its doors for good. And even harder to believe that Sam, Thomas, Max, and Pippa had nearly lost their lives to Nicholas Rattigan: scientist, fugitive, and monster, whose crimes included the murder of Sam's own parents. It was hard to believe in *anything* other than the beauty of the day and the cozy, shabby comfort of the museum, which was as familiar to all the performers as a pair of ancient slippers, battered over time into the exact shape of the wearer's foot. Even Caroline and Quinn, the albino twins, were in a rare state of harmony, and sat side by side, their foreheads touching, braiding each other's long white hair and humming alternating portions of "Happy Days Are Here Again."

For Sam, the pain of knowing he'd once had a mother and father who loved him was tempered by the relief of knowing for sure that he had not been to blame for their deaths, as he'd always secretly feared. Besides, now that they had names—Priscilla and Joe—he could actually grieve for them. And he had, until grief was nothing but a dull throb, as if his heart were a shoe and his parents' memory a pebble lodged deep inside of it.

In a weird way, it even felt good. Because losing someone meant you'd had someone to lose.

"Whose turn was it?" Sam said to Thomas, plopping down on the rug. Thomas was winning the latest round of DeathTrap. In a brilliant move, he had used the feathered quill pen (supposedly the same one Thomas Jefferson used to signed the Declaration of Independence) to temporarily rewrite the rules, allowing him to capture Sam's pirate hook with a much less powerful U.S. army pin.

But Thomas had apparently grown bored with the game. An enormous book was now open on his lap. Sam just caught a glimpse of the title: *Chemical Compositions and Their Practical Applications*. "Forget the game," Thomas said irritably. "We can't play without a Reverser. We'll have to call a draw."

"Finally." Max spoke up from the corner. She was sitting in her favorite armchair—large and exceptionally comfortable, except for a few protruding springs—and polishing her knives. "If I had to listen to you two squabble about the rules anymore, I might have lopped off my own ears."

Sam felt his face heating up, as it often did these days whenever Max spoke to him—even though she rarely had anything nice to say. Ever since Howie the Human Owl, who could rotate his irritatingly perfect head a stunning 180 degrees, had arrived and then promptly quit (or more accurately, been kicked out of) the museum, Max had been even more snappish than usual. Sam didn't know whether Max was embarrassed that she'd briefly had a crush on Howie, furious about Howie's betrayal of them, or still sad that he had left. He really, really hoped it wasn't the latter.

"Be quiet, all of you." Pippa was draped across a sofa, this one covered in a coarse woven blanket that had supposedly belonged to Geronimo. "I can't hear a thing." And she reached over to turn up the volume knob on the old radio.

". . . You've been listening to *Woodhull's Music Lover's Hour*," said a patchy voice from the speakers, "sponsored by Woodhull Enterprises. *When you need it done well, you need it done by Woodhull.*"

"Did you know," Thomas said, without looking up, "that the human body contains enough carbon to provide lead for nine thousand pencils?"

"Shhh," Pippa hushed him sharply. "I'm trying to listen."

". . . interrupt the program for a special announcement, coming to you straight from Edward T. Woodhull IV, president of Woodhull Enterprises. On September fifteenth, the company will launch the world's largest dirigible. The mammoth airship will fly from a factory on Staten Island to midtown Manhattan, where it will be moored on top of the Empire State Building for a full week . . ."

"Hey, Sam." Max's mouth was hooked into a smile. Sam ducked, trying to conceal a new, furious round of blushing. It felt as if someone had lit a fire underneath his skin. "What's wrong with Freckles? He's scratching like crazy."

She was right. Freckles was furiously scratching his left ear, meowing, whining, and craning his neck to nibble his fur.

"I'll tell you what's wrong with him." The door to the attic slammed, and Danny the dwarf came stomping in from the hall. The tall cowboy hat he had recently taken to wearing—a gift from William "Lash" Langtry, the museum's world-famous rodeo star—was just visible over the bookshelves. "It's those fleas!"

And he rounded the corner into the small common

area where the children were gathered.

Instantly, Pippa gasped. Thomas dropped his book. Even Max stopped polishing her knives and instead stared at him, gape-jawed.

"Wh—what happened to your beard?" Sam stammered.

"What happened to your *eyebrows*?" Thomas blurted out.

Danny, who for as many years as the children had known him had sported a long red beard, thick as copper wire, and a pair of bushy eyebrows so pronounced they looked like russet caterpillars tacked to his forehead, was completely and totally clean-shaven. He looked like an overgrown baby.

"Enough!" General Archibald Farnum stomped into the attic behind Danny, panting a little and leaning heavily on his cane. "I said enough, you hear me? I won't have you mouthing nonsense about my highly trained, highly intelligent—"

"Vermin!" roared Danny, spinning around to face General Farnum. "Awful, bloodsucking, itch-crazy vermin!"

"Vermin? *Vermin?*" Farnum's long white beard wiggled, as if it, too, were enraged. "You listen to me, you sprout. I should have you thrown into jail for slander.

I handpicked each one of those fleas myself, and every one has more intelligence in its speck of a brain than you have in your fat skull!"

"Say that again, you big windbag, and I'll bop you right in the nose," Danny cried, waving a fist—which, unfortunately, only came up to Farnum's kneecap.

"You," General Farnum said, his face by now so red he looked like an ancient, wizened tomato, "are not fit to be a flea on the back of one of my fleas! You are nothing but a—an ear mite! You are a vicious, lying dust mite!"

"Hey now, enough hooting!" Lash Langtry appeared and stepped between the two men only a fraction of a second before they could come to blows. "There are ladies present, don't forget."

Both Caroline and Quinn popped off the bed in unison. "Hi, Lash," they crooned. And then, glaring at each other: "Jinx."

Lash tipped his hat to them and returned his attention to Danny. "What's all this about, anyway?"

"What this is *about*," Danny huffed, "is our so-called General—"

"So-called! I'll have you know I commanded a platoon of Rough Riders while you were still in diapers—"

"—and his collection of miserable skin-feeders! Look at me! Just look at me! I haven't slept a wink in a week."

"All one hundred and two of my fleas are present and accounted for," General Farnum said. "I did roll call just this morning." He gestured with a sweep of his cane toward the miniature circus set, equipped with tiny balance beams, swings, and trapezes, in which his performing fleas were kept. Even from a distance, Sam could see the tiny dark shapes darting between various pieces of equipment.

"Then why"—Danny's voice was cresting again dangerously—"can't I stop ITCHING?"

General Farnum let out a noise that sounded suspiciously like a growl. "Have you considered the possibility of *lice*? Oh, during the war we saw plenty of lice. The dirtiest soldiers were always the most affected."

"You rotten scoundrel, I bathed not four days ago—"

"My point exactly. You stink!"

"Fellas, fellas." Lash once again intervened. "No reason to get so riled up. Danny"—he turned to the infuriated dwarf—"I hate to say it, but General Farnum's got a point. You don't exactly smell like a bouquet of daisies. And General Farnum"—Lash turned to the general before Danny could burst into a renewed round of fury—"ain't it possible that one or two of your, er, *specimens* may've made a break for it?"

"No," General Farnum said stiffly. "I do not lose

men, Langtry—or fleas, as the case may be."

"Well, now," Lash said quickly, before the argument could resume, "what say you both go ahead and shake on it? Come on," he added, when neither man moved. "We're all family here, right?"

After a long second, Danny extended his hand with a grunt. General Farnum clasped it quickly, then immediately turned away, muttering.

"Well, see?" Lash said cheerfully, even as the general stomped off. "All's well that ends—"

"Thomas. Pippa. Sam. Max. Dumfrey wants you in his office." Gil Kestrel, the museum's new janitor, had materialized in the doorway.

It was as if the voice carried with it an arctic chill. Instantly, all the lightness and ease was blown from Lash's face. Slowly, Lash pivoted to face Gil. Everyone was frozen, as if stilled by the sheer force of electric tension in the room.

Gil's eyes flicked to Lash. "Langtry," he said shortly.

"Kestrel," Lash said tightly. As far as Thomas could tell, these were the only words the two men ever exchanged. *Langtry. Kestrel.* And they would pass each other in the hall sticking as close as they could to opposite walls, as if convinced the other one carried an infectious disease.

12 🐾

Lash and Gil had known Mr. Dumfrey from the old days, back when they all traveled the country together, performing for massive crowds in towns across America. But whereas Lash was always telling stories about that time, Gil hardly spoke at all, unless it was to give orders or ask whether anyone had moved the mop. Thomas knew no more about him than he had on the day Gil first appeared at breakfast, clutching a weathered rucksack and moving his ever-present toothpick back and forth in his mouth, like it was an idea he'd been chewing on for decades.

One time, Max had worked up the courage to ask Dumfrey about why Gil and Lash hated each other, but Dumfrey had merely waved off the question.

"Bygones, my dear, bygones!" he'd said cheerily. "Old bones laid long ago to rest."

But it was obvious that whatever the reason for the tension between them, it was anything but gone.

Finally, Gil turned away, and the electric spell that had bound them all in place was broken. Instantly, the air came whooshing back into Thomas's lungs.

"Some family," Max muttered as they followed Gil out into the hall and down toward Dumfrey's office.

2

Mr. Dumfrey's office was accessible only from the performers' staircase, which corkscrewed up the back of the museum before belching its travelers into the attic. As usual, his door was closed, though even from several feet away Pippa could hear Dumfrey's deep, rumbling chuckle emanating from within.

"Well, now, look at that," he was murmuring. "Would you believe I'd completely forgotten . . . and Miss Annie Priggs! How time flies. What a dear she was, what an absolute dear. I wonder whatever happened to Miss Annie Priggs, and whether she ever got the solo act she wanted. Perhaps I ought to . . . no, no."

Kestrel rapped once and, without waiting for a reply, swung the door open. "Delivery for you, Mr. D," he said.

Seated at his desk, his small round spectacles perched on the end of his nose, Mr. Dumfrey was bent over an enormous book so overstuffed with pamphlets, photographs, and loose papers, it looked like an accordion. Instantly, Mr. Dumfrey jumped, slamming shut the book. But as he did, a yellowed photograph was expelled from between its pages and floated down toward Pippa's feet. She snatched it up and nearly choked.

"Mr. Dumfrey," she said. "Is this you?"

"Let me see," Max said, and grabbed the photo from Pippa's hands.

In the picture, Mr. Dumfrey was standing in front of a peaked circus tent between two lean, tall men: Kestrel and Langtry, both instantly recognizable, although Kestrel's face was transformed by a dazzling grin, so different from his usual scowl.

Mr. Dumfrey had a dark mustache, a full head of dark brown hair—somehow, Pippa had just assumed he'd always been as bald as a newborn baby—and, most incredibly, most unbelievably, was about sixty pounds lighter. With one hand raised to his eyes to shield them from the sun and a corner of his mouth quirked into a

15 ☞

smile, it was almost, almost possible to see the resemblance between him and his half brother, Nicholas Rattigan.

Except that Rattigan rarely smiled, as Pippa knew too well. And when he did, there was no humor or life in it. It was the smile of a snake as it opens its jaw to swallow a mouse.

Dumfrey pushed up from his desk and leaned over, snatching the photograph back from Max and upsetting a collection of pens with his stomach in the process. "Yes, yes. All very silly. Took a trip down memory lane, I'm afraid to say. Can't blame me . . . having all these old friends around . . . a bit of vanity, I suppose. . . ." His face was the color of a stop sign.

Kestrel's mouth flattened into something less than a frown. "Dumfrey here was the star of the show."

"Mr. Dumfrey, you *performed*?" Pippa squeaked. She had seen Mr. Dumfrey onstage, of course. He often made announcements during the performances of the museum's newest attractions—most recently, General Farnum and his world-famous flea circus. But as far as she knew, Mr. Dumfrey had no special talent beyond his ability to fudge the truth by claiming, for example, that a bunch of dolls with insect wings pinned to their backs was actually a family of Irish fairies; or that an old broomstick decorated with seashells and feathers was in fact an aboriginal Polynesian spear, used in rituals of sacrifice. *Faith begets fact*, Mr. Dumfrey was fond of saying.

"Performed?" Kestrel worked his jaw, left to right, moving the toothpick back and forth in his mouth. In the three weeks he had worked for the museum, Pippa had never seen him without one. Even when Kestrel ate, he merely shoved the toothpick to one corner of his mouth and shoveled food into the other. "Wasn't anybody east of the Mississippi better than Mr. D at what he did, and nobody west, either."

"But . . . what did you do?" Sam asked, a little awkwardly.

"It doesn't matter now," Mr. Dumfrey said quickly. He shot a pointed look in Kestrel's direction, as if cautioning him to stay silent. "It's all in the past."

Unsatisfied, Pippa focused her attention on the scrapbook, closing her eyes. Almost immediately she inhaled the smell of old, sunbaked leather and ink, of tobacco-stained fingers and photographs drying to the consistency of leaves. A second later, various images flashed in her mind: of a young woman, squinting, holding an enormous white cone of cotton candy; of Kestrel and Lash with their arms around each other's shoulders, laughing; of a dusty circus tent and a bearded lady standing in the entryway (not, Pippa thought critically, as fine a bearded lady as Betty; her beard was much patchier and not nearly so long). It was as though her mind had fingers and could riffle through all the pages, one after the other—she was scanning fliers, hopping over notices advertising the Best Variety Show in America, flipping past a dozen pictures of the Priggs sisters, Famed Contortionists and Human Pretzels, fumbling for some evidence of Mr. Dumfrey's special skill. Suddenly, an image of the young Dumfrey began to form. He was holding something over his shoulder, a broomstick, or a shovel, or—

Slam.

All at once, a dark wall came down in her mind and she could no longer see. Mr. Dumfrey had shut the scrapbook away and, furthermore, wedged an ornate Victorian cabinet directly in front of it. When she closed her eyes now, all she saw was a confusion of papers and a miscellany of objects—rubber bands, paper clips, old bills.

"I'm sorry, Pippa." Mr. Dumfrey looked anything but sorry as he returned to his desk and sat down with a little, satisfied sigh. "But it really isn't nice to stick your mind into other people's business." He carefully righted the cup of pens he had reversed earlier, slotting each pen back in its rightful spot. "Thank you, Kestrel. That'll be all for now. I do believe Miss Fitch may need your help turning out the Bloody Baron exhibit. That old guillotine is terribly hard to maneuver."

Kestrel's toothpick once again hopped from one corner of his mouth to the other, and without another word, he turned and left the room. Dumfrey turned a beaming smile on the children. "So," he said, "you wanted to see me?"

There was a brief pause. Once again Pippa wondered, somewhat guiltily, what special talent Mr. Dumfrey might possibly have possessed. In his cage, Cornelius preened his feathers and let out a prolonged squawk.

"Actually," Sam said, again apologetically, "you wanted to see us."

Mr. Dumfrey struck his forehead with the palm of his hand. "So I did, so I did. Don't know what's wrong with my mind nowadays. Old age, children, old age. Never say I didn't warn you!" His face turned serious.

"I'm about to entrust you with an enormous responsibility," he said, lowering his voice, as though worried that the large bust of Thomas Jefferson occupying one corner of his desk might come to life just to eavesdrop.

"As you know, the poor Monsieur Cabillaud has taken ill."

"Let's hope it's the plague," Max muttered. Pippa elbowed her sharply, trying to arrange her face into a fitting expression of sympathy.

Monsieur Cabillaud was the museum's resident tutor, and ever since September 1 had insisted that school was back in session. It seemed he had spent the whole summer brainstorming new ways to torment them with agonizingly boring lessons on every subject, from the correct conjugation of the French verb for *somersault*, to the proper application of Epsom salts to cure stiff muscles, to the names of all the Chinese dynasties from 2000 BC to the present day. He had even conscripted Smalls the giant, an aspiring poet, to give weekly two-hour lessons on literature, during which Smalls read aloud from his newest unpublished work, "How Sweetly Doth the Pigeons Coo," and railed against the stupidity of every literary magazine that had rejected it.

"Normally," Mr. Dumfrey continued, having failed to hear Max's comment or chosen to ignore it, "Monsieur Cabillaud takes care of all our expenditures and deposits." Mr. Dumfrey coughed—perhaps because there were usually far more expenses than deposits, if there were any deposits at all. "But this week I must ask you to take his place."

"You want us to go to the bank?" Max asked, in her typically blunt style.

Mr. Dumfrey looked vaguely irritated to have been interrupted. He coughed again. "I would do it myself," he said, "but I'm expecting an important phone call. A once-in-a-lifetime opportunity—a specimen so rare it doesn't yet even have a name."

Pippa and Thomas exchanged a look.

"I would hope that this goes without saying, but it is absolutely imperative that the money go safely into the accounts"—Mr. Dumfrey emphasized the word *safely*, peering at each child in turn over the rim of his glasses—"especially in light of recent . . . events."

In the past two months—ever since Professor Rattigan had vanished, seemingly into thin air, from a shuttered trolley factory into which he had lured them— the number of bank robberies in New York City had spiked a record 250 percent. There was no doubt, at least in Pippa's mind, that the two factors were linked. Rattigan had made no secret about the fact that he was planning something big. And something big meant something expensive.

Unfortunately, there was no way to prove it.

Half the New York City police department and a whole team of special agents were combing the city for Rattigan, with absolutely no success, and every robbery had so far gone off seamlessly, leaving no indications behind of who might be responsible.

Pippa, Max, Sam, and Thomas knew that Rattigan must be behind the bank heists. And deep down, *very* deep down, Pippa was the teeniest bit . . . relieved. Of course she would never admit to it: her friends wouldn't understand, and most of the time she joined them in hoping that he had simply vanished from the face of the earth.

But if Rattigan died, then she would have no chance of asking him about *her* parents. Tom, she knew, felt that the museum was his true home. Max thought having parents sounded like more trouble than it was worth and proudly declared herself an orphan to anyone who would listen. Sam knew that his parents were named Priscilla and Joe and seemed satisfied.

Pippa wanted more. Not just names, but pictures, and facts, and stories. Knowing that she might have had parents who loved her had opened up a need she hadn't known existed, just as the smell of sizzling bacon will awaken a sudden hunger.

Mr. Dumfrey removed the metal cashbox from a desk

drawer and handed it to Thomas. Once again, Pippa couldn't help herself. The contents of the enclosed metal box floated up to her consciousness, as if the material that separated her from them had been suddenly dissolved.

"Three dollars and seventy-five cents?" she blurted out, even as Mr. Dumfrey counted the money into a large envelope. "That's it?"

Mr. Dumfrey had the grace to look embarrassed. "Ah, yes, well. . . . I might have deducted a certain fee for museum development and expansion. Rare specimens don't come free, you know!"

"And"—Thomas took the cashbox and peered into it—"a set of false teeth." He made a face.

"Aha!" Mr. Dumfrey leaped to his feet and, cupping the teeth carefully in a palm, transferred them to one of the many glassed-in cabinets that cluttered his office. "I've been looking for these everywhere. Do you know these fine specimens once belonged to George Washington? An excellent man, and very careful about his dental hygiene. Really, they're in beautiful shape, don't you think? Especially considering his diet—all starch. Really no fresh vegetables or fruit to speak of; I don't know where that business about the cherry tree came from. Now go on," he said, turning businesslike again.

"Straight to the bank and no stopping. Miss Fitch has threatened to serve my head on a platter if we go one more week on cabbage stew."

Max zipped the envelope into her jacket, which was several sizes too large, so as to accommodate the knives and blades she always carried with her. Almost automatically, Pippa counted four of them tucked into various pockets. Just then, the phone began to ring.

"That's your cue." Mr. Dumfrey snatched up the receiver with one hand and waved them good-bye with the other. "Is that you, Sir Barrensworth? Excellent, excellent. Dumfrey here, of Dumfrey's Museum of Freaks, Oddities, and Wonders." As Thomas, Sam, Max, and Pippa retreated from his office, Mr. Dumfrey pulled his mouth away from the phone and whispered, "Be careful."

"Now," he said, returning his attention to the call and gesturing for Pippa to close the door behind her. "About the price we were discussing . . ."

3

A small crowd was gathered just outside the
museum, waiting for admission. Hanging
over the entrance was a garishly painted ban-
ner advertising *General Farnum's World Famous Flea Circus* and
showing vastly magnified fleas wearing elaborate circus
costumes while bouncing on trampolines, riding tiny
tricycles, and performing various acrobatic routines.
The eager customers would likely be disappointed by
the real thing—the fleas were so small it was hard to
tell where they were, much less whether they were actually backflipping—but Pippa was just grateful that the
new attraction had taken much of the attention away
from the living wonders of Forty-Third Street, as she,

Thomas, Sam, and Max had briefly been known.

For a short time, they had become unlikely—and largely *unliked*—celebrities, and nearly every day a new article, many of them unflattering, had appeared in the newspapers about them. They had found it difficult to move through the streets without someone shrieking an insult in their direction or whispering or merely staring. But now they slipped into the street happy, unnoticed, and undisturbed.

It was a beautiful fall day, warm but crisp, with the sun sitting high in the sky like a perfectly cooked egg. Across the street, Barney Bamberg was sponging the windows of his new delicatessen, while the smell of pastrami, corned beef, and sauerkraut issued from the open front door. Jumbled displays of wrenches, nails, keys, and hammers gleamed in the windows of Majestic Hardware. Henry, the day porter at the St. Edna Hotel, was napping on the job, as always.

"Hey," Thomas piped up. "Want to hear a joke?"

"No," Max and Pippa said together.

Thomas ignored them. "What do you do with a dead chemist?"

Sam made a face. "Not now, Thomas. You know science makes my head hurt."

"Come on. Just play along."

"Leave him alone, Thomas," Max said. Sam turned so red, Pippa was sure his whole face would combust. When, she wondered, would he 'fess up to his enormous, obvious crush on Max?

"Barium," Thomas said. When no one said anything, he sighed. "Bury him. Get it?"

Sam groaned.

"I'll bury *you*, unless you shut it," Max said, glowering.

"No sense of humor," Thomas mumbled, but fell silent when Max moved a hand threateningly toward her pocket.

Despite the new, sharp-toothed curiosity that nibbled at Pippa whenever she thought about her past, she was happy. She was happy to be walking here, in the sun, side by side with her friends—even Max. She let her mind wander and skip like a stone across the river of people flowing toward Broadway, skimming through pockets and purses, the knowledge coming to her easily now, with hardly any effort, as if the whole world were an origami figure unfolding itself to reveal its secrets. She could see the melted taffy gummed to the bottom of a woman's pocketbook and the man with a sandwich in his pocket; she could see card cases and money folds, loose change and gold-tipped pens.

She could even, occasionally, slip into other people's

minds. These images came to her in brief bursts, like camera flashes that left a lingering image, a quick impression of shape and meaning. There! A pair of darned socks strung from a wash line. And there! A memory of a little girl whose fingers were sticky with jam. There! A narrow office space in a tall gray building; the smell of ink and paper. They bubbled up to her consciousness and then vanished again, like items bobbing on a tide.

Then, suddenly, a new image intruded: the breath went out of her, and she felt as if she'd been hurled against a rock. A factory, dimly lit, and someone screaming . . . Rattigan's face, twisted into a cruel smile . . . an arm pinning a wide-eyed girl to his chest . . . pinning *Pippa* to his chest . . . .

She let out a short cry of pain, spinning around, searching the teeming crowd.

Someone—one of the men and women on the street— had been there that night at the factory, the night they had last confronted Rattigan and Pippa had been sure she was going to die.

Almost immediately, however, she began to doubt. She saw no one who looked suspicious or even faintly recognizable: just the usual mass of scowling businessmen and street vendors, women herding their small children, theatergoers craning their necks to look at the billboards. Had she imagined it? Maybe her own memories had intruded—it was hard to distinguish, sometimes, between her mind and other people's, as though they were two sticky masses that sometimes gummed together.

"Move it." A fat man elbowed her roughly, and she realized she'd stopped walking in the middle of the sidewalk. She hurried to catch up to her friends, who had just reached the corner.

"Hey." Sam pointed at the far corner, where a boy with straw-colored hair sticking out of his hat was squatting on an overturned milk crate. "Isn't that Chubby?"

It was. There was no mistaking Chubby's thatch of unruly hair, his nose as thin and long as a pencil, or his bizarre style of dress. Today he was wearing battered boots, unlaced, tongues lolling out; red-and-green striped socks; pants several inches too short for him; and several shirts layered over one another, all of it topped with a floppy woolen cap, so he looked rather like someone who had selected his outfit by diving headfirst into a laundry basket.

They crossed the street, dodging a clattering trolley car. Chubby was sitting with his elbows on his knees, surrounded by various pots and brushes. A sign written in shaky black letters on cardboard next to him said: *SHEW POLISH OR SHINE.*

"Hello, *Leonard*," Pippa said sweetly. Chubby scowled at her. For years, Chubby had been tormenting her by using her full name, Philippa, which she hated. But she had recently learned that Chubby had been born *Leonard* and wasted no occasion to remind him.

"What are you doing?" Sam asked, surveying Chubby's various materials.

"What's it look like I'm doing?" Chubby said, scrubbing his nose with a finger and leaving behind a large streak of black shoe polish. "Read the sign." He gestured to it proudly.

"But what about selling papers?" Thomas asked.

Chubby was an orphan, and proudly so. For years he had ruled all the corners between Herald Square and Forty-Second Street, selling papers and also collecting bets on everything from whether or not the Yankees would win their next home game to the quantity of pigeons that would roost on the Pepsi sign at any time. For a short while he'd even lived with a group of petty thieves and had made his living picking pockets.

But after Rattigan had kidnapped Chubby to try to blackmail Thomas, Pippa, Sam, and Max into cooperating with him, Chubby had vowed to change his ways.

Chubby waved a hand. "I gave Tallboy my corner," he said, pronouncing the name *Tallboy* the way someone might say President Roosevelt or Mickey Mouse, as if everyone should know him. "I got tired of slinging news all day for peanuts. I make twice as much right here, plus I don't got to stand all day."

"Don't *have* to stand all day," Pippa corrected him.

"Will you lay off?" Max said. "You sound like Cabillaud."

"Cabiwhat?" Chubby scratched his head. "So what do you say? Ten cents for a polish, five cents for a shine." He brandished a filthy brush in their direction.

"What's the difference?" Thomas asked.

Chubby grinned and hawked a wad of spit onto the toe of his shoe, then rubbed it in with a thumb. "See?" he said proudly. "Good as new."

Max laughed. Pippa shot her a dirty look. "You're disgusting," she said, turning back to Chubby.

Chubby seemed to take that as a compliment and only shrugged. "Who wants to go first?"

"Err, maybe next time," Sam said quickly.

"How's Von Stikk?" Thomas asked, deftly changing the subject. "She manage to get you in school yet?"

The word *school* provoked an explosion of rage. "It should be illegal!" Chubby burst out, clutching his head as if the very idea of education pained him and leaving a long trail of smudgy shoe polish across his face. "The woman's prosecuting me."

"You mean persecuting," Pippa said. "Sorry," she added, when Max shot her a look.

Chubby frowned. "That's what I said. Prosecuting." He looked over his shoulder, as if worried Von Stikk might be hiding somewhere in the crowd, prepared to jump out at him. "No matter where I go, she's there. It's like she's following me. Yesterday I had to hide in a crate of sausages to avoid her. I smelled like pork for the rest of the day. A dog nearly took my hand off."

Pippa was tempted to point out that Chubby often smelled a bit like pork, but remained silent.

"Tough break," Thomas said, clapping Chubby on the shoulder. Pippa knew, however, that he was relieved that Andrea von Stikk had found a new target. Von Stikk had overseen the Von Stikk's Home for Extraordinary Children until it was closed because children kept disappearing, presumably because they had run away. Her newest project was the Von Stikk School for Underprivileged Youths, and in the summer, she had briefly attempted a legal campaign to remove Thomas, Pippa, Max, and Sam from Dumfrey's care and enroll them at her school. "Take it easy, okay, Chub?"

"I always do," Chubby said cheerfully. "Wait!" he called out as they started to move on. His face turned serious. "Listen. I, ah, never thanked you guys for, you know, saving my life." He extended a hand solemnly to Thomas. "And I want you to know if you ever need anything, I'm your guy."

"That's all right, Chubby," Thomas said with feeling, reaching out to clasp Chubby's hand. "There's no need to thank—ahhh!"

There was a loud buzz. Thomas jumped back with a yelp, shaking his hand as though he'd been burned.

"What *was* that?" Thomas said, his freckles darkening as they did when he was angry: like a small, furious constellation.

Chubby only hooted with laughter. He opened his palm, revealing a small, circular device. "Superdeluxe joy buzzer. I got it from the new joke shop on Fifty-Seventh Street. They got everything—stink bombs and itch powders, dribble glasses and whoopee cushions, loaded dice and fake decks."

"Can I see?" Max said, staring at Chubby with renewed interest.

"Get your own," he said coolly, slipping the joy buzzer back into a pocket that contained—Pippa blanched—one quarter of an old bologna sandwich. "But really," he said, once again extending a hand toward Thomas, his face turning serious. "Thank you."

Thomas cast an infuriated glance at Chubby's outstretched palm. "I'll pass," he said. "See you next time, Chub." He continued scowling as they kept on toward the bank, muttering something that sounded very much, to Pippa, like "revenge."

Located at the corner of Broadway and Sixty-First Street, the New York Federated Savings Bank looked like an ancient Greek temple. It looked like a temple inside, too, with its soaring ceiling, vaulted windows, and a marble floor so beautifully polished that you felt slightly guilty for walking on it. Gray-faced men sat behind enormous gray desks, sorting gray documents into gray folders, all of them moving so mechanically that Pippa thought at first she was looking at the same man replicated over and over.

It was obvious that the bank had taken recent precautions against robbery. An armed guard was stationed next to the front doors, and a second guard paced the room, evaluating customers and keeping one hand on a holstered gun.

A line of people snaked up toward the counters. Pippa, Thomas, Max, and Sam joined the back of the line. Normally, Pippa enjoyed the bank, but she kept thinking of the vision she'd had in Times Square, of Rattigan's leering face and her own mouth open in a scream. He was out there, somewhere, and the key to her past was locked inside of him . . .

She was jolted from these thoughts when the man behind her stepped hard on her heel, nearly sending her sprawling onto the floor. She whipped around.

"That's the third time you've trampled on my . . . ," she started to say, but the words got tangled in her throat. Cold fear gripped her, as if the floor had just dropped away and she'd plunged into freezing water.

The man was wearing a long overcoat with the collar turned up and a low-brimmed fedora hat that concealed his eyes. He had his gloved hands in his pockets.

And in one of them was a gun.

Slowly, the man raised his eyes to hers. They were dark brown, nearly black, and cold as stone. He drew his lips back into a grin, and she saw that beneath his straggly mustache, his teeth were yellowed and rotting.

"Pardon me, your highness," he said mockingly.

"Forgiven," Pippa squeaked. She turned around, her heart beating very fast. She nudged Max with an elbow.

"Stop bumping me," Max said lazily, without looking

up. She was using a gold-tipped penknife to clean her fingernails. Pippa nudged her again, a little harder. Still, Max didn't look up. "I *said* keep your elbows to yourself."

Thomas had just reached the counter.

"Hello," he said to the gray-faced man blinking at him from behind the glass, looking like a somber fish staring out from the murky depths of an ocean. "We'd like to make a deposit."

"Thomas," Pippa hissed.

"Hold on a second, Pip," he said, waving her away. "You have the money, Max?"

"Gave it to Sam," she said, still concentrating on her fingernails.

"I gave it to you," Sam said, turning to Thomas. "I'm *sure* I gave it to you."

"Step aside, please, if you aren't ready to conduct your business," the gray-faced man said in a voice that sounded as if it had been piped out of a tin can.

"You didn't," Thomas said to Sam.

"Did."

"Didn't."

"Sirs, I must ask you to step aside so that our other customers . . ."

"Thomas," Pippa tried again desperately. The

38 ☞

man shifted behind her. She could feel his growing impatience—could see the barrel of the gun, inching upward in his pocket, pointing directly at her lower back.

"Not now, Pippa." Thomas glared at Sam. "You don't think I would remember if—"

He didn't get any further. The man shoved Pippa roughly out of the way, at the same time yanking the gun from his pocket. In an instant, he'd seized Thomas by the collar and jammed the revolver to his neck, lifting Thomas clean off his feet and pressing his face to the window that divided him from the bank clerk.

"Nice and easy now and no trouble," he said in a low voice. The bank clerk's face had gone from gray to sheet-white. "Or else *this one's* brains get splattered on the counter, understand?" He shook Thomas so hard, Thomas's teeth clacked together. "A thousand dollars, small bills, in an envelope. *Now.*"

As the trembling bank clerk began counting out bills, Pippa felt a desperate desire to scream. But she couldn't risk it—not when Thomas was in danger. Max started to reach into her pocket but Sam shook his head.

The man would have to release Thomas, or set down the gun, in order to take the money. And then Pippa would scream. . . .

39 ☞

The clerk sealed the envelope and slid it beneath the glass, drawing his hand away quickly, as if the man were a poisonous snake who might bite.

"Nice try," the robber snarled, and Pippa's heart sank. "Put it in my pocket."

The clerk did as he was told, sliding open the little glass window, reaching forward with trembling hands to stuff the envelope into the robber's coat pocket. And still the guards hadn't noticed or moved, though the customers in line were starting to get impatient.

"P—please," the clerk stammered, keeping his voice low, nervously licking his lips. "L—let the boy go. You got what you wanted."

"I'll think about it, just as long as you don't make a peep," the robber snarled, and Pippa's heart sank. And she knew, in an instant, with that intuition that was more than feeling, but vision, that the man didn't intend to release Thomas—not until he made it free and clear of the bank.

Keeping Thomas in a choke hold, the man spun around.

Pippa didn't have time to think. He was nearly on top of her. She could see Thomas's eyes, big as moons, trying to communicate a message. But she didn't understand. And without thinking, she dropped to the ground, jutted out a leg, and tripped the man as he barreled headlong for the doors.

The robber went flying, releasing his hold on Thomas. They both tumbled to the ground, hard, and the gun skittered out of the robber's hand and discharged with a thunderous—

Bang.

The bullet ricocheted off the wall and left a fine web of cracks in one of the glass doors as the guard, letting out a cry of surprise, stumbled backward, fumbling for his own gun. Suddenly, everything was chaos. Women were screaming as they pulled their children to the ground. Clerks cowered under their desks.

By then both Thomas and the robber were back on their feet. Their eyes fell on the gun at the same time. Thomas dove for it first.

At that moment, one of the guards came charging across the floor, roaring for the robber to put his hands up. Pippa watched, horrified, as time seemed to slow down, to grow soupy and almost still: Thomas was in the air, reaching out a hand, sailing, sailing—directly into the path of the oncoming guard.

"Watch out!" Pippa screamed. But it was too late.

The guard knocked the fallen gun with the toe of his boot, spinning it back toward the robber. A fraction of a second later, Thomas hit the ground, colliding with the guard's shins, and the two of them fell into a hopeless tangle of limbs.

The robber bent over to snatch up his gun, his long fingers outstretched, only inches from the weapon—

Thwack.

The thief let out a high-pitched scream as a knife—Pippa recognized it as one of Max's favorites, with a fine, needlelike blade and a bone handle—nicked him perfectly between his outstretched fingers. He drew back, cradling his injured hand, leaving a trail of blood across the front of his coat. He must have decided the gun wasn't worth the trouble, because in the next instant he was barreling toward the doors again, easily knocking aside the lone trembling guard who stood between him and the exit, shaking too hard to draw his weapon.

"Quick!" someone screamed. "He's getting away!"

"Sam!" Pippa called desperately.

Luckily, Sam understood. He lunged for the nearest desk—an enormous, hulking thing made of heavy oak—and hefted it in the air, revealing a small knot of people clustered beneath it, whimpering, like mice crammed into a hole. With a grunt, Sam heaved it toward the doors . . .

. . . just as the robber slipped through them onto the street.

Crash.

The desk tumbled through the thin glass and spun across the stone steps. Pedestrians leaped out of the way, screaming. An alarm began to wail, so loud that Pippa had to cover her ears. Several curious faces appeared beyond the shattered doorway, peering at the inside of the bank from behind the remaining jagged teeth of glass, so that Pippa had the sudden impression of being an animal in a zoo exhibit.

Outside, the robber had already disappeared into the crowd.

"I should have known," was the first thing Assistant Chief Inspector Hardaway said when he spotted Thomas.

Max groaned. Sam cast a longing look at the door, as if he were thinking of making a run for it. Only Pippa managed to respond.

"Hello, Mr. Hardaway," she said.

"*Assistant Chief Inspector* Hardaway," he snarled. Pippa didn't blink. Thomas was sure the insult was deliberate. He felt an unexpected surge of affection for her. Pippa might act like an overcooked noodle sometimes, but when push came to shove, there was nothing soft about her.

"All right." Hardaway spun around in a circle, hitching up his belt, addressing the room at large. "Does someone want to tell me what the h—"

"Sir." Hardaway's underling, Lieutenant Webb, coughed the word, indicating with a jerk of his chin all the little children just emerging from behind overturned tables and countertops, and Hardaway swallowed back the curse, barely.

"Does someone want to tell me," he said through gritted teeth, "what in the name of my aunt Tillie happened here?"

"We were robbed, sir." An ashen-faced man sprouted from behind his desk, like a particularly fast-growing and colorless flower. He smoothed and resmoothed his tie with hands as plump as dumplings. Thomas immediately identified him as the bank manager.

"Poor Mr. Abner was at the counter—" He gestured toward the ashen-faced clerk who had delivered the money into the robber's hand.

Now that the danger was over, however, Mr. Abner seemed considerably recovered—cheerful, almost, as if invigorated by the whole affair and by his role in it. "That's right, Inspector," he said with great solemnity, puffing up his chest. "He came pushing to the front of the line and grabbed hold of that boy"—he indicated

45 ☞

Thomas—"and that's when I saw the gun." One of the witnesses let out a low moan, as if even the memory was too much. "He told me to put the money in an envelope. I was hoping he would have to put down the gun, or release the boy, to take the money, but he was clever. He made me tuck it into his pocket."

"What did he look like?" Hardaway said, and Lieutenant Webb removed a pad of paper and pen from his back pocket. Beneath the brim of his fedora, Lieutenant Webb's eyes were as hard and dark as two very old raisins.

Now Mr. Abner appeared uncomfortable. "I—I didn't get a good look at him."

"You didn't get a good look at him?" Hardaway repeated. "He was standing less than six inches from you!"

"He was wearing a hat, pulled very low, and a high-collared coat," Mr. Abner said, removing a handkerchief from his pocket and swiping agitatedly at his nose. "He looked a bit like your lieutenant, actually . . ."

Lieutenant Webb let out a low growl.

"In the manner of dress, I mean," Mr. Abner said quickly. "That's all. Like I said, I didn't get a good look. He had a gun . . ."

"I see." Hardaway's frown deepened to a scowl. "So he scared the wits straight out of you. Anyone else?" He looked around the room at the assembled crowd. When no one spoke, he let out a little huff of impatience. "Give me something. Was he tall? Short? Dark? Fair?"

"Tall," a short woman said, shivering. "Very tall."

"Not so tall," a tall man said, disagreeing. "Quite average, really."

"He was wearing a hat, but I could see his hair was dark," said someone else, just as an older woman holding a squirming poodle said, "He was quite fair. Blond, practically white."

"He was ugly," Max said.

"He had a betting slip in his pocket," Pippa said, "and a book of matches."

"He had a mustache," Sam added. "An ugly one."

"Wonderful." Had Hardaway been a dog, Thomas was sure he would have bared his teeth. "So we're searching for a man who may or may not be tall, has either light or dark hair, sports a mustache, likes to gamble, and occasionally requires a match." He wrenched off his hat as though tempted to throw it—instead, he settled for mashing it back onto his head. "That narrows it down to half the population of New York."

"We tried to stop him," Sam said, somewhat defen-sively.

"I can see that," Hardaway said, shooting a glance at the shattered door and the splintered desk beyond it, around which a crowd was still buzzing like ants over the remains of a picnic. "How much did he make off with?"

Mr. Abner hung his head. The manager spoke up. "A thousand dollars, sir."

"Not exactly." Thomas spoke up for the first time. He dug a hand into the inside of his jacket and revealed a slightly crumpled envelope.

Pippa gasped. "You didn't."

"'Course I did," Thomas said proudly. "You didn't think I'd let that lunatic half strangle me for no rea-son, did you?"

Thomas wasn't built like other people. His bones were *flexible*. They could bend. As a result, he could squeeze himself into a shape hardly larger than a child's suitcase. He could escape a pair of handcuffs or a thick cable of chains. And he could certainly escape a head-lock. As soon as the robber had seized him, however, he knew he would have the chance to recover whatever money the clerk handed over to him.

"But—how?" Pippa said as Thomas gave the envelope

to a still-scowling Hardaway, who looked as if he would have actually *preferred* the money to be gone.

"Max taught me," Thomas said, shrugging. Max grinned and gave him a thumbs-up. Pippa folded her lips together and for once had nothing to say about Max's old habit of picking people's pockets.

Hardaway opened the envelope and peered inside. When he looked up, his dark eyes were glittering dangerously. "Is this some kind of a joke?" he said softly. "There's less than four dollars here."

"See? I *told* you I gave you Mr. Dumfrey's money," Sam grumbled.

"Wrong envelope," Thomas said, digging in his other pocket and producing the correct one.

The bank manager looked as if he was about to swoon from joy. "Miraculous!" he exclaimed. "Amazing! Wonderful!"

"Lucky," Hardaway growled, before dismissing them.

If Thomas was hoping for a peaceful afternoon, he was to be disappointed. Even before they reached 344 West Forty-Third Street, he could hear a commotion from inside. A small group of their neighbors had assembled just outside of the museum, doing a terrible job of trying to appear casual while craning their necks to see inside. The noise had drawn out even the reclusive Eli Sadowski, who lived next door and ventured outside only rarely, and then typically only for a few minutes, to procure another stack of newspapers to add to his vast collection or to visit a doctor for medications to combat everything from dust sensitivity to a fear of cucumbers.

"Hello, Eli," Thomas said as he slipped through the knot of people and put his hand on the gate. Thomas had a soft spot for the man, despite or maybe because of his eccentricities. It was in Mr. Sadowski's cluttered apartment that Thomas had decoded the mystery of one of Rattigan's many pseudonyms and realized his connection to a series of murders that had occurred earlier in the summer.

Eli touched a finger to his hat distractedly but kept his eyes glued to the museum doors. Through them, Thomas could hear the squabbling of angry voices. The crowd scattered slightly when Sam cut through it, allowing Thomas to get the gates open and slip inside.

But before he could reach the doors, they flew open, and a woman in a feathered hat scurried out, gripping the hand of her wide-eyed daughter. Simultaneously, the sound of angry voices crested.

"How dare you?" General Farnum was shouting. "How dare you come in here and—?"

The doors closed with a soft *whoompf*, so Thomas couldn't hear the rest of what he said.

"Come, Delilah," the woman said, when her daughter stopped to suck on her fingers and stare at Thomas. She gave the girl's hand a tug. "I knew we should have gone to Coney Island instead," she muttered, casting a disapproving look at Thomas, as if he were to blame for all her troubles. "*Very* unprofessional, if you ask me, even for a freak show. Such *language* . . ."

Now desperately curious, Thomas flew into the museum, followed closely by Sam, Pippa, and Max.

He was relieved to see that Farnum and Danny hadn't resumed their earlier argument. Instead, a very tall man with the squashy face of a somewhat overripe sweet potato was distributing business cards to the crowd gathered around Farnum's flea circus, even as Farnum lunged after him, trying to snatch the cards back. A card ended up in Thomas's hand before he could refuse it.

"Ernie Erskine's Professional Extermination," the squashy-faced man was saying jovially. "Fumigation and cleansing. Best flea killer in the business for over forty years."

51 ☞

"Flea killer?" General Farnum grabbed back the card from an alarmed-looking old woman. "You murderous monster, I'll have you brought up on charges—I'll have your head mounted to my door—"

"Don't be fooled, ladies and gentleman," Erskine continued, as if Farnum hadn't spoken, working the crowd like a politician on a press tour. Thomas couldn't help but think that if he didn't look so normal, he'd make a very good performer. "Dress 'em up like ballerinas or rodeo clowns, these aren't nothing but pests, pure and simple. Breed like bunnies and itch like poison ivy. Even now, they're probably jumping and skipping all around us, making nests in pocketbooks and pant creases."

"How awful," an old woman said loudly, above the dismayed muttering of the crowd.

"It makes one feel positively filthy," agreed the man next to her.

General Farnum's bushy eyebrows looked as if they might spring off his forehead and launch an attack. "The only *filthy* thing in this room—" he began, but he didn't get to finish his sentence.

Erskine was still talking over him, even as the crowd began backing toward the door, casting suspicious glances at the small black blurs moving within their colorfully decorated terrarium—which, only a minute ago, had been their main reason for paying the twenty-cent admission. "No doubt about it," he said. "Only good flea is a dead one! Call Ernie Erskine's Exterminators, before it's too late!"

And with that, Ernie followed the last customer out the door, leaving the furious General Farnum yelling after him.

"Handpicked—best fleas from San Francisco to Syracuse—slander—"

"Let's go." Thomas nodded to the others. He felt sorry for General Farnum. Farnum was at least twenty years older than Mr. Dumfrey, and even though he often repeated the same stories about his time fighting for Teddy Roosevelt during the Spanish-American War, about the fleas that had infested their sleeping bags, and Farnum's discovery of the insects' remarkable intelligence and acrobatic ability, he reminded Thomas somewhat of the late Siegfried "Freckles" Eckleberger, the closest thing Thomas had ever known to a grandparent. Besides, General Farnum had reason to be obsessed with his fleas. His first wife was long dead, and his second had left him for a French lion tamer. He had no children. Before joining the museum, he'd had no family at all—except, of course, for his fleas.

Halfway up the stairs to the attic, they could still hear the general raging.

"World famous!"

"Poor General Farnum." Pippa sighed. "And the flea circus was doing so well."

"Well," Max said, "that's what you get when you go around teaching bugs to do backflips."

B ANK ROBBERY—FOILED!

When Thomas went out to get the paper the next morning, he found that nearly every headline was the same. Returning to the museum just as the other residents were waking up, he found Pippa in the kitchen, blowing steam off a mug of tea.

"Hello," she said. "Where'd you go?"

"Paper delivery," he said, and slid the newspaper between them. He sat down, and they huddled together and began to read.

There's no doubt about it: New York City is in the grips of a crime wave. A spate of recent bank robberies has the

New York City Police Department spinning in circles, and yesterday, at 11:55 a.m., the New York Federated Savings Bank became the most recent target. As in previous instances, a single man entered, waited on line before producing a gun, and demanded the clerk hand over cash. This time, however, there was an unexpected twist to the story: when the robber attempted to take a boy hostage, he instead got a whole lot more than he bargained for.

"They looked normal-like," said Fred Genovese, who was on security duty at the time, "just like any other kids. But one of 'em—a skinny kid, looked like someone who'd get his teeth kicked in at school—chucked a desk straight through the doors. Musta cleared forty, fifty feet. And those desks are heavy. Solid oak with brass claw feet, probably a hundred, a hundred ten pounds."

Miss Eliza Niefenager, who had come to the bank to withdraw a sum for her monthly meeting of the Women's Midtown Cotillion, added: "And there was a girl—at least, I'm pretty sure she was a girl. She was wild-looking, like an animal. She had on an enormous jacket. And pants! In any case, she threw something—I think it was a knife, but she moved so fast, it was hard to see—and nicked that awful man right in the hand before he could snatch up his gun."

Mr. Gould, the bank manager, was overjoyed. "That small boy got all the money back!" he told *The Daily Screamer* exclusively. "Every penny!"

"Harumph," Pippa said. "Not a word about me."

"Cheer up," Thomas said, giving her a thump on the knee. "At least they didn't say you looked like a wild animal."

"To Max, that's a compliment," Pippa grumbled.

They continued reading:

Not everyone, however, approved of the intervention of these four young Samaritans. Assistant Chief Inspector Hardaway of the New York City Police Department, who has been spearheading the effort to track down the perpetrators of the recent spate of robberies, emphasized that the children's actions may well have endangered the investigation.

"This is police business," he said. "The details are confidential, but let's just say that the NYPD has launched a complex and delicate plan to bring the thief—or thieves—to justice. Now that they've had a scare, they'll take extra care next time to cover their tracks." He added: "Besides, those kids could have got someone killed. Like I always say, leave the job to the professionals."

"Piddle," Pippa said. "They've got a plan like I've got a third eye."

"I knew a woman with a third eye once," Smalls said with a sigh, turning away from the stove. He was holding a large wooden ladle that in his enormous hand looked more like a teaspoon. "Rebecca was her name. A most exquisite creature. I wrote a poem for her. 'Triclops of My Dreams' it was called. I still remember the first line. *O hadst thou three eyes wide to see, the love and care I have for—*"

Thomas cleared his throat and read the last paragraph of the article out loud, so that Smalls couldn't continue.

"'This was not the first time that these four "living wonders," Thomas Able, Philippa Devue, Sam Fort, and Mackenzie (last name unknown), all of whom reside at Mr. Dumfrey's Dime Museum of Freaks, Oddities, and Wonders, have had run-ins with the law. In August, they were on scene when the notorious fugitive Nicholas Rattigan made a dramatic escape from a West Side factory. And earlier this year, they made headlines after a string of murders baffled police and made a former reporter at this very newspaper an overnight sensation.

"'"Born criminals," Hardaway said, when asked for further comment.

"'The renowned educator Andrea von Stikk—'"

"Not her again," Pippa interrupted. "I thought she'd finally gone on to making Chubby's life miserable."

Thomas shrugged and continued reading. "'—von Stikk was quick to stress that it is the fault of the children's education, and not the children themselves.'"

"'"It's that madman, Mr. Dumfrey," she stated firmly. 'How many times do those poor children need to end up in mortal danger before the state agrees to remove them from the clutches of that charlatan? The children need discipline and a proper education.'"'"

"Proper education, *ma foi!*" As Thomas finished reading, Monsieur Cabillaud was just entering the kitchen. It was the first time he'd been on his feet in days, and though he still looked quite pale, he was dressed impeccably as always in a fine tailored suit, a silk cravat, and a thin-brimmed hat (which had been designed to unique specifications to fit his pin-sized head). "I shall write to zat terrible lady and give her some *education* of her own."

"Thomas, look," Pippa said, pointing to the bottom of the page, where a smaller headline read: *Police Still on the Hunt for Fugitive Rattigan. For full story, turn to page 12.*

Thomas turned the page—but before he could continue reading, his attention was attracted by an advertisement that dominated the better part of the page. Pippa saw it at the same time and inhaled sharply.

"Is that . . . ?" she said.

"Howie," Thomas confirmed.

The advertisement showed a group of performers clustered in front of a stately old building, above which a giant neon sign indicated the *Coney Island Curiosity Show.* The text, which was liberally sprinkled with capitalization and exclamation points, trumpeted: *New York City's BEST and ONLY LEGITIMATE Freak Show and Dime Museum! Don't be FOOLED by imitators! Don't be FLEECED by impostors! All freaks are 100% AUTHENTIC and you won't BELIEVE your eyes! Come see Howie the Human Owl and Alicia the Armless Knife-Throwing Wonder!—and much much MORE!*

In the photograph, Howie was standing front and center, wearing a typical expression of self-satisfaction and looking, as always, irritatingly perfect. Thomas noted that he had one arm around a girl who could only be Alicia. Like Howie, she had the same kind of chiseled physical perfection typically found only among dolls: cloud-blond hair; big, staring eyes; lips that looked as if they had been drawn on by someone trying to imitate a rosebud. Only the empty sleeves of her blouse, tied loosely at her chest, and the knife handle clutched between the toes of her bare feet betrayed her uniqueness.

"I don't believe it." Pippa's face had grown flushed.

"They practically call us frauds."

"At least they don't mention Mr. Dumfrey by name," Thomas said.

"They might as well," Pippa said. "New York's *only legitimate* freak show? It's offensive. I'd like to find that little worm and twist that great big head of his right off."

Earlier in the summer, Howie had briefly joined up with Mr. Dumfrey's Dime Museum. His startlingly good looks and ability to swivel his head a full 180 degrees had made him a temporary sensation, but Thomas had never quite trusted him. Howie was sly and rude and arrogant, and had boasted constantly of his connections to famous performers on the circuit and even to the United States government: his uncle could supposedly rotate his entire torso without moving his feet, and had worked as a bodyguard to a US president.

Eventually, Howie had revealed his true nature: all along, he'd been looking for opportunities to sabotage the museum. Despite his superficial politeness, he hated Thomas, Max, Pippa, and Sam—despised them not for being different but for having been created. Somehow—they still could not figure out how—he knew that they'd been made, born by Rattigan and his sick experiments. Howie had even started an organization called SUPERIOR: Stop Unnatural Phony Entertainers from Ruining and/or Impairing Our Reputation.

Thomas couldn't help but crack a smile. "You sound just like Max."

She glared at him. "Careful," she said. "Or it'll be your head, too."

"Speaking of heads, we'd better get rid of the evidence." Thomas stood up. "I'd like to keep mine, and if Max sees this, she'll go absolutely—"

"If I see what?"

Thomas froze. Max had just appeared in the doorway, yawning, rubbing an eye with her palm. Her hair was so wild, it looked as though she had styled it by attempting to electrocute herself.

"Nothing," Pippa and Thomas said quickly, at the same time.

Max narrowed her eyes. "What's the matter with you?" she said. "What's the big secret?"

Thomas moved for the trash bin. But Max was too quick. She darted across the room and snatched the paper from his hands. It didn't take her long to find the advertisement.

Thomas braced himself for an explosion of curses or a violent demonstration of temper. Even Monsieur Cabillaud, huddled in the corner over a steaming cup of chamomile tea, had gone still, with one hand tremblingly clutching the spoon he had been using to stir. Only Smalls was oblivious, still lumbering around the stove, mixing and stirring, humming to himself.

After a minute, Max merely folded the paper, her lips pressed tightly together, crossed to the trash can, and stuffed the paper so deep inside of it, her arm all but disappeared.

"What's for breakfast?" she said with a toss of her hair, and Thomas let out the breath he'd been holding.

"What's for breakfast?" Smalls repeated, turning away from the stove with a flourish, holding a dented saucepan in one enormous hand. "Only the sweetest ambrosia! The nectar of the gods! *To taste the gentle moon, and freshening beads/Lashed from the crystal roof by fishes' tails.*"

Seeing the children's blank faces, he coughed. "Oatmeal," he said, setting down the saucepan to reveal its lumpy contents, and shrugged. "It was all we had."

Just then, the heavy creaking of the floorboards announced Mr. Dumfrey's approach. A moment later he stomped down the stairs into the kitchen, leaning heavily on the banister and clutching a handkerchief in one hand. "Well, come on," he said immediately, with an impatient wave of the handkerchief, as if he'd been waiting there for hours. "I've got something to show you. Most extraordinary thing . . ." And he turned and began clomping up the staircase, which was so narrow it barely accommodated Mr. Dumfrey's stomach.

"*What's* the most extraordinary thing?" Thomas called after him. But when Mr. Dumfrey didn't respond, muttering instead about the absurdity of a system that required you to climb down only to climb up again, he shrugged and stood up. Pippa and Max got to their feet and went after him.

When they entered his office, they found Mr. Dumfrey standing beside his desk, which had been cleared of its usual clutter and was now dominated by a large dome-shaped object, covered with an embroidered shawl. Sam was already waiting for them there, but he just shrugged when Thomas gave him a questioning look.

Beckoning them closer, Mr. Dumfrey grasped one corner of the shawl. Then, with a dramatic flourish, he yanked it away.

"Ta-da!" he cried.

The shawl had been concealing a birdcage. Inside was one of the most amazing creatures the kids had ever seen—an enormous bird with dazzling red feathers and a coal-black beak shaped like a parrot's. A golden crest topped its head and its tail blazed with every color of the rainbow.

"Behold," said Dumfrey, his face beaming with delight. "The last living example of the magnificent species *Aviraris igneous*! The Exotic Black-Billed Ethiopian Firebird," Mr. Dumfrey added, when the children only stared at him blankly. "I named it myself."

"A Firebird," Sam said thoughtfully, approaching the cage and stooping down for a closer look. "I've never heard of a Firebird before."

The Firebird turned to face Sam, tilting its head side to side with an air of condescension. For a moment, Sam could see himself reflected in its dark, intelligent eyes.

Then, without warning, the Firebird cried out: "Step away, step away! Big lug, step away!"

Sam stumbled backward, shocked by the voice, which sounded nearly human.

"Oh, yes," Mr. Dumfrey said serenely. "It speaks as well."

"Ugly crow!" Cornelius squawked from his cage, ruffling his feathers in annoyance.

"Now, now, Cornelius," Mr. Dumfrey said, waggling a finger in the cockatoo's direction. "Be nice."

"Where'd you get it?" Thomas asked, taking Sam's place in front of the cage, but staying a good three feet from the bird. Once again, the Firebird looked at

Thomas appraisingly, like a man coolly considering his options at a buffet.

"This magnificent creature is the one I've been waiting for all week," Mr. Dumfrey said. "It was hand-delivered by the fellow who captured it—a celebrated explorer, famous throughout the world, a legend in his own time."

"What's his name?" Thomas asked.

Dumfrey frowned. "Hmmm, seems to have slipped my mind. Wait a moment," he said, patting his pockets. "He left his card somewhere . . ."

Pippa had approached the cage as well. "Check your vest," she said, without turning around.

"Aha!" Mr. Dumfrey extracted a crumpled card from his vest pocket and adjusted his glasses with two fingers. "Here it is. Sir Roger Barrensworth. Funny. Sounds like an English name, doesn't it? But his accent was more Italian. . . ."

The Firebird had apparently made a decision about Thomas. "Shrimp!" it screeched, still in that weirdly human voice. "Silly shrimp! Nosy, noggin-headed noodle!"

Thomas blushed all the way to his ears and backed away quickly. "Not very friendly, is it?"

"Let me see," Sam said, holding out his hand to Mr.

Dumfrey. The card had been folded in half. Inside was a crumpled Tendermint gum wrapper, which Sam flicked off with a fingernail, noting several others like it in the wastepaper basket. Even the card smelled vaguely like mint.

"Sir Barrensworth really likes his chewing gum," Sam said.

"Sir Barrensworth lived for years alone in the wilderness," Mr. Dumfrey said. "If that is the worst habit he acquired, he should consider himself lucky."

Beneath Sir Barrensworth's name was an address, 1270 Park Avenue, and the words: *Explorer. Adventurer. Collector of Rare Speecies.*

Sam frowned. "*Species* is spelled wrong," he said.

Mr. Dumfrey snatched the card back. "Probably a printer's error," he said, waving a hand. "Don't you see how lucky we are? We're saved! The Firebird will be the star of the show—and all for the bargain price of fifty dollars."

Sam nearly choked. "*Fifty dollars?*" That was more than the museum made in a month.

"Cheap!" the Firebird squawked, ruffling its feathers. "Cheap! Cheap!"

"It would be worth more if you wrung its neck," Thomas mumbled.

It was Max's turn to receive an appraisal from the Firebird. This came even quicker than it had for the others.

"Animal!" the bird screeched. "Beastly, untrained animal!"

"You're one to talk," Max said, without seeming the slightest bit offended. And she stuck out her tongue.

Suddenly, with a yowl of pure rage, Freckles bounded into the room and, claws outstretched, leaped directly for the cage on Mr. Dumfrey's desk.

"Freckles, no!" Sam yelled.

Max just managed to catch Freckles by the scruff of his neck and haul him backward before he could work a paw between the cage bars. Even after Max deposited him on the floor, Freckles continued to growl, circling the desk, watching Mr. Dumfrey's newest acquisition with an expression of pure greed.

Cornelius ruffled his feathers in such a way that he appeared to be chuckling.

"Clever cat!" he squawked. "Very clever cat!"

"On the bright side," Pippa said as soon as Mr. Dumfrey had dismissed them and they'd managed to shoo Freckles out into the hall, "if the museum folds, at this rate we can just open a zoo."

6

ven though there was no morning performance scheduled, Max headed straight for the
Odditorium after excusing herself from Mr.
Dumfrey's office. As always, the big hall smelled faintly
of old popcorn and bubble gum. The floor, despite
daily scrubbings, was sticky as she made her way down
the aisle toward the stage. The lights were dimmed,
and in the shadows she saw Kestrel moving between the
seats, searching for trash discarded by previous audience members and giving the faded felt cushions the
occasional scrub with a large shoebrush.

Max cleared her throat. Kestrel straightened up. His
large, dark eyes seemed like holes seared into his face,

and Max felt suddenly uncomfortable. She crossed her arms.

"Miss Fitch wants you upstairs," she lied. The museum's seamstress and general manager was so severe that even Mr. Dumfrey didn't dare contradict her. The first and last time Max had made the mistake of seeking Miss Fitch out to ask a question, she had spent *five hours* in the costume shop, getting poked with needles and strangled with yards of taffeta.

Kestrel didn't say a word, but loped immediately toward the door. Max held her breath until he was gone. There was something about Kestrel that made her think of graveyards, or lost cats, or the vacant buildings of the Bowery, sad and skinny and dark. Like he was absolutely *contagious* with tragedy.

Once she was absolutely sure she was alone, she hefted herself onstage. The Odditorium looked different when there was no audience to fill it—sadder but also more beautiful, like an exotic flower wilting behind glass. She moved backstage, blinking in the gloom, and located the large, spinning board she occasionally used in one of her most successful tricks, the Spinning Pinnacle of Death. The wheel was fitted with leather arm- and ankle-straps by which Danny would normally be restrained. While the wheel spun, Max would throw a series of knives—eight or ten, depending on how she felt—so that by the time Danny was released, she had re-created him in metal silhouette.

Today, however, she was interested in a different kind of target practice.

She shoved the wheel across the stage, grunting a little. Finally, satisfied, she stepped back, counting off fifty feet. From her position, the Spinning Pinnacle of Death, with its multicolored rings, looked just like an oversized dartboard.

It was perfect.

After once again checking to make sure that the Odditorium was completely empty, she kicked off her shoes and then, hopping to maintain balance, peeled off both socks in turn, wiggling her toes to get the blood working. Then she removed a knife from the back pocket of her blue jeans—a pair Lash had given her, which fit almost perfectly after she'd cuffed the hems several times—and set it on the floor.

The first difficulty was in merely picking the knife off the floor. She tried with her right foot, and then with her left. She switched back to her right foot. She spread her toes as wide as they would go. She stomped down on the handle. Still, the knife kept slipping.

It was all much harder than she'd thought. And the

harder it was, the angrier she got, and the more desperate to succeed.

Finally, by wedging the knife handle in the space between her big and second toes, she managed to get the knife airborne. Now she was standing on one leg, and she briefly pinwheeled her arms and hopped a little from left to right. When she could finally balance without wobbling like a top on a floor made of Jell-O, she took a deep breath, keeping her arms outstretched, and tried to imagine Howie's face sitting directly in the middle of the colored wheel, pinned there like Danny was during their act. That black hair, practically shellacked in place. That smile that was like the blinding-white grin of a predator. The bright blue of his eyes.

How had she ever believed, even for a single second, that he might be the teensiest, tiniest bit cute?

Suddenly energized by a wave of fury, she let out a half-mangled cry and threw. Or kicked.

The knife arced through the air . . .

Then clattered and skidded toward the wings, landing at least ten feet away from the target.

She tried again. This time the knife slipped from between her toes too early and went skittering across the floor like a giant, rotating insect. Her next try was even worse. She released too late, and the knife soared into the air at a nearly vertical angle, so she had to dive out of the way to avoid getting sliced in two by its descent. The more frustrated she became, the worse her throws (or kicks; she couldn't decide)—until at last, with a short scream of rage, she snatched up the knife with her hand and hurled it straight into the very center of the wheel, and then, for good measure, threw another three knives after it, *thwack*, and *thwack*, and *thwack*, so that the four blades aligned in the approximation of a deeply scowling mouth.

Hearing a step behind her, she whirled around, gripping the last of her knives in one raised hand.

"Don't shoot!" cried a pale, skinny man standing in the door to the Odditorium, holding up both hands.

"Who are you?" Max demanded, keeping her knife raised and hoping that in the dim light the man didn't notice her furious blushing. She wished she hadn't taken off her shoes. It seemed somehow to place her at a disadvantage. "What do you want? How long have you been standing there? Why are you spying on me?"

"I—I'm not," he said. "I mean, I wasn't. I've got a letter, that's all. For delivery to 344 West Forty-Third Street." He held up an envelope as proof, and at last Max lowered the knife, returned it to her pocket, and

73 ☛

jumped lightly off the stage.

The man took a step backward as she approached, and she saw that his face was covered with light stubble. He was wearing old clothes that were patched, sewn, and brushed, treated with care that only the very poor give to their belongings. The man's eyes traveled nervously over the room with its vaulted ceiling, speckled with mold; and the low-hanging banner trumpeting the Freak Show to End All Freak Shows!; and the large props visible on the stage, including the Spinning Pinnacle of Death but also a large coffin that Goldini sawed in half during his act.

"Don't be a baby," she said as she reached for the letter in his hand and he gasped and jerked away. "I'm not going to cut your fingers off."

The man looked unconvinced, but he at last allowed Max to take the letter, immediately backing up several paces, safely out of reach.

Despite all of Monsieur Cabillaud's lessons, Max was not yet a very good reader. She didn't understand why *whole* and *hole* sound the same but could be spelled differently, or how *bill* and *bill* could be spelled the same and mean different things. How come *sign* was pronounced *sine* and yet *signal* wasn't pronounced *sine*-al?

Still, she had no trouble recognizing the names written precisely in black ink on the front of the envelope.

For Thomas, Pippa, Max, and Sam.

Instantly, she got a very cold, very *icky* feeling, as if someone had just dribbled mud down her spine.

"Where did you get this?" she croaked out. But when she looked up, the man was gone. Obviously, believing his duty done, he had fled the museum and its strange inhabitants.

She opened the envelope with shaking fingers. The *ripppp* of the paper seemed very loud in the empty space. But she could barely make out the words on the page in front of her. It was as though, in an instant, she'd forgotten all of Cabillaud's lessons. Her heart was pounding. Words swam around on the page like fish in a pool of white water. She couldn't get her mind to focus long enough to try to tack them down into any order.

One word, and one word only, jumped out at her, clear as a flashlight beam in the middle of the night.

Max was suddenly overly aware of how alone she was, here, in the vast Odditorium, with all its strange shadows. . . .

She hurried out into the lobby, where the large paneled windows at least gave the room a bright, busy look, and nearly collided with Monsieur Cabillaud.

"Watch where you are going!" he huffed out, in a French accent made even more pronounced by his stuffy nose.

Mumbling an apology, she hurried to the performers' staircase and took the stairs two at a time, stopping on every floor to check for Pippa, Thomas, and Sam. She found them in the attic. Sam was still wearing his pajamas, and he blushed a deep scarlet when he saw her, for a reason she couldn't fathom.

"Look," she panted out, shoving the letter at Thomas and nearly tripping over Freckles, who gave a reproachful meow.

Thomas read the letter and his face darkened. Pippa, who was reading without even looking over the page, went white. Sam took the letter from Thomas, holding it carefully between two fingers.

"Out loud," Max said in a strangled voice. She already knew who it was from. She just needed to know what it said.

Sam read, in a trembling voice:

"'Congratulations, children, on another inspiring display of the powers I gave you. I'm so proud. Soon, I hope, you'll be very proud of me.'"

It was signed with a single name; the word that Max had seen and immediately recognized:

—*Rattigan.*

N-U-M-O-N-Y-A.
N-U-M-E-O-H-N-I-A.
K-N-E-U-M-O-N-I-A.

Max gnawed on the end of her pencil. Her brain ached from the effort of thinking. Why did spelling have to be so ridiculously complicated? And why did certain words have to be so much longer than other words? If Max ever became president, she would mandate that no words could be longer than two syllables.

Of course, then she couldn't be president. She'd have to be the *present*. Or the *predent*.

Monsieur Cabillaud thwacked a ruler down on Max's paper. "Eyes on your test," he said with a severe glare. "Five more minutes."

It was no use. She couldn't concentrate. Not after the news she'd seen this morning, about Howie and stupid amazing armless Alicia, and certainly not after the letter they'd received.

Pippa had, predictably, wanted to go to the police. "This proves it," she'd squawked, sounding exactly like Mr. Dumfrey's pet cockatoo, Cornelius. "This *proves* that Rattigan was involved in what happened at the bank. That means he's in New York."

Thomas shook his head. "All it proves is that Rattigan reads the newspaper," he'd said. "Look," he added, when Pippa opened her mouth to protest, "*I* know Rattigan's to blame. *You* know Rattigan's to blame. But that doesn't help us, not as far as the cops are concerned."

Sam was still staring down at the page with an expression of disgust, as though the paper was covered not with words but crawling insects. "What about the last bit," he said, "the part about making us proud? What's that supposed to mean?"

Thomas's face was grim. "It means he has something planned," he said. "Something big."

"Three minutes," Monsieur Cabillaud announced, and then sneezed loudly.

Max sighed and gave it one last shot. P–N–E–U–

M-O-N-I-A. She shook her head. Now that *definitely* wasn't right. But before she could erase it, someone began to scream—a high, anguished wailing that rattled up through the floorboards and made Max's teeth hurt.

Monsieur Cabillaud leaped up from the edge of his desk, where he had been perched. "Stay here, children. Keep your eyes on your—*oof*." He didn't finish his sentence. Already, Max had barreled by him, practically knocking him off his feet as she sprang toward the spiral staircase. Pippa and Sam followed quickly after her.

Monsieur Cabillaud fumbled to restore his glasses to his small, sloped nose. "As your tutor, I *demand* zat you all get back here *zees instant*!" he screeched.

But it was too late.

He was speaking to an empty classroom.

From various corners, closets, and rooms, the residents of the museum materialized, pouring down the stairs toward the source of the sound like bits of paper swirling down a giant drain. Lash appeared with a lasso looped over one shoulder. Betty came out from the bathroom with her beard wet and set into pink rollers. Caroline and Quinn, who had been squabbling over a particularly pretty spangled dress, came down the stairs with the item in question still gripped between them.

Max nearly collided with Mr. Dumfrey as he emerged from his office wearing red-toed slippers and an expression of deep irritation. From the faint lines crisscrossing his face and the large ink stain marking his chin, she judged that he had once again fallen asleep on his desk while attempting to sort out the monthly financial reports.

"What in Houdini's name is that awful racket?" he said as first Max, then Sam, then Pippa, then Lash, then the twins, bounded by him.

"Sounds like a prairie dog choking on a prickly pear," Lash shouted back, and Mr. Dumfrey, joining the back of the line, allowed himself to be swept up by the current of motion and carried downstairs toward the lobby.

On the second floor, Miss Fitch, with a thimble on her thumb and several pins in her mouth, emerged from the costume department, neatly dodging a wax replica of the Tree of Knowledge, behind which the door to her quarters was concealed. She was followed by a shirtless Danny, who was being fitted for a new tuxedo to use in the ballroom dancing act.

In the lobby, they found Smalls and Gil Kestrel

already gathered. Thomas had taken his usual shortcut through the walls, and was just brushing a fine layer of dust from his clothing.

General Farnum was on his knees in front of his flea circus, both hands pressed to the glass, leaving smudgy fingerprints. His face was contorted with grief.

Mr. Dumfrey shoved through the crowd. "General!" he cried. "What's gotten into you? What's the matter?" Dumfrey had very little tolerance for dramatics, unless he was the one performing. "Speak, for God's sake."

For a moment, General Farnum's mouth worked up and down, as if he were trying to chew through an invisible bit.

"Go on, General," Lash said, giving him a nudge.

With a deep, shuddering sigh, Farnum finally managed to speak.

"Dead!" he choked out. "All of them—*dead!*"

For the first time, Max noticed that the glass terrarium, usually full of zipping dark shapes, was perfectly still. Peering closely, she saw hundreds of miniature specks freckled across the sand: dead fleas, small as the point of a pencil, piled on the floor of the circus.

Betty gasped. Smalls put a massive arm around her and hung his head.

"Good night, sweet fleas, and may flights of angels

81 ☞

sing thee to thy rest," he said solemnly, wiping a tear from one eye.

"Maybe they're only napping," Caroline suggested.

"Don't be an idiot, Caroline," said Quinn. "Of course they aren't napping." She turned to General Farnum and laid a hand consolingly on his shoulder. "Maybe they've just come down with a bad cold."

Mr. Dumfrey bent forward to more closely examine the fallen insects. "This is *very* unfortunate. And the circus was doing so well . . ." He shook his head and then brightened. "Good thing about the Firebird. With just a little training, it'll be shipshape for the show."

General Farnum seemed not to hear. "All those years of training . . . Handpicked them myself, from Tennessee to Tallahassee and all the way to Tahoe. I'll never find a better group of fleas, *never*."

"Hmmm." Lash removed the top of the terrarium, scooped up a handful of the dead fleas, and began to prod them with a finger. "Nope," he said, depositing the fleas back into their tank. "Nothing doing. Dead as a doornail, each and every one of them."

"It was an ambush." The general sounded as if he were choking on a large and very dry baked potato. "A cowardly sneak attack." Then, in an instant, his face transformed. Gone was the grief, replaced by an expression of such utter rage that Max felt almost frightened. He rocketed to his feet and spun around, pointing a knobby finger at Danny.

"It was you," he spat out. "You killed them, didn't you? To punish me."

"Get your sausage out of my face," Danny said, swatting at Farnum's finger. "And stop talking nonsense."

"You practically admitted it yesterday," General Farnum thundered. "You said you wanted them dead!"

Danny puffed himself up to his full three foot seven. "You better shut your mouth, Farnum, before I shut it for you."

"Oh, yes? You think I'm afraid of you, you murderous sad sack—?"

"That's it, you blundering bag of—"

"Erskine's Exterminators," Thomas said loudly. Max saw he was reading from a business card and remembered that she, too, had received one.

General Farnum and Danny both turned to stare at him.

"What did you say?" General Farnum said.

"Ernie Erskine's Exterminators," Thomas repeated, and then read from the additional message printed on the back: "'New York's Number One Flea Exterminator. You Got 'Em, We Gas 'Em.'"

83

"I told you I had nothing to do with it," Danny grumbled.

Mr. Dumfrey cleared his throat. "Would someone kindly explain to me," he said, blinking, "what you are all babbling on about? What exterminators? Who's Irksome?"

"Erskine," Thomas corrected, and explained how the exterminator had visited the museum the day before, distributing business cards and trying to convince the crowd that the fleas would infest their clothing.

General Farnum squeezed his hands into fists. "That coward," he muttered. "That *criminal*. I'll make him pay for this."

"It might have been an accident," Thomas said. "Some of those chemicals can kill a rat from a distance of a hundred feet. If he touched the glass, even for a minute—"

"No such thing as accidents, sonny," the general cut in, before Thomas could finish, "not when it comes to war."

And before anyone could stop him, he pivoted on his heel and, whacking the floor so hard with his cane even the walls shuddered, stormed out the door.

8

There was a momentary pause.

"Cowards die a thousand deaths," Smalls quoted somberly, removing his hat and placing it to his heart. "The valiant taste of death but once."

"Oh, will you just shut up?" Quinn burst out. "For goodness' sake. They're just *fleas*."

Max had turned to the windows to watch General Farnum stomping angrily down the street, his coat flapping behind him, like the leathery wings of a bat in flight. "Don't tell Farnum that," she said.

While the other residents of the museum dispersed, Sam volunteered to help Kestrel relocate the flea circus, since it now provided an unsavory picture to anyone who might choose to enter the lobby: all those pathetic little black dots strewn motionless across the sand, in front of miniature balance beams and saw-horses.

"One, two, three, *heave*," Kestrel instructed. But no sooner had Sam laid a hand on the glass than a pane cracked under the pressure of his fingers. He drew back quickly, horrified, as a spiderweb of fissures appeared across the glass.

"Sorry," he said, blushing so hard he could feel it all the way to the very tips of the pimples on his fore-head. "I'm—clumsy—I didn't mean to—" He still didn't know whether Gil Kestrel, the newest addition to the museum, understood what made Sam, Pippa, Thomas, and Max so different.

Who had made them so different.

"S'all right," Kestrel grunted, as if he hadn't noticed. "Move aside. I'll get it myself."

When Kestrel braced to get a firmer grip on the large glass terrarium, a rolled-up magazine fell from his back pocket. Eager to help, Sam bent to retrieve it. *Modern Aeronautics* was written in large font across the cover, and, in slightly smaller type: *The Joy and Beauty of Flying*.

"Wow." Sam squinted at the cover photograph, which

86 ☞

featured a man, arms wide, standing on the wing of a small aircraft in flight. "Funny he doesn't get blown clear off the—"

"Gimme that." Kestrel snatched the magazine back from Sam with such force that Sam took a startled step backward. "Keep your eyes where they belong and mind your own business."

With a final glare, Kestrel turned, heaved the glass terrarium into his arms, and teetered off into the darkness of the galleries, leaving a bewildered Sam staring after him. Sam was positive that Kestrel was upset because Sam had seen the magazine. But what was so embarrassing about an interest in airplanes? A few years ago, Thomas had gone through a flight phase. Read about a hundred and fifty books about the physics of flying and went around annoying everyone using words like *propulsion* and *aerodynamic.*

"Don't worry about him, Sam-O."

Sam jumped when Lash laid a weathered hand on his shoulder. When he turned, he saw that Lash's face was grim.

Lash shook his head. "That man's got blood in his veins sour as a lemon and cold as a Rocky Mountain snowdrift."

"What's the matter with him, anyway?" Sam said.

"What's he so upset about?"

Lash sighed. He shoved his cowboy hat back on his head, revealing a long red forehead, grown even longer as his fine blond hair had begun to retreat. "I've known Kestrel a long time," he said, and then stopped, chewing on his lower lip.

Sam was now desperately curious. Lash was many things—but he was never, ever at a loss for words. In fact, it was nearly always impossible to get him to *stop* talking. Even after all the other residents of the museum had gone to bed, Lash was often still chuckling over some past performance or hilarious incident featuring people no one else knew: Sally the human seal, who preferred to eat raw fish and could balance a beach ball on her nose; Jolly Jimbo McCrae, the Minnesota fat man, who consumed 14,000 calories a day to maintain his physique and had to be moved from place to place in a specially designed wheelbarrow; Droopy Dan, the clown who never smiled, and dozens more.

"And?" Sam prompted. "You've known Kestrel a long time *and*?"

"Well, I guess there ain't no harm in telling. Kestrel and me used to work the same circuit, along with Mr. D," Lash began. Sam wondered again what Mr. Dumfrey's act could possibly have been. But now wasn't the time to press for information. "Me and ol' Kestrel were friends, you would say. Good friends."

Sam held his breath. There was something so strange about the way Lash was speaking, about the way he looked—lips tight, face drained of all color, eyes focused on somewhere in the far distance. Sam was gripped by a sudden sense of cold, as if a winter wind had sprung up from nowhere. "So what happened?" he asked.

Lash started slightly, as if he'd forgotten Sam was in the room. "Kestrel was a pilot," Lash said. "Best stunt pilot there was."

So that explained the magazine Kestrel had been reading: Kestrel must miss flying. Sam wondered how Kestrel had ended up here, sweeping up candy wrappers and popcorn kernels, plucking chewing gum from beneath the seats of the Odditorium. He stayed quiet, waiting for Lash to go on.

"We were working the traveling route then. Carny style, set up just south of Indianapolis for a week and a half. One of the tightrope walkers was a girl named Claudette." His voice caught and he cleared his throat. "Prettiest girl south, east, or north of the Mississippi, with a heart of solid gold. She wanted to go up in Kestrel's plane. Wouldn't quit bugging him about it, morning,

89

noon, and night. Finally he said okay." A muscle worked in Lash's jaw, like a miniature heartbeat. In and out. "I'll never forget that day. May twenty-second, bright as bluebells, all clear sky. The kind of day that makes you think nothing bad could ever happen."

Once again, Lash paused. Sam's heart had begun to speed up. He could hardly control his impatience. "So what *did* happen?"

"He took her up, all right. Higher and higher, until the plane was just a little white bird in the sky." Lash's voice had grown very quiet. "Then he started pulling his usual tricks. We were all watching, you know. Free show, and wasn't anybody in the circus who didn't like to watch Gil Kestrel fly. Only . . . only . . ." Once again, his voice broke.

"What?" Sam said.

Lash's face was the color of curdled milk. "Only it turned out poor Claudette wasn't strapped in right," he said. "When Kestrel went into an upside-downer . . ."

Sam's breath got tangled up somewhere behind his tonsils. He could picture it so vividly: the shrill cry of terror, the small dark figure of a girl tumbling through the sky.

Before speaking again, Lash fished a dented silver flask from his front pocket and took a long swig. He drew the back of his hand across his mouth to wipe it. "After that," he said, "Kestrel swore off flying forever."

Now Sam wished he hadn't judged Kestrel so harshly. He tried to imagine what he would do if anything ever happened to Max. But even thinking about it made a space the size of a bowling ball open up inside his chest. And Max barely even spoke to him, except to snap at him for breaking things. "I don't blame him," he said heatedly. "It must be awful, losing your girlfriend like that."

For the first time since starting in on his story, Lash looked at Sam. His eyes were bloodshot, as if he'd gone days without sleeping. "Claudette wasn't Kestrel's girlfriend," he said quietly. "She was mine."

"Can anyone tell me," Thomas said, tugging at his collar, "why funeral clothes have to be so uncomfortable?"

It was the following day, and the residents of Mr. Dumfrey's museum were gathered in the courtyard, dressed in their Sunday clothes despite it being only Tuesday, to mourn the loss of General Farnum's extraordinary and internationally famous fleas.

Sam scanned the assembled crowd. "Max hasn't come back yet," he whispered.

"Shhhh." General Farnum, looking extremely regal in a high-collared military jacket with polished brass buttons, hushed them loudly. He was standing next to Smalls—who was similarly dressed in an ill-fitting black suit—in front of a small hole that had been dug between two paving stones in the courtyard behind the museum, a few feet away from the garbage cans. Mr. Dumfrey, sweating in the afternoon sun, was busy lining the small hole with silk flower petals taken from Goldini's trick bouquet.

"You don't think she got into trouble, do you?" Sam lowered his voice even further.

Thomas shook his head. "Max knows how to take care of herself."

"I said quiet," General Farnum said gruffly. But Sam thought he detected a tremor in the general's voice.

At that moment, the door to the kitchen swung open and Max slipped out into the courtyard. She'd left the museum soon after breakfast to try to find out whether anyone among her vast acquaintances of street urchins and message boys knew the person who had delivered Rattigan's note to them. If they could find Rattigan's delivery boy, they might be able to find Rattigan.

But as soon as Sam saw Max's face, he knew she'd failed.

"No luck?" he whispered as she took a place between him and Thomas. She shook her head.

"All right." Mr. Dumfrey straightened up, mopping

his face with a handkerchief. "We're ready to begin." He raised his voice. "Bring out the deceased."

Nothing happened. Miss Fitch—who hadn't bothered to change, since she nearly always looked as if she was going to a funeral—rolled her eyes heavenward. Goldini, shifting in his patent leather shoes, leaned his head toward Mr. Dumfrey and murmured something too low for Sam to hear.

"Bring out the deceased," Mr. Dumfrey said, a little louder.

Behind Sam, the door to the kitchen swung open a crack. Lash poked his head out. "What's all this yim-yammin' about a disease?"

"The bodies," Sam whispered. General Farnum, though doing his best to conceal it, looked absolutely swollen with grief. Even his mustache was droopier than usual. "Bring out the bodies."

"Gotcha." Lash disappeared again.

There were the faint sounds of scuffling from behind the door, followed by a few tentative bleats of a bagpipe. Suddenly the door burst open as the music swelled and became a rhythmic, up-tempo march. Danny came first, face red, his cheeks puffed out around the bagpipe, having set aside his deep dislike of General Farnum just to have an excuse to play his beloved instrument—though Sam couldn't help but feel that his choice of song, "When Irish Eyes Are Smiling," might be inappropriate under the circumstances.

Caroline and Quinn came next, heads bowed, looking quite striking in their identical dark dresses, their skin nearly translucent in the sun, their long white hair threaded with flowers, elbowing each other only occasionally.

Last came Lash. He had removed his ten-gallon hat for the occasion and was wearing, in addition to the beat-up blue jeans and checkered shirt he was very rarely without, a very ill-fitting jacket he must have gotten from the costume department, with tasseled shoulder pads and elbow patches. On his upturned palm he carried a small kitchen matchbox, into which Farnum had previously siphoned all of the bodies of his beloved fleas.

The procession flowed around the miniature grave and quickly filled the courtyard. Sam was forced backward to accommodate the group and wound up placing his foot in a very squishy, pulpy, smelly pile of trash that had somehow gravitated out of the garbage can—a substance, from the looks of it, that might have been either a disintegrating sock or the remains of Goldini's cooking from the night before. On the street level, a couple strolling hand in hand paused to gape.

Danny finished the song, extending the last note so it trembled prettily in the air. In the resulting silence, Caroline let out a dramatic sniffle and touched her face with a handkerchief. Quinn rolled her eyes.

Smalls cleared his throat. "Dearly beloved," he began. "We are gathered here today to pay our respects to the great, the incomparable, the *extraordinary* fleas of General Archibald Farnum's World-Famous Flea Circus. They were friends—"

"They were *fleas*," Quinn muttered. General Farnum glared at her.

"—and, though their time was cut tragically short, our memory of them will be long. In the words of the poet, 'Death be not proud of thyself for killing these fleas—'"

"Yes, yes," Mr. Dumfrey said hastily, before Smalls could really get going. "Very good. *Very* moving. Lash, would you be so kind?"

Lash stepped forward, his face composed in an expression of great solemnity, holding the matchbox. Sam couldn't help but look to Kestrel, who was standing as far from the group as possible, arms crossed, hat pulled low so that his face was in shadow.

What would it be like, Sam wondered, to be

responsible for killing someone else, even—or especially—if you didn't mean to? How were people like Professor Rattigan able to sleep, eat, shave, stroll with the sun on their faces, wiggle their toes in the morning, and watch baseball, knowing all of the pain and suffering they had caused? Sam's earliest memory was of seeing his mother and father, open-eyed and staring, their arms curled around each other as if they'd died in an embrace. Rattigan believed he'd had a good reason to kill them, just as he thought he could end war by creating the most powerful army on earth. All the people he murdered and crimes he committed, he said, were for a greater good.

Despite the fact that the September air was surprisingly warm and he was wearing an old magician's suit, complete with tails, mandated by Miss Fitch, Sam shivered.

Would it be possible that they might someday have to kill Rattigan in order to stop him? Would Sam, too, become a murderer?

That was the problem with violence. Despite what Rattigan believed, it couldn't simply be stamped out. It was a bacteria, a disease. It spread on contact.

Lash kneeled, wincing a little, and deposited the small matchbox in its grave. Caroline let out a little sniffle. The couple had moved on down the street, and for a moment, Sam felt as if he were standing inside a lightbulb, held in a fragile glass container, in the light, with all the people he loved, in the only home he'd ever known.

"Good-bye, good soldiers," General Farnum said, his voice thick with feeling. "You were brave. You were honorable. You—"

"*There* they are."

A voice from the street made everyone turn. Just like that, Sam's sense of peace and calm shattered. Max emitted a noise that could only be described as a growl.

Police officers Schroeder and Gilhooley were standing on the street above the sunken courtyard. Sergeant Schroeder, stuffed into his uniform like a turkey straining within a sock, was staring down at them with a gloating expression, as if he'd caught them in the middle of a crime. Officer Gilhooley, as always, looked as if a hard wind might suddenly blow him elsewhere— looked, in fact, as if he wished that it would.

"Ah, our old friends," Mr. Dumfrey said, imbuing the words with a tone of great sarcasm. "To what do we owe the pleasure?"

"Save it, Dunley," Schroeder said. He came plodding down the steps, huffing, holding up his badge as if it were a talisman that might keep him protected from great evil. "Move aside, please, move aside. Is there an Archibald Farnum here?"

"I'm General Farnum," General Farnum said, drawing himself up. "What's this about?"

Schroeder drew his lips back over his teeth. It was a horrible smile—like the smile of a shark just before it eats you. "Turn around, please, and hands behind your back."

There was an immediate outcry. Everyone began to shout.

"What's the meaning of this?" General Farnum spluttered, even as Schroeder knocked the cane from Farnum's hands and spun him around. In one fluid motion, he unclipped a pair of handcuffs from his belt. "You can't be serious."

"Lay off of him!" Max shouted.

"He didn't do anything," Pippa cried.

Schroeder ignored them. He was obviously enjoying himself. "Archibald Farnum," Schroeder announced, speaking loudly so that he could be heard over the din. "You're under arrest"—here there was a collective intake of breath, and just for a second, it got very still, and very silent—"for the murder of Ernie Erskine."

10

There was a new explosion of shouting and protestation. Speaking over the din, Schroeder continued: "You have the right to remain silent . . ."

"Remain silent!" General Farnum burst out. "I will *not* remain silent, sonny. You're talking to a decorated war veteran, do you know that? It's an outrage!"

"Mistake," Betty said softly. "There must be a mistake."

Schroeder went on, undeterred: "Anything you say may be used against you in a court of law. You have the right to an attorney. Should you be unable to afford one—"

At the mention of money, Cabillaud paled and made the sign of the cross.

"—one can and will be provided for you."

Thomas watched it all with a growing sense of nausea. He felt as he sometimes did when he turned a corner in the city and could suddenly, miraculously predict what he would see, as though it had all happened to him before: a woman in a red coat walking a three-legged dog, a blind beggar with a tin cup and a cardboard sign pinned to his coat. Déjà vu—that's what it was called.

But this déjà vu was all too real. Instantly, he was transported back to the spring, when Gilhooley and Schroeder had stormed the museum with handcuffs and accusations. That time, it was Mr. Dumfrey who had been arrested on suspicion of murder.

And Thomas knew in that moment that it wouldn't end. They would always be harassed, accused, mistreated. The police would find any excuse to make their lives difficult, Hardaway and his group of mindless, suited-up zombies especially. Hardaway was furious at them for being different: he wanted them to pay.

"Gentlemen, gentlemen," Mr. Dumfrey spoke up. "Let's not rush to any hasty conclusions. General Farnum is an upstanding citizen and, as he mentioned to you, a veteran of the Spanish-American War, in which he served with great bravery and gumption."

"Look at the man," Danny said. When he was angry his Irish accent became more pronounced. "He's ancient! He's older than a tree stump and twice as useless. Takes him twenty minutes just to get on and off the kettle in the morning, if you catch my drift. He *couldn't* have killed anyone."

"Thank you, Daniel," General Farnum said stiffly.

"Nice try," Schroeder practically snarled. His eyes glinted. He had been trying to pin a bad reputation on the museum for months. This was obviously his big chance. "But we got eyewitnesses who say this creep"—he shoved General Farnum roughly toward the stairs—"was the last person going into Erskine's place."

"Witnesses?" Mr. Dumfrey huffed a laugh. "Louts! Liars! Lowly libelous frauds! We'll have them brought up on charges! You should be arresting these so-called witnesses, not interrupting flea funerals—"

Gilhooley worked a long, skinny finger in his long, skinny ear and spoke for the first time. "Could you speak up, sir? I—I thought I just heard you say flea funeral."

Mr. Dumfrey, who had never once turned down the occasion to give a monologue, barreled on, "—and beating down doors to harass perfectly innocent—"

"Wait," General Farnum said, and Mr. Dumfrey abruptly shut up. It was something about the tone of Farnum's voice. He appeared, far from hysterical, perfectly calm. But that was the terrible thing; he was like a man who, having driven off a cliff edge, relaxes on the plunge toward the rocks. "Wait," he repeated. Even Schroeder released his grip on Farnum slightly, so he could at least straighten up, though he winced in his handcuffs as if they hurt. "Your witnesses weren't lying. I *did* go to see that crook Erskine. I was worked up."

"That's enough, Farnum," Danny growled. "Keep your mouth shut if you know what's good for you."

"That's right." Kestrel spoke up for the first time. His arms remained crossed. He was leaning against the kitchen door, his eyes still shaded by his hat. "These half-wits got nothing on you."

At the same time, Lash said, "These numbskulls couldn't pin a tail on a donkey." For a second, the two men looked at each other, as if acknowledging the similarity of their thinking. Then they both looked away.

"I've got nothing to hide," General Farnum insisted. He directed his words over his shoulder, toward the still-scowling Schroeder. "I did go and see Erskine, like I said. I was mad as a horned devil. But"—this as the babble of voices rose up again—"I never meant to hurt him. I only wanted to have a word about the fleas."

Gilhooley scrubbed at his ear more vigorously. "Sorry," he said, in response to Schroeder's glare. "I keep thinking I hear the word *fleas*."

"There are fleas and there are *fleas*, Sergeant," General Farnum continued. "And my fleas were the special kind. I wanted him to 'fess up to what he'd done—a dastardly ambush when my boys were outflanked, outclassed, and outmaneuvered."

There was a long pause. Schroeder stared at Farnum. Finally, Betty cleared her throat.

"He'd poisoned all the fleas," she explained.

"Aha!" Schroeder cried. "I knew it. A motive!" and he seized Farnum by the wrists.

"No!" General Farnum protested, even as Schroeder propelled him up the stairs and to the street. "I swear on my stars, I never laid a hand on him! He was breathing when I left the building!"

"Save it for the judge, Farnum," Schroeder said, even as they disappeared from view.

Gilhooley hesitated for just a second longer. He removed his hat from his head and pressed it to his chest. Even his hair, Thomas noticed, was long and lanky, like noodles plastered to his forehead.

"I'm, er, very sorry for your loss," he said, and then, replacing his hat, scurried after his colleague.

For a long minute, no one said anything.

"Well." Miss Fitch spoke first. She looked even more unhappy than usual, which—considering the fact that she had once actually modeled for the illustrated dictionary under the word *displeasure*—was saying a lot. "This is very unfortunate."

"I knew no good could come of those fleas," Danny said, stroking his smooth chin. "But did anyone listen?"

"He won't go to prison, will he?" Goldini asked in a whisper. Goldini had a terrible fear of enclosed spaces ever since he had accidentally locked himself in a trick box for three whole days. They'd eventually been summoned by a furious banging and discovered he'd eaten an entire handkerchief for sustenance. "They won't—lock him in a cell?"

"Now let's not get our lasso in a loop," Lash said decisively. "He'll be out in a jiff, you'll see."

"Will he?" Betty shook her head. Her auburn hair glinted, halolike, in the setting sun. "You heard what Sergeant Schroeder said. He had motive *and* opportunity."

"She's right." That was Kestrel, speaking up from

his position by the door. "How do we know he *didn't* do it, after all?"

"Now hold on." Lash pointed a finger at Kestrel. In an instant, his face had darkened with fury. "General Farnum may be a lot of things, but one thing he's not is any kind of murderer. Unlike *some* people I know."

Although the sun was still shining, it was as though an enormous cloud had swept in overhead. Thomas half expected a clap of thunder to erupt over their heads, for sheets of rain to materialize from the blue sky.

Though Kestrel and Lash had finally quit glaring at each other, the sensation of cold discomfort stayed with Thomas. "It doesn't matter whether General Farnum did it or not," he said. "The police will do everything they can to pin it on him."

"Enough." Mr. Dumfrey held up a plump hand. "Enough," he repeated, staring hard at Thomas when he began to protest. "The best offense is a good defense, as they say. I'll just ring up my lawyer, Bill Barrister, and have him scoot down to the station—"

"I don't think he'll be of very much help in this instance," Miss Fitch said. "Mr. Barrister died last January."

"Dead," Mr. Dumfrey repeated, stroking his chin.

"No wonder he never answered my Christmas card. Is it too late to send flowers, do you think?"

Miss Fitch inclined her head as if to say yes, it very much was too late.

Mr. Dumfrey exhaled loudly. "Well, no matter." He squared his shoulders. "We'll just have to find a new lawyer."

"And pay him with what?" Monsieur Cabillaud huffed. "We can barely keep ze lights on!"

"I know a lawyer," Betty said. "She's very good. Remember the Romberger case? That German butcher shop owner, accused of bludgeoning his brother-in-law to death with a meat mallet? Everyone was convinced he was guilty until she proved it was the victim's wife using a frozen leg of lamb."

"*She?*" Mr. Dumfrey's face darkened. "Wait a second. You're not talking about—"

"ROSIE BICKERS!" Quinn and Caroline chorused together. "She'll be perfect," Quinn added.

"She'll be brilliant," Caroline chimed in.

"She'll say yes," Betty said gently.

"Absolutely not," Mr. Dumfrey said firmly. "I refuse to go to that wretched woman. Do you know she once served me with a warrant? Andrea von Stikk tried to have me brought before the courts on a health department violation!"

"Oh, right," Pippa said, making a face. "The Incident of the Three-Legged Chicken."

"That stew was perfectly fine," Dumfrey said irritably. "You're still standing, aren't you?"

"Come on, Mr. Dumfrey," Pippa said. "Think of poor General Farnum."

Mr. Dumfrey only scowled.

"Think of the fleas," Sam added.

Mr. Dumfrey scowled deeper.

"It'll be free publicity for the museum," Betty pointed out. "Everyone loves reading about Rosie."

The words *free publicity* acted on Mr. Dumfrey like a jumper cable to a lifeless battery. Instantly, his posture changed. He straightened his shoulders. He neatened his bow tie, which had begun to gravitate left. He cleared his throat.

"Well," he said, with great dignity, "I suppose for the sake of our friend General Farnum, I can afford to let bygones be bygones. It's settled, then. Rosie Bickers it is, first thing tomorrow!"

11

Rosie Bickers's office was almost directly across town, on a bustling portion of Lexington Avenue just north of the Chrysler Building. Pippa, Max, Thomas, and Sam quickly volunteered to go with Mr. Dumfrey, and Max was relieved when he agreed.

They passed through Times Square, which even in early morning was flooded with tourists. Enormous billboards boasting *Broadway's Best Musical!* and *America's Brightest Stars!* loomed high overhead, eclipsing the sun and casting the streets in shadow, so Max felt almost like a bit of debris floating on a canyon river, tugged along by the current of the crowd. She was comfortable in the buzzing streets, happy to observe without being observed, as she had learned to do during her years on the streets.

Occasionally, she saw something that brought her back to those times: a familiar corner where she had occasionally swiped some oranges from a fruit seller; a beat cop who'd once chased her off the steps of a church; a palatial movie theater where she had occasionally stolen in to watch films for free and sneak bites of popcorn from the theatergoers sitting next to her.

Every so often she missed the freedom that came from belonging to no one—from *being* no one. But for the most part, her life on the streets already seemed vastly distant, as if it had happened to someone else. Mr. Dumfrey, the museum, Thomas and Sam and even Pippa—she belonged to them now and they belonged to her, and she wouldn't have had it any other way.

"We'll have to be sharp around Rosie," Mr. Dumfrey said as they neared Fifth Avenue. "Made a name for herself as the best criminal defense lawyer this side of the Atlantic. Do you remember the Case of the Stinking Mackerel? No? Hmmm. You were too young, I suppose." Mr. Dumfrey sighed. "I was a fan of Rosie's, one of her first admirers—that is, until she threw in with Andrea von Stikk and tried to get me brought up on charges. Ah, here we are, 551 Lexington Avenue."

Max was immediately disappointed. She'd imagined that the best criminal defense lawyer in New York City would have offices that reflected her reputation, in a gleaming skyscraper with marble floors and bodyguards flanking the entryway.

This was a dreary five-story building, its shabby exterior stained with soot. The lobby was narrow, dim, and musty-smelling, and a filthy carpet ran toward a single flight of stairs, at the top of which was a glass-paned door marked *Bickers, Attorney at Law*. Max squinted at the words written underneath the company name, puzzling them out slowly.

Criminal Investigations, Domestic Defense, and Private Security.

Then:

Hopeless Cases Welcome.

And finally:

No Solicitation, Suck-ups, or Silliness.

Max had a feeling she might like Rosie Bickers.

"Remember what I said about Rosie," Mr. Dumfrey said in a whisper, touching his nose. "Keep your wits about you."

Before he could knock on the door, however, it flew open, and a man came barreling out, forcing Mr. Dumfrey to take a quick step backward. His face was very red and his jacket was on in reverse, as though he'd been forced to put it on in haste. Even as he started down the stairs, an outraged female voice carried out into the hall.

". . . And for the last time, if I ever see you in these offices again, I'll take your tonsils out through your nostrils! I'll snip your tongue with a pair of gardening shears! I'll wear your eyeballs as earrings! I'll—"

The door swung shut, swallowing the rest of her words. But almost immediately it opened again, revealing a short, squat, coarse-complexioned woman with a knot of frizzy dark hair, wearing a purple suit that made her resemble nothing so much as a very angry eggplant. She stopped abruptly in the midst of her monologue when she saw Mr. Dumfrey standing on the landing.

Instantly, her demeanor changed. She gave Mr. Dumfrey a toothy smile, stepped forward, and began vigorously pumping his hand.

"Ah, what a surprise. The great Mr. Dumfrey," she said. Her accent was wide and flat and recalled the sailors who unloaded cargo at the Fulton Fish Market. This, too, was not what Max had expected. "I see you brought your little wonders with you, too." Her eyes swept appraisingly over the small group. "Come on in, come on in. Sorry about the greeting. I was just having

a friendly little chat with the tax man. Something tells me he won't be bothering me again this year." She let out a husky laugh.

"Miss Bickers," Mr. Dumfrey said primly as she led them into her office—which, though very large, was just as dingy as the lobby had been, and filled everywhere with stacks of paperwork and overflowing files. In one corner, a secretary with the complexion of a dirty mop and blond hair pinned at the nape of her neck was doing her best to disappear into a typewriter. "You're looking well."

She waved a hand. "Save it, Mr. D. Or did you forget I can sniff out a lie like a bird dog on a duck hunt?" She had to shuffle past various file cabinets and an assorted miscellany of bewildering objects—a pair of crutches, an old-fashioned wicker baby carriage, an umbrella stand in the shape of an elephant's foot, a suitcase plastered with stickers from Niagara Falls—just to get to her desk. She didn't sit down, however. She just leaned over her desk to face them.

"So," she said, her eyes gleaming. "What can I do you for?"

Mr. Dumfrey wasted no time. "You perhaps read about the murder of the unfortunate Ernie Erskine in this morning's paper?"

"Hmmm. Was he the one found half-submerged in the East River, or the body chucked into a cement pourer? No—forgive me. He was the exterminator. Strangled in his office."

"Correct," Mr. Dumfrey said. "And unfortunately, our own General Farnum has been accused of doing the strangling."

Rosie whistled and sat down in her chair. "Has he been arrested?" Mr. Dumfrey nodded. "Is there evidence against him?"

This time, Mr. Dumfrey hesitated. "Witnesses," he said finally. "General Farnum went to visit Mr. Erskine and was apparently the last person to see him alive."

"Except for his killer," Max put in. Rosie raised an eyebrow at her, as though surprised that Max could speak.

"Except for his killer," Mr. Dumfrey agreed.

Rosie whistled again.

"But," Mr. Dumfrey hastened to add, "General Farnum couldn't have killed him. Honor and duty. That's what he lives for."

"And fleas," Thomas muttered.

"Mmm." Rosie spread her palms wide. "What else?"

Mr. Dumfrey started. "What do you mean?"

Rosie leaned forward. "Let's be frank with each other, Mr. Dumfrey," she said. "I'm not one of the half-brained gidbits that wander into your museum, gaping and gawping over a fake mermaid or doctored photograph of an English garden gnome."

"All of my natural specimens are one hundred percent authentic," Mr. Dumfrey said stiffly.

Rosie raised her eyebrows but didn't argue with him. "My point is," she said. "We both know you're here for one reason and one reason only. I take the hard-up cases. The hopeless cases, like it says on the door." She leaned back in her chair. "So what else? The cops must have more ammunition than that."

Mr. Dumfrey cleared his throat and tugged on his bow tie. "General Farnum and the dead man had a disagreement earlier that afternoon. The fight was witnessed by a sizable crowd." Mr. Dumfrey looked deeply uncomfortable. Max didn't blame him. Hearing the evidence out loud made General Farnum's position seem much worse. "General Farnum was in an extreme state of emotional distress. He stomped off, swearing revenge."

This time, Rosie didn't whistle. She sat in moody silence, spinning a fountain pen on her desk. Finally, she roused herself. "I'll take the case," she said. Even as Mr. Dumfrey rushed to thank her, however, she cut him off. "But I'm warning you, I'm not a miracle worker. The truth is the truth. Not my fault if you don't like it. But I'll poke around a bit, see what I find out."

"We can help you," Max said. "We could scout for you."

Rosie smirked at her. "Thanks for the offer, sweetheart," she said. "But I've got it covered."

Max felt her face blush a deep red and decided she didn't like Rosie at all.

Rosie stood up, signaling that the meeting was over. "You can find your way out, can't you? Watch out for the boxes—had a client in here the other week tripped and went headlong down the stairs. We're suing the box manufacturer. Hazardous, if you ask me." She plastered on her toothy grin again and began pumping Mr. Dumfrey's hand, even as she led him toward the door.

"We haven't—erm—discussed the issue of payment," Mr. Dumfey said. "I'm afraid that at this very moment, the museum is in just a bit of a tight spot."

Rosie waved a hand. "Consider it a favor. It's the least I can do for an old friend, isn't that right?" She clapped Mr. Dumfrey so hard on the back he stumbled. "Besides, this kind of case makes publicity you can't buy for the world. No, no. This one's on me. Don't you

117 ☞

think another word about payment."

"Wonderful woman," Mr. Dumfrey said, once they were back on the street, blinking in the sunshine.

"Harumph," was all Max said.

12

When they returned to the museum, they found the street even noisier than usual. Two enormous moving vans, parked up the block, were obstructing the flow of traffic. Angry truckers, cabbies, and drivers were blowing their horns and shouting curses out the windows of their vehicles, while men in blue overalls unloaded box after box from the vans, ignoring the deafening din.

"Looks like someone's taking over Cupid's Dance Hall," said Thomas.

"Maybe a decent restaurant," Mr. Dumfrey said hopefully. "We could use one around here."

Drawing closer to number 344, they noticed a

woman standing at the entrance. She unfolded a piece of paper from her pocket, squinted at it, and then stared up at the museum's double doors, as if to verify she had the right address.

"Can I help you?" Mr. Dumfrey said. She started and turned to them.

She was, Sam thought, one of the prettiest women he'd ever seen in his life. Some people, Sam knew, thought that Caroline and Quinn were beautiful, and he judged that this woman must be about their age. But whereas Caroline and Quinn had the soft, pale skin of uncooked dumplings—at least in Sam's opinion—this woman had a complexion of fine ivory, with a strong nose and dark, cascading hair, heavy eyebrows, and a mouth that looked as if it had been stained with strawberry juice.

When Max grew up, Sam thought, she would look a little like that. Immediately, he pushed the idea of Max and her lips away, just in case Pippa decided to drop in unexpectedly on his thoughts, an irritating habit she'd recently been cultivating.

"I'm looking for Mr. Dumfrey," she said, and smiled, showing off white teeth that were just a tiny bit uneven.

"And you've found him," Mr. Dumfrey said cheerfully. Ever since Rosie had agreed to work for no pay, he'd been in a remarkably good mood. "To what do I owe the pleasure?"

"I saw an article about the museum in the newspaper," the woman said. She was wearing a camel-colored coat that reached from her chin practically to her ankles. She tugged on the collar, and Sam wondered how she wasn't burning up. "I was hoping you might have an open position."

"And you are . . . ?" Mr. Dumfrey said.

"Emily," she said, smiling again, "Emily Bellish."

"Well, you see, Miss Bellish," Mr. Dumfrey said apologetically. "Just now the museum is experiencing a few *complications* of the financial variety. That is to say, we're in absolutely no position to . . ."

He trailed off as Emily's whole face transformed. Her smile evaporated. She looked suddenly wide-eyed and helpless, like a child lost without parents in a crushing crowd. The effect was so terrible Sam would have rushed to her and given her a hug, had he not 1) been by nature painfully shy and 2) been likely to crush her ribs by doing so.

Mr. Dumfrey coughed, as if choking back the words he'd been about to say. "But there's always room for more talent! Come, come." Mr. Dumfrey gestured her up the steps toward the doors. "Let's go up to my office.

We'll have more privacy there." And they were gone, disappearing together into the museum.

Thomas shook his head. "She must have an act," Thomas said. "I wonder what it is?"

"I don't know," Sam said musingly. "She doesn't look like a freak, that's for sure." He was still struck by the woman's dark eyes and low voice, and by the idea of Max smiling at him like the woman had, all warmth and twinkle. Then he became aware that the real Max was scowling.

"Did you see that coat?" she said. "Maybe she has scales."

"Or maybe she's a human owl, like your old boy-friend, Howie," Sam blurted out, before he could regret it. He was expecting Max to yell at him—she had expressly forbidden any of the others from mentioning Howie's name, on pain of having their tongues plucked out of their heads—but instead she merely narrowed her eyes at him and then turned, flouncing into the museum.

Pippa sighed. "Did you have to go and mention Howie?" she said. "Now she'll be even nastier than usual."

"Just ignore her," Thomas said.

Pippa glared at him. "Easy for you to say. I share a

corner with her. Last time she got in a bad mood about Howie, she used my favorite hat as target practice."

"I don't know why she's so upset," Sam grumbled. "It's been almost two months."

Pippa looked at him pityingly. "You really don't understand anything, do you?" she said. Then she, too, followed Max into the museum.

Thomas shook his head. "Girls," he said, in the tone of someone who knows all about it. "So what do you think? You going in?"

"Nah." Sam stuffed his hands in his pockets—which weren't, technically, pockets, since the lining had long ago given way to the pressure of his fingers. "Don't feel like it yet." In reality, he was already deeply regretting what he'd said to Max. In his most honest moments, Sam admitted to himself that he had a teensy, tiny crush on Max—but he was also terrified of her, and in no mood to be on the receiving end of one of her rages.

"Come with me," Thomas said. "I'm going to run up and say hi to Mr. Sadowski. You remember how he has all those old newspapers?"

Sam nodded. In addition to old newspapers, Sadowski also had old radios, old coffee mugs, old grocery lists, old socks, old photographs, old piles of furniture . . . In fact, there was very little that Sadowski *didn't* have crammed into his apartment.

"*That's* where we have to look for Rattigan," Thomas said firmly. "Years ago, his arrest was big news. What do you want to bet we find names of the people who tried to spring him?"

"Sure." He was more than a little relieved to have an excuse to delay returning to the museum for a bit. And if the last time he'd accompanied Thomas up to Mr. Sadowski's apartments was any indication, they might be busy for hours. Mr. Sadowski had quite a library. The problem was that he could never seem to find it.

As soon as they started down the street, however, Sam saw something that made him stop dead.

That *something* was a hat—a large, feathered hat, worn by a large, elaborately dressed woman standing in front of the moving trucks, giving orders to the men in suspenders. Her face was concealed by the enormous straw brim, and she was too far down the street for Sam to make out what she was saying, but he recognized her fat bejeweled hands and the sharp cadences of her voice, like an enraged canary.

He felt as if all the blood in his body had pooled into his feet. "Is that—?" he gasped out, but found he couldn't say her name. "That can't possibly be . . ."

Thomas had spotted her, too, and he let out a short,

anguished cry. "Von Stikk," he said. "What's she doing here?"

But it was painfully obvious: both Sam and Thomas stood, stricken, as she hefted a wooden crate in her arms and disappeared inside the old Cupid's Dance Hall, followed by several movers, who'd obviously been ordered to work faster. Thomas started across the street immediately and Sam followed after him, feeling queasy, hoping there must be some mistake, some innocent explanation for the trucks and the cartons and Von Stikk's presence on West Forty-Third Street.

There was, however, no mistake. Many of the cartons were labeled with Von Stikk's name. And the old tin sign that used to hang next to the doors of the dance hall, the one that listed various rules, such as no cursing, spitting, or gambling, had been replaced by a sign that said simply, in elegant cursive: *Von Stikk School for Extraordinary Underprivileged Youths.* It seemed she had combined her two latest educational projects.

Andrea von Stikk was moving in.

Eli Sadowski's apartment might have doubled as a museum for all the broken, useless, and bizarre objects, including old costume mannequins and sawhorses, sewing machines and picture frames, cracked mirrors and grandfather clocks missing their hands—much of it stacked in enormous towers that seemed a bare nudge from toppling over. As usual, Eli greeted them with the offer of milk tea, which they quickly and emphatically declined.

"Well, nice to see you, always very nice to see you," he said, but he seemed even more agitated than usual and Sam noticed he had not taken the time to finish dressing. Normally he wore a suit that might have been lifted from the last century, complete with a top hat and even a cravat. "My brother Aaron sends his regards, as usual."

Thomas and Sam avoided looking at each other. Aaron Sadowski had been dead for several weeks, but Eli insisted on consulting him about matters, such as what to serve for tea and whether it was a good time to begin tidying the apartment (the answer was always no).

"You'll forgive me," Eli said, with an aggressive sweep of his hand that threatened to topple an enormous stack of empty milk bottles, "but I have business outside. A terrible thing, really—I would avoid it absolutely if I could—but very urgent. I've just read that an abandoned rocking chair has been sitting for days on Seventy-Second Street. So you see there's not a moment to lose."

Sam couldn't help but note that Sadowski already had several broken rocking chairs wedged beneath broken card tables and armchairs whose stuffing was largely missing. "Do you need another rocking chair?" he couldn't help but ask.

Eli didn't seem to hear. "Shameful, what people waste," he said, putting one foot into a dress shoe and another into a galosh without seeming to notice the difference. "Shameful," he repeated, grabbing what looked like a constable's hat and wedging it down over his head. "In any case, stay as long as you like. You know the way out." And without another word, he hurtled into the hall, slamming the door shut so that all the towers of objects in the apartment gave a faint, ominous shudder. Dust filtered down from the ceiling, and Sam sneezed.

"Well," Thomas said with fake cheer. "Let's get started."

For hours, they worked their way through stacks of mildewing and yellowed newspapers, looking for news stories about Rattigan and clues about the identities of the people who'd helped him after he made his first, infamous break from prison. But it was no use. The newspapers weren't organized by year—they weren't organized at all—and although they found plenty about

Rattigan, it was nothing they didn't already know.

Finally, Thomas stood up. "This is pointless," he said.

Sam agreed only too happily. His knees ached from sitting cross-legged, and his back was sore from bending over decades-old print. Besides, it had started to get dark, and Sadowski's twisted towers of belongings cast heavy shadows over the floor and reminded Sam of warped fingers, reaching for something.

They retraced their path to the door only to find themselves in an unfamiliar room filled almost entirely with birdcages.

"Hmmm." Thomas frowned. "Maybe we should have made a left at the plaster bust of Beethoven?"

They tried again to find the door, only to end up in yet another unfamiliar portion of the vast apartment: a bathroom, the entire tub filled with bottle caps.

"I told you," Sam said, getting frustrated, "to go straight at the stack of old gramophones."

This time, he took the lead. But barreling around the corner, eager to get out of Sadowski's apartment as soon as possible, he let out a shout: a terrible face was staring back at him, an insect's face with a long, deformed snout, its enormous eyes reflecting his look of terror.

Thomas stepped around him, reached up, and unhooked the thing from the coatrack where it had been hanging. When he swung it in Sam's direction, Sam took a step backward.

"What is that thing?" Sam asked. Even though he saw now that it was not, in fact, a gigantic insect, it was as terrifying as ever to him.

"Gas mask," Thomas said quietly. "From the war. They killed thousands of people with gas." He began to move as though to hook the gas mask over his head.

"Don't." Sam reached out a hand to stop him, and Thomas dropped the mask before he could. "Don't." In the quiet sifting of the dust and the darkness settling all around them, it was all too easy to imagine the ghosts of old soldiers passing nearby.

Thomas replaced the mask carefully. Two more right turns, and they saw the door at last. They hurried home in silence, to the warmth and noise and safety of the museum.

13

¿**A**s soon as they revealed that Miss von Stikk's School for Extraordinary Underprivileged Youths had relocated to just down the block, Max let out a screech so loud it stunned the other three into silence.

The Firebird, which had been relocated to the attic to help it "integrate" with the other performers—Mr. Dumfrey was hoping that his investment might at last be persuaded to learn words that weren't insulting— came awake with a squawk. Even Freckles, who had been hungrily eyeing the bird from a distance, darted under Sam's bed.

"*WHAT?*" Max sprang to her feet and began

rummaging through the collection of objects piled around the attic. She opened old steamer trunks and closed them again, cursing. She shoved aside a set of leather-bound books and even overturned a waste-paper basket, which thankfully contained only a single crumpled tissue and a coffee-soaked playing card.

"What on earth are you looking for?" Pippa asked.

"Matches," Max responded, without looking up, as if it was the most reasonable answer in the world. She was on her hands and knees now, feeling beneath the sagging sofa cushions.

"Why? So you can burn the place down?" Sam said it as a joke—but when Max glared at him, he knew she was dead serious.

"Don't be stupid," Pippa said. "It's brick. A fire would never catch."

Max sat back on her heels, seeming to accept the reasonableness of this line of logic. But her face stayed dark and her eyes were flashing like railway signals. *Danger, danger.* "It's all that woman's fault," she practically spat. "Rosie Bickers."

Pippa sighed. "You're just mad that Rosie called you *sweetheart*."

Max whirled on her, and Sam was grateful that, for once, somebody else had been the one to say the exact wrong thing. "I'm *mad*," she said, her voice getting dangerously quiet, "that Rosie was the one to set up Von Stikk in our backyard, and then *forgot* to tell us about it." She shook her head disgustedly. "What do you want to bet that fat hyena will be banging down our doors morning, noon, and night? What do you want to bet she'll be making up stories about us in the papers?"

"Max is right," Pippa said, gnawing on her lower lip. "She'll never leave us in peace."

"We'll never be in peace, *period*." Now Max's voice was rising again, climbing up a scale of rage. "If it's not Von Stikk coming after us, or the papers calling us monsters, it's the police accusing one of us of trying to bump off a stranger and locking up poor General Farnum, when really they should be trying to keep Rattigan from bumping *us* off."

She lingered on the last note, and Sam had a sharp, painful memory of Rattigan's voice, like the whisper of a silk cord around the throat.

In the end, you see, your father was weak . . . far too weak to stop me . . .

He forced aside the memory, but couldn't so easily get rid of the cold feeling that had overtaken him.

Max was right. Even if they miraculously tracked down Rattigan, there would never be a stop to the accusations, the attention, the constant needling feeling of being looked at and judged. They were growing stronger, smarter, more skillful by the day.

But that only meant they were getting further and further from normal.

Everyone settled into a gloomy silence. Thomas sat, frowning deeply, staring glumly at his shoes.

But after a while, he straightened up. "You know, Max," Thomas said slowly. "You're not totally right. There *is* something we can do."

"Do-do!" the Firebird squawked. "That's about all you'll do-do!"

Everyone ignored the bird.

Pippa looked at Thomas. "About Rattigan?"

"I wasn't thinking of Rattigan," Thomas said.

"About Von Stikk?" Despite her turbulent expression, a note of hopefulness crept into Max's voice.

"No, not about her, either." Thomas scrubbed the side of his nose. "I meant that we can help General Farnum."

Sam stared at him. "But the police—"

Pippa immediately made a noise of protest, as if Sam had cursed.

"The police always go for the most obvious solution," Thomas said, shaking his head. "Farnum didn't

133 ☛

kill Ernie Erskine. We're agreed on that, right?"

Everyone nodded.

"But he *did* go see Erskine," Thomas continued. "Which means that the murderer must have seen Erskine after him. Maybe he left some evidence behind."

"Like what?" Max scoffed. "A bloody handprint?"

"Not likely!" the Firebird squawked, ruffling its feathers and giving a convincing impression of laughter. "Not bloody likely!"

"Oh, shut your beak," Pippa said crossly.

Thomas shrugged. "Like *anything*. It's worth a look, isn't it?" No one said anything. "Well, isn't it? Or should we trust Rosie Bickers to do the job?"

"No," Max said emphatically. "No way."

There was another long moment of silence, during which Thomas looked at each of them expectantly. Finally, Pippa sighed. "All right, Tom," she said. "Tell us what you're thinking."

It wasn't difficult to sneak out after dinner. The museum's residents, especially Mr. Dumfrey, had been temporarily distracted by the arrival of Emily. By dinnertime, it became clear what her special feature was.

Every single inch of visible skin—from her anklebones to collarbone, wrist to wrist—was covered in

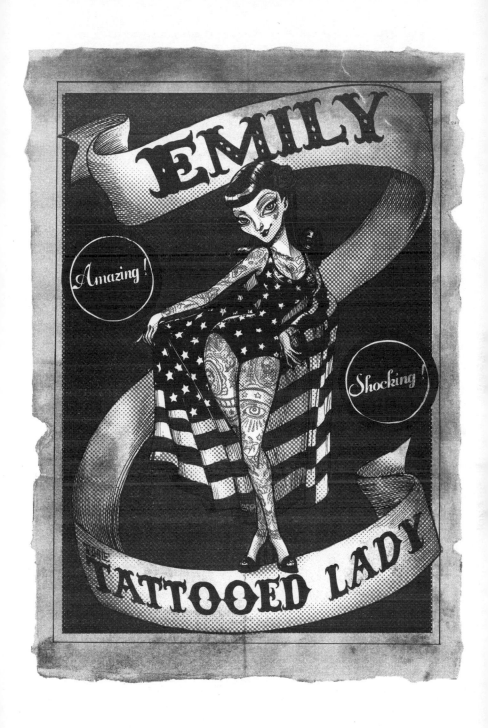

brightly colored tattoos, so that it looked as if a patterned dress had become grafted to her skin.

Sam caught himself staring at her left forearm, where a woman was cupping a hand to her ear, listening to the whisperings of a snake coiled in a tree. The tableau looked surprisingly similar to the Adam and Eve exhibit in the Hall of Wax, behind which the entrance to Miss Fitch's quarters was concealed.

"That's all right," Emily said, before he could look away. "I'm used to people staring. That's kind of the point, isn't it?"

But Sam couldn't look at her for the rest of the meal.

After dinner, while the other residents argued about how the attic should be rearranged to accommodate Emily and whether Smalls really needed *three* beds laid end to end, Sam, Max, Thomas, and Pippa simply slipped out the front door.

The moving vans were gone from the street, and lights burned on all floors of Miss von Stikk's new school. At the old Cupid's Dance Hall, music might have been piping into the streets through the open window, and women might have been trailing in and out through the doors, laughing and tottering on high heels. But now the street was still, the music forever silenced.

Erskine's store was just off the Bowery, a rough portion of New York, home to pawn shops, saloons, and flophouses. The sun was just setting when they emerged from the subway at Second Avenue and made their way toward the address listed on Erskine's card, and Sam felt a hard squeeze of anxiety: big men leered at them from open doorways, and a whisper followed them down the street like the faint hiss of a snake. He didn't want to fight tonight. He didn't *ever* want to fight, really. He didn't want to be here, period—he would much rather have been sprawled out on the bed next to Freckles at the museum, or laying out a game of DeathTrap with Thomas. Unfortunately, it was starting to seem to Sam that the right thing to do was almost always the thing that was least comfortable.

He wondered where Rattigan was tonight.

They paused at the corner of Chrystie and Stanton, from which they had a clear view of the entire street. There was a single policeman watching over Erskine's shop. He looked as sorry to be there as Sam was himself.

"All right," Thomas whispered. "Pippa, you go distract the policeman—"

Pippa snorted. "And how do you expect me to do that?"

Thomas sighed. "I don't know. Pretend to be lost or something."

Pippa scowled at him, and Thomas rolled his eyes.

"Fine," he said. "I'll do it. Sam, you get us in. But try not to break down the door this time, will you?"

He trotted off before Sam could protest and approached the policeman, gesturing wildly and looking much younger and more confused than he had even a second earlier. Sure enough, after a minute the policeman was guiding Thomas in the opposite direction, leaving the entrance to the shop clear.

"Come on," Max said.

They hurried down the street to Erskine's building. Sam took a deep breath, wiping his palms on his blue jeans, and carefully tested the front door. The lock was old, and the wood groaned beneath the pressure of his hand. It would be nothing for Sam to break down the door, but that would bring the police in after them. He tested the doorknob next and was shocked when it snapped off cleanly in his hand.

"Oops," he said.

"What'd you do?" Pippa whispered.

He turned around, holding up the doorknob. "I didn't mean to," he said.

"That's all right. It isn't your fault. And besides,

it worked." She pushed the door open with an elbow, revealing a dark hallway that smelled like paint and chemicals.

They moved into the shop, closing the door behind them and trusting that the police officer wouldn't look too closely at the doorknob when he returned. It was pitch-black. Sam tried to turn around and Max let out a yelp.

"That was my foot," she whispered. He could feel her warm breath on his cheek and he took a step backward.

"That was *my* foot," Pippa said.

"We need a light," Max said.

"Give me a second," Pippa replied, and Sam heard her footsteps move off. He stayed perfectly still, terrified that if he so much as twitched he would stomp on Max's foot again or break something. A moment later, Pippa had located a lamp, and the room was illuminated in a soft white glow. Sam immediately checked the windows. Luckily, the blinds were drawn. Hopefully the light wouldn't attract attention. Just to be safe, however, Pippa unwound her scarf and draped it over the lamp, dimming the light.

Erskine had three rooms on the ground floor: the first, a kind of reception area with a smelly carpet and a cheap laminate desk; the second, what looked to be a storage room full of cartons labeled with chemical names; the third, a small bedroom with a single very small window fitted high up in one wall.

"Check this out," Sam said, pointing to the bed, which was unmade. "Maybe that means his killer surprised him while he was asleep?"

"Maybe," Pippa said. "Or maybe he didn't like to make his bed."

"Shhh." Max hushed them sharply. "Did you hear that?"

"Hear what?" Sam said. She waved a hand, silencing him. And then he did hear it—a series of soft and muffled thuds from somewhere inside the walls, as if a heavy fist were banging, trying to get out. Sam's mouth went very dry.

Pippa screwed up her face in concentration, and Sam knew she must be trying to see, to feel her way in through the plaster. She was getting better. They *all* were, actually. Sometimes, even lying down, Sam could *feel* his strength pulsing through him, shimmering in his blood and even his fingertips.

Pippa's face cleared. "It's only Thomas," she said, and a second later, there was a rattle and a pop, and an air duct came away from the wall, and Thomas emerged, covered in dust.

"Oof." He swung easily and silently to the ground, dropping the last few feet, and then sneezed. "I need to find a better way to travel."

"How'd you get in?" Pippa asked.

"I had to loop around the back so the cop wouldn't spot me," he said, shrugging. "I went through the heating ducts."

Together, they returned to the storage area, which was piled with boxes. Thomas reached inside and extracted a bottle of something called Fleas-B-Gone, giving it a shake. "Empty," he said. He reached for another one. "All of them empty." He spun the bottle around and let out a low whistle. "No wonder this stuff works. The main ingredient's ethyl parathion."

"Ethel who?" Max said.

Thomas looked up. "Ethyl parathion," he said. "It's a kind of poison. Could flatten an elephant with the right dose."

A chill went down Sam's spine. "What about a man?" Sam asked. "Could that whatever it's called kill a man?"

Thomas shrugged. "Definitely, if he inhaled enough of it. During the war it was used as a nerve gas. Reaper gas, it was called."

"But Erskine wasn't poisoned," Pippa reminded them. "He was strangled."

"That's right." Sam frowned, trying to recall what he'd learned from Rosie Bickers. "He was sitting at the desk."

They returned to the office. The desk was piled with invoices, orders, and unopened mail—stacks and stacks of it, over-spilling the drawers and haphazardly tacked beneath makeshift paperweights: horseshoes, bricks, and empty bottles of Fleas-B-Gone.

"What are we supposed to be looking for again?" Max said as Thomas and Pippa began to sift through the accumulation of paperwork in the drawers.

"I don't know," Thomas said. "But we'll know if we find it."

Half the desk was dominated by an ink-stained blotter, which was covered with a miscellany of mail and newspaper cuttings. Sam began sorting through it, but with every second he became increasingly convinced that they were on a hopeless mission. He thought of General Farnum and the way his mustache quivered when he was upset, how soft his voice became as he coached his fleas through their training exercises, the precise way he polished his boots every morning, and felt a sudden panic. He hadn't known General Farnum for long, but already Sam had grown to think of him as a friend. The museum wouldn't be the same without

142

him. Sam wouldn't be the same.

He'd lost so many people already.

He shifted a stack of invoices and saw a letter, half-finished, penned in handwriting he already recognized as Erskine's.

Don't threaten me, were the first words he saw, and his heart jumped into his throat.

Don't threaten me, he read again, and then:

You're nothing but a swindler and the next time I see you I'll be sure and say it to your face. If I don't get either my order or my money back I swear you'll regret it, Benny. He stopped reading. The name *Benny* rang alarm bells deep inside his mind. It was familiar to him. But the connection eluded him, and so he continued: *Enough with your stories and excuses, you'll drive me out of business and over my dead body will you—*

The letter stopped abruptly, as if he'd been interrupted before he could finish it.

Which, Sam thought with a tiny shiver, maybe he had.

"Guys." Sam's voice squeaked. *Over my dead body.* Poor Erskine hadn't realized how literal the words would prove to be. "I think—I think I found it."

"Found what?" Max said.

Sam took a deep breath. "*It*," he said. "The thing we didn't know we were looking for."

14

ϟ**A**fter the letter had passed hands, there was a moment of silence.

"So," Thomas said. "Looks like Erskine had an enemy."

"Benny," Pippa said. "But who's Benny?"

They returned their attention to the desk, this time searching specifically for references to a Benny. They sorted through piles of mail both unopened and opened—it seemed Erskine *was* in danger of going out of business, since he'd received multiple complaints for failing to keep his appointments—and even sifted through the contents of the wastepaper basket, carefully avoiding the crumpled wads of used Kleenex.

Pippa spent a whole ten minutes standing very still, breathing calmly through her mouth, focusing on the name *Benny* and trying to see her way into the desk drawers and file cabinets to find its twin.

But it was useless. Erskine's shop was *too* full, too crammed with papers and files. It was as if someone had upended an enormous library inside of her mind, and she was left feeling confused and overwhelmed, with the beginnings of a headache.

"Nothing," Thomas said disgustedly, after he'd removed the final drawer from Erskine's desk. "Nothing but junk and junk and unpaid bills."

"And more of this stuff," Pippa said, holding up another empty bottle of Fleas-B-Gone.

Suddenly, Sam straightened up, white-faced, as if a phantom hand had passed down his back. "I knew it," he whispered.

"Knew what?" Max had given up the search long ago and was instead trying to pry loose a quarter that had somehow gotten wedged between two floorboards.

Sam reached into his back pocket and withdrew the battered wallet that was a twin of Thomas's. Pippa knew that Siegfried Eckleberger had bought them each a wallet for Christmas the same year Pippa got a small necklace with a four-leaf clover on it, which unfortunately Freckles the cat had consumed not long after his arrival. From his wallet, Sam extracted a small newspaper clipping. Then he looked up, eyes shining.

"I knew I recognized the name," he said. "Benny Mallett, of Chemical Compounds Incorporated. I wrote to him after Freckles wouldn't stop scratching."

Max stood up, dusting off her hands, having apparently abandoned her attempts to retrieve the money. "What are you talking about?" Max said, snatching the clipping from Sam.

Knowing Max would take forever to tease out the words, Pippa closed her eyes and felt her way down through Max's hand and into the grainy paper. It was as easy now as sliding down a banister—it was as if she could send her brain out to grab hold of objects in the real world. She read out loud: "'Cat Can't Stop Scratching? Try Fleas-B-Gone, the Number One Most Effective Flea Killer in the World.'"

There was a cartoon beneath that, of a happy cat giving the thumbs-up, and then beneath that, in smaller letters: "Send all inquiries, orders, and complaints c/o Benny Mallett, Chemical Compounds Inc., 660 Neptune Avenue, Sheepshead Bay, Brooklyn."

"So let me get this straight," Max said. "Erskine was getting his supply from some guy named Benny."

"And then the supply stopped." Thomas rubbed his forehead. "But why would the supply stop?"

"It doesn't make any difference, does it?" Pippa said. "Maybe Benny decided he didn't like Erskine. Or maybe he went into business for himself and decided to cut out the middle man. Either way, Erskine was *mad*. He started threatening Benny Mallett—"

"So Mallett decided to kill him," Tom finished. He was still frowning. "Seems like a pretty weak reason to kill somebody."

"Maybe he didn't do it on purpose," Sam said. "Mallett came to confront Benny, they started arguing—"

"And Mallett accidentally strangled him?" Thomas shook his head. "It doesn't make sense."

"Look, we don't have to prove that Mallett *did* it." Sam's voice was edged with exasperation, and Pippa knew he was eager to leave the room where Erskine had been killed. He kept casting longing glances at the door. "Just that Farnum *didn't* do it. Right?"

"Right." Thomas nodded slowly. "I guess so." But he sounded unconvinced.

"Tomorrow we'll go to Sheepshead Bay and talk to Mallett," Pippa said, taking the lead.

"Where's Sheepshead Bay?" Max asked.

"Near Coney Island," Pippa answered automatically,

and then immediately wished the words back into her mouth. Coney Island was where Howie had gone and joined up with another, rival freak show. She hoped Max wouldn't remember.

But obviously, Max did. She smiled meanly, narrowing her eyes. "Count me in," she said.

15

They had planned to sneak off to Coney Island just after breakfast the following morning and return to the museum by the one o'clock matinee show. But the day was a busy one. First, Monsieur Cabillaud demanded that they spend several hours listening to his lecture about the brilliant and misunderstood Marie Antoinette, and on the damaging effects of too much butter in the diet, which he claimed had been her downfall.

Then, when Mr. Dumfrey, beaming, announced that Miss Bellish, the pretty tattooed woman who'd been standing outside the museum doors the day before, had agreed to join the show at a reduced salary—a blessing, especially since they still couldn't get the Firebird to do anything but insult anybody who came near it—Thomas was charged with making a last-minute trip to the printer's office twenty blocks away to order new brochures advertising *Emily the Tattooed Wonder*. Caroline and Quinn, meanwhile, upon learning that Emily would precede them in the show's lineup, huffily threatened to quit the museum entirely, and both Pippa and Betty had to spend nearly forty-five minutes soothing their egos.

To further add to the mess, Sam couldn't locate a single steel bar he had not already twisted into a balloon-animal shape or a single concrete block he hadn't split by the light application of his pinkie finger, and Max's costume had several rips in the seam where her knives had been improperly stored. All of this meant that by the time the matinee show was due to begin, Thomas, Pippa, Sam, and Max had no time to do anything but throw on their costumes and hurtle onstage.

The performance, however, went smoothly. Nearly every seat in the Odditorium was full, and the crowd burst into appreciative applause after Pippa had an audience member write down the first and last names of her father's parents on a piece of paper and then successfully guessed them, all from a distance of one hundred feet. It was an old standby, and by this time the paper wasn't even necessary. Pippa could have known about Irma and Egbert Ziegenfelder merely by concentrating, allowing her mind to slip like a hand into the mind of the audience volunteer. But she wasn't certain of her abilities yet. The ability to read minds, really read them, was so far unreliable at best. Besides, she wasn't sure she was ready to reveal it.

Max and Thomas were a big hit, too. They'd recently collaborated on an act that involved a hatbox and half a dozen knitting needles sharpened to daggerlike precision. Max, too, had gotten better. Faster, if that were possible, and even more deadly accurate. Sometimes it seemed that when she threw, she wasn't even releasing her knives: they were simply her fingers, extensions of her body.

Even though Pippa had seen them practice the trick before, she still couldn't watch, and she heaved a sigh of relief when it was all over and Thomas emerged, unharmed, holding the hatbox now perforated with a half dozen holes. Sam performed his tearing-a-phonebook-in-half trick with his usual air of gloomy embarrassment, hurrying offstage as quickly as he could manage it despite a standing ovation and various cries of "Bravo!" returning to the wings with his face flaming scarlet and shedding his costume so quickly he ripped his vest clean in two.

"That's the third one this week," he said glumly, eyeing the torn costume.

Lash did his famous bullwhip act, successfully knocking a pen out of the hand of a man in the front row and a lollipop out of the mouth of a child in another, and receiving a standing ovation for both efforts. He came off the stage with tears of joy in his eyes.

The only trouble came when Gil Kestrel wheeled out the famous Firebird for its inaugural performance. Pippa held her breath as the bird was uncovered and sat preening, seemingly unconscious of its audience, in the middle of the spotlight.

"Behold." Mr. Dumfrey's voice resonated from a concealed portion of the backstage. "The one, the only, the last remaining bird of its species: *Aviraris igneous,* the Ethiopian Black-Billed Firebird!"

The audience gasped as the bird raised its head and shook out its feathers, revealing more fully its remarkable plumage and colorful tail and the dark eyes that appeared to be staring sharply at everyone and everything in turn. Even Pippa found that she was holding her breath—the bird did look remarkable, like something out of an old fairy tale.

Later, Pippa could not have said where Freckles came from. One second he wasn't there and the Firebird was basking in the warm glow of the audience's attention; the next second, the white furball was darting across the stage, fangs bared, claws extended, hissing.

"No, Freckles, no!" Mr. Dumfrey shouted, plunging onto the stage, waving his arms frantically, as the audience roared with laughter and the Firebird began screeching bloody murder. "Stop him! Stop that beast!"

"Oh, no you don't." Suddenly Lash appeared with a lasso circling overhead, expertly hooking Freckles around the tail and tugging the cat backward before he could reach the bird. Pippa exhaled as the Firebird, now squawking curses, was hauled quickly offstage, even as the audience shouted and clapped and stamped their feet, clearly believing that it was part of the show.

Luckily, the performance got quickly back on track. Emily the Tattooed Wonder proved to be a sensation. Even Pippa was mesmerized by her presence, the way she glided silently into the spotlight, clutching her coat to her chin, and then in an instant disrobed—revealing nothing but a swimsuit and skin bursting with color. She did nothing but stand there and slowly revolve, and yet Pippa couldn't tear her eyes away. It seemed to her that the vivid tattooed images were moving ever so slightly, that the horses might break free of Emily's skin and gallop through the air and the fish might wriggle their way after them, that the American flag might start waving in the breeze and little George Washington might lay down his hatchet and start singing "The Star-Spangled Banner." It was beautiful and terrifying at once. When Emily retrieved her coat from the ground and put it back on, there was a sigh from the audience, and then a thunder of applause.

"She's a hit, a smash, an absolute triumph!" Mr. Dumfrey had materialized in the wings to watch Emily's first performance, and he applauded loudly along with the audience. "I knew she would be. The crowd loves her."

Miss Fitch, who was watching, too, only sniffed. "Not much to it," she said, and Pippa wondered whether the coolness of her attitude had anything to do with the fact that earlier, Lash had complimented Emily on the very realistic depiction of a rodeo cowboy riding a bucking bronco on her right forearm. "It's practically indecent, if you ask me. A shame, too. She would have been a very pretty young woman. But now she's painted up like an Easter egg."

"It's the furthest thing from indecent," Mr. Dumfrey said. "On the contrary. Her tattoos are highly educational. Have you looked closely at the scene pictured on her right shoulder? A magnificent depiction of the signing of the Declaration of Independence."

Just then the albino twins took the stage, putting a firm end to the argument.

After the performance, Pippa and Max scrubbed off their stage makeup and went to find Sam and Thomas. This was their opportunity to get to Sheepshead Bay and talk to Benny Mallett, and Pippa knew that they might very well be on their way to speak to a killer. But after coming face-to-face with Rattigan—twice—no killer could scare her.

Rattigan was quite a different breed. He had made Pippa, Sam, Thomas, and Max into monsters— engineered them that way, worked them over in his laboratory like samples of experimental bacteria. But he was the real monster. Even now, she could sense him hovering somewhere just out of reach, like a person waiting backstage to make an entrance—taunting them, plotting his next move.

But where was he? And what would he do next?

There was still quite a crowd milling around the entry hall, many of them clustered around Emily, who was cheerfully signing autographs. Pippa spotted Rosie Bickers in the corner, near the giant stuffed Tasmanian emu, conversing earnestly with Mr. Dumfrey. Mr. Dumfrey had his arms around the Firebird cage, and every so often turned to coo in its direction, apparently trying to calm it after its disastrous appearance onstage. Judging from the way it screeched, flapped, and attempted to nip his nose off, he wasn't having much success.

Before they could make it to the door, Mr. Dumfrey turned and spotted them. "Sam! Thomas! Pippa! Max!" He jerked his chin toward the ceiling, and Pippa didn't have to be a mind reader to know what it meant: *in my office, now.*

"You know, that foul-tempered feather duster wasn't part of the deal," was the first thing Rosie said in Mr. Dumfrey's office as he deposited the Firebird cage onto his desk with a heavy sigh.

"Who you calling feather duster, scrub lug?" the bird screeched. He did have a point, Pippa thought: today, Rosie was wearing a blazer and a skirt that looked as if they'd been assembled from the kind of material used for scouring pots and pans.

"He just needs a bit of training," Sam said optimistically.

Rosie jerked her chin in the children's direction. "I

never said yes to your kid wonders, either," Rosie said. "I'm not here to play babysitter."

"Oh, yeah?" Max fired back, eyes flashing. "Well, we don't need any help from a suited-up loudmouth like you, either."

Rosie turned to Max. Instead of seeming offended, she squinted at Max with renewed interest. "You don't, do you?" She raised an eyebrow.

"All right, Max, that's enough," Mr. Dumfrey said, even before Max could open her mouth. He was seated, as always, in his leather armchair. Rosie was perched on the edge of his desk, having shoved aside the full-scale replica skull of an adult *habeascorpusaur*, a dinosaur said to have existed all the way into the early Renaissance— at least, according to the sign that Mr. Dumfrey had written to accompany the model. "And Rosie, have some faith. I think you'll find that information often comes from unexpected sources."

"So it does!" the Firebird crowed gleefully. "Pretty smart for a fat man!"

Mr. Dumfrey rubbed his forehead. "I'm beginning to have fantasies," he said wearily, "of a roasted bird for dinner. Not you, Cornelius," he said, when Cornelius ruffled his feathers.

That shut the Firebird up, at least temporarily.

Rosie, obviously resigning herself to the children's presence, removed her hat and gave her head a good scratching. "I did some digging. Turned up two locals who say your man Farnum wasn't the last person to visit Erskine on the night he died." She reached into her back pocket and produced a little notebook, like the kind Hardaway had his sergeants carry around for him. "Around ten thirty p.m.—give or take a quarter of an hour—a man slipped out the front door. Skinny, medium height, low-brimmed hat, scraggly mustache. Seemed jumpy." She flipped closed the notebook and replaced it in a pocket.

"Funny," Pippa said slowly. The mention of the straggly mustache had set off alarm bells in her head. "That sounds kind of like the robber at the bank."

"What robber?" Rosie asked, and Pippa explained how she and the others had been witness to one of the recent bank robberies.

"Bank robbery *attempt*," Thomas clarified, swiveling around. He was standing in the corner next to Cornelius's cage, pushing food pellets through the bars. "I got the money back, remember."

"Probably a coincidence," Rosie said. "Lots of men have straggly mustaches. My second husband, for example. Looked like he had a clot of seaweed tacked to his upper lip. Half the time I was tempted to yank it clean off."

"Maybe," Pippa said. But she wasn't convinced.

Rattigan had been like a shadow, passing across their lives, darkening everything he touched. Could he be involved in Erskine's death, too? But for what possible reason? It didn't make any sense.

"The cops will have to spring Farnum now." Sam looked around the room hopefully. "We'll prove Erskine was alive when he left. All we have to do is bring in your witnesses."

"Yeah, about that." Rosie made a face. "Look, I'd trust my guys with my life. Never let me down and always give it to me straight. But the cops may not see it that way. One spent a few years in Sing Sing for forgery, and the other got called up for stealing apples off a grocery cart. It was Thanksgiving," she added. "Nothing makes for a better pie than stolen apples."

Sam groaned. "Great," he said. "Our star witnesses are a forger and a thief."

"Criminals!" the Firebird screeched. "Misfits! *Losers!*"

Mr. Dumfrey hauled himself out of his chair, snatched a woven Navajo blanket from one of his many shelves, and tossed it unceremoniously over the Firebird's cage, muffling the bird's continued shrieks.

"I've done more with less," Rosie pointed out. "And if we go to trial, I'll make sure everyone on the jury thinks those two men never leave church except to help old ladies across the street."

"We're hoping it doesn't come to that," Mr. Dumfrey said, easing himself back into his chair. "Time is, unfortunately, not on General Farnum's side. The sooner we can get him out, the better." He turned to Pippa, his blue eyes bright behind his glasses, and Pippa had an uncomfortable *shoving* feeling deep in her mind, as if Mr. Dumfrey were trying to read her thoughts and not the other way around. Could that have been his secret talent, all those years ago? Was Mr. Dumfrey a mentalist, too? "Pippa, why don't you tell Rosie Bickers what you found at Mr. Erskine's apartment?"

There was a moment of shocked silence, and for a second, Pippa was sure Mr. Dumfrey *had* read her thoughts. Thomas and Sam exchanged a look. Max busied herself carefully examining a pen cap she'd snatched from Dumfrey's desk as if it were a precious artifact she'd never seen before.

"We didn't . . . ," Pippa started. "I mean, why would you think we—?" She swallowed hard. "We've never even been to Chrystie Street."

"Philippa, please." Mr. Dumfrey removed his glasses

and set them down on his desk, leaning back in his chair with something approaching a smile. "I've known you since you were a child—I've known *all* of you, even if I lost track of our dear Mackenzie for a while."

Max made a face, no doubt because of the combination of *dear* and her full name.

"You don't think I know when you've been up to something?" Mr. Dumfrey continued. "The four of you have been skulking around and whispering in corners for days. It doesn't take a brain like Monsieur Cabillaud's to figure out you might have decided to help General Farnum on your own. Besides"—Mr. Dumfrey did smile now, and spread his hands widely—"you've just confirmed it."

Pippa's face went hot. That, she thought, was Mr. Dumfrey's true talent: even with no special magic, he always understood. Thomas nodded very slightly. She took a deep breath. "We did go to Ernie Erskine's apartment," she said. "We were looking for evidence."

Rosie crossed her arms. Pippa couldn't tell if she looked mad or not. "How'd you get in? Didn't the cops have a guard outside?"

"Well, he was slightly . . . distracted," Pippa said. She didn't mention that Thomas had been the one to distract him by claiming to be searching for a fictional street address on the equally fictional Elmore Street and confusing the cop so entirely that by the end of the conversation he couldn't even point in the direction of the East River. "And then Sam, um, noticed that the doorknob was broken."

"Things are often spontaneously breaking in Sam's presence, I've found," Mr. Dumfrey remarked.

Rosie raised her eyebrows but said nothing. Pippa thought she looked ever so slightly impressed.

Thomas cut in with the rest of the story: "We found boxes of a poison called Fleas-B-Gone. But all of the bottles were empty. Erskine must have been out of the poison." He proceeded to explain about the threatening letter they'd found on the blotter, how Erskine had seemingly been interrupted in the middle of writing it, and how Sam had put together that Benny was Benny Mallett, who manufactured Fleas-B-Gone from his storefront in Sheepshead Bay.

When he was finished, Rosie was silent for a moment.

"Might be something to it," she grunted at last, as if she didn't like to admit it. "Got a full caseload and enough paperwork to start my own newspaper. I'll get down to Sheepshead Bay when I can," she added, rising from the desk and sticking her hat back on her head.

"Actually," Thomas said, scrunching his nose, "we

were thinking of going to see Benny Mallett this afternoon."

Pippa held her breath. It was a gamble. Mr. Dumfrey had previously forbidden them from getting involved in police business, and he'd been touchier than ever since Rattigan had escaped their capture. Of course, even if he forbade them from seeing Mallett, they would go. Still, she didn't like lying to Mr. Dumfrey.

Rosie paused in the act of crossing to the door. She swiveled to face them again. "You may be extraordinary," she said softly, "but it looks like your hearing is below average. I said I'll handle it. Murder's no business for children, extraordinary or not, and I won't—"

"Oh, let them go, Rosie," Mr. Dumfrey said with a little sigh. "They'll go anyway, whether we give our permission or not."

Rosie stood there for a moment, examining each of the children in turn. Pippa found she couldn't even begin to make progress into Rosie's mind. It was particularly well guarded—sharp and spiky and angular. Reading it was like trying to grab a porcupine barehanded. She knew she should be offended by Rosie's attitude—Rosie obviously didn't think much of them—but she actually found Rosie's blunt speech refreshing.

"Fine," she said at last. "But don't expect me to come

and clean up the mess if you make a bungle of things." And with that, she turned and barreled out into the hall, moving like a linebacker with his gaze fixed on the end zone.

As soon as the door had swung shut behind her, Mr. Dumfrey's expression turned serious. He leaned forward, clasping his hands on the desk.

"Rosie's right about one thing," he said. "As I've told you before, this isn't a game. Mallett may be dangerous. He *is* dangerous, if he killed Erskine. I'm trusting you to tread carefully."

"Why are you trusting us at all?" Pippa asked.

Mr. Dumfrey sighed and stood up, moving toward the narrow window, which looked out over the small courtyard toward the dingy gray faces of the buildings on the opposite side of the street. Absentmindedly, he stuck a finger in Cornelius's cage, and the bird gave it an affectionate nibble. For a long moment, Mr. Dumfrey was quiet.

Finally, he spoke. "Years ago, when I set out to find you—you four, the last of the children my brother kidnapped, or stole, or bought for his *experiments*"—it was rare to see Mr. Dumfrey angry, but he practically spat the word—"I swore that I would keep you safe. That I would protect you."

A shiver went down Pippa's neck, as if a ghost had breathed on her from behind. "The last of the children?" she repeated. "Does that mean . . . ?"

Mr. Dumfrey didn't turn around. But she could see his shoulders sag. "There were others, yes," he said softly. "Dozens. Maybe more."

Pippa felt as if an invisible hand were pressing on her chest. Suddenly, she could hardly breathe. She thought of the nightmares she'd had since she was a child, of a long hallway filled with cages, and a child in every one. Not nightmares, she knew now. Memories.

She'd always believed they were the only ones. Or maybe she'd hoped they were.

"Mr. Dumfrey," Sam ventured, "Rattigan knew my parents' names. He knew all sorts of things about them. He must have had some connection to the people he chose—"

"If he did, I don't know of one," said Mr. Dumfrey shortly, "as I've told you before."

Pippa swallowed. "But why us?" Pippa persisted. "Why any of us? There must be a reason."

Mr. Dumfrey hesitated for only a fraction of a second. And yet in that pause, Pippa wedged herself quickly, seamlessly, into his mind and felt it seize like a muscle, or an animal in front of headlights. "There was no reason," he said quickly. "It was random."

She withdrew quickly from his thoughts, bringing a hand to her chest. It felt as if she'd inhaled ice. Mr. Dumfrey had just lied to them. She was sure of it.

"But that doesn't make sense." Thomas was frowning. "Why would he have gone to all the trouble to get rid of Sam's parents if—"

"I'm telling you, I don't know." Mr. Dumfrey thumped the windowsill so hard with a fist that the glass pane rattled. "I don't know why he picked any of you."

"Wait a second," Max said. "You said there *were* dozens of others. So what happened to them?"

Mr. Dumfrey sighed and brought up a hand to rub his eyes beneath his glasses. He was still turned to the window. Pippa could see his reflection, slivered by the panes.

"His so-called work was dangerous. Playing with blood and brains. Splicing animal parts into humans, and strangers into one another, and more. Playing God." Now Mr. Dumfrey's voice had an edge Pippa had never heard before—a raw, wounded quality, like someone in physical pain. "He treated humans like lab rats. And like rats, they died." Mr. Dumfrey's voice broke a little and he cleared his throat. "That's why I vowed to find the four of you, even if it took a lifetime.

166 ☞

I was hoping you would never have to know about Rattigan and his experiments, never have to know about the past. I failed."

"You didn't—" Thomas started to protest.

Mr. Dumfrey turned away from the window at last, holding up a hand. "Don't argue with me, Thomas. It's true. I failed in my original goal—to keep you safe. To keep you protected. But maybe, after all, that's not such a terrible thing." He looked older, in that moment, than Pippa had ever seen him, and she felt a pain deep in her chest, a quick flash of intuition: they couldn't possibly stay at the museum forever. Someday, they would have to leave Mr. Dumfrey behind. But who would take care of him then?

"You're getting older," Mr. Dumfrey said, as if he'd read her mind. "The world is full of Rattigans, just as it is full of beautiful and wondrous things. You will have to see all of it, and you will have to see it on your own. So go." His smile didn't quite touch his eyes. "Soon, I fear, I will not be able to keep you safe anymore. I will do my best. You should know that. I will always do my best." His glasses were slowly misting over. "I fear that soon, you'll have to look out for one another."

16

Mr. Dumfrey's speech left Thomas with a lingering unease, a heaviness in his chest and stomach, as if he'd just eaten too much of Smalls's lumpy, overcooked porridge. He didn't want to think of a day when he would have to leave the museum. Sure, the roof leaked, and someone was always snoring, and half the time the cashbox was empty and they had to make do with dinners of fried bologna sandwiches.

But the museum was so much more than that. It was Danny playing the violin or, on special occasions, the bagpipes, and singing ballads about heroic dwarfs of yore. It was Betty combing out her long beard, and

Caroline and Quinn linking arms to demonstrate the newest dances (when they could be convinced to stop fighting). It was Lash showing off by wrapping his whip around a mop handle to make it skid across the floor and Smalls reciting his awful poetry and Goldini turning cards into goldfish and goldfish into pennies he sank to the bottom of the tank. It was playing DeathTrap with Sam on rainy days or setting up apple-bowling in the Hall of Wax, using empty soup cans for pins. It was Pippa sprawled out on the sofa listening to the radio and Max doing an impression of Sergeant Schroeder by smooshing her cheeks together with her hands.

It was, in other words, home.

Leaving the museum by the front door, now thankfully clear of lingering audience members, Thomas had a shock that soon drove all thoughts of Dumfrey from his mind. Across the street a tall, skinny boy dressed neatly in a school uniform had just slipped out from Von Stikk's doors and was now moving quickly down the street, loosening his tie as he went and shrugging off his sweater. He would have been totally unrecognizable except for his signature straw-colored hair, which was now plastered to his head with liberal amounts of pomade.

Thomas could hardly believe it. *"Chubby?"*

"No," Pippa said wonderingly. "It can't be."

Chubby turned and winced, as though it pained him to have been recognized. For a second, he looked as if he was considering bolting.

"Chubby." Thomas lifted a hand and waved, though they were standing only about twenty feet from each other. "What are you doing?"

"What are you *wearing*?" Max asked.

Chubby jogged across the street, looking quickly left and right. "Shhhh," he hissed. "Stop yelling my name. You want the whole neighborhood to hear you?" He was still struggling out of his sweater, and for a brief second his head disappeared and he was all pointy elbows distorting the wool. Then he extracted himself again. His tussle with the sweater had left a portion of his hair pointing skyward.

Sam was obviously trying very hard to keep a straight face. "Your hair's messed up," he said.

"Good." Chubby raked his fingers across his head, leaving him looking as if he'd recently been electrocuted. "You wouldn't believe all the rules in that place. Clean your fingernails. Tuck in your shirt. Wash your hands after using the toilet." He shook his head disgustedly. "It's like being in jail, but boring."

"You haven't really joined up with Von Stikk, have you?" Thomas asked. It was impossible to imagine Chubby—who had not only run an illegal betting ring when he wasn't selling papers, but briefly crashed in Chinatown with a bunch of amateur pickpockets—learning multiplication tables and practicing penmanship.

"I had to." Chubby looked tortured. "You hear about that big old dribble they're going to float over the city next Saturday?"

"You mean the *dirigible*?" Pippa said.

"That's what I said." Chubby shot her an exasperated glance. "Anyway, Von Stikk's got the corner on the best seat in town. Roof of this office building right across from the Umpire State Building."

"Empire State Building," said Thomas.

Chubby ignored him. "Half the city's turning out to watch." He scratched his neck, looking slightly embarrassed. "Anyway, I got some, er, interests in the landing."

"Chubby," Thomas said, "are you gambling again?"

"No, no," Chubby said, far too quickly. "Nothing like that. More like . . . estimating probabilities."

Pippa rolled her eyes.

"Don't tell anyone about me going to school, okay?"

172

Chubby looked around the group anxiously. "I don't want to ruin my reputation."

"Oh no," Pippa said. "We wouldn't want anyone to know you're finally learning to read."

Chubby, who evidently hadn't picked up on her sarcasm, exhaled with relief. "Thanks, Pip," he said, thumping her on the shoulder. "I knew I could count on you."

"It's *Pippa*, Chubby," she said through gritted teeth. "Or should I call you *Len*?"

"But you aren't really learning to read," Max said, before Chubby could respond. From the expression on her face, she might have been saying *you aren't really learning to wrangle poisonous snakes with your bare hands.*

"Nah." Chubby hooked his thumbs into his belt loops, practically preening with pride. "Von Stikk says I'm one of the worst students they ever had. But you know," he continued thoughtfully. "It ain't so bad. Sure, there's lots of learning and numbers and teachers yakking away all day long. And they suit you up like a preacher on Sunday. But the grub ain't half bad and I got my ways of keeping things interesting."

His face took on a crafty expression.

As if on cue, the doors to Von Stikk's institute banged open. Students barreled into the streets, covering their noses, coughing into cupped palms. A high-pitched scream announced Von Stikk herself. White-faced, tears streaming down her cheeks, hair disarranged from its typical pouffy bun, she plunged outside after her students.

"Horrors!" she screeched. "SCANDAL!"

Chubby grabbed Thomas's arm and tugged him around the corner. The others followed.

"Stink bomb," he clarified in a low voice. "Two of 'em, actually, detonated at the same time. I had help on the inside. The Extra-Stink Dirty 5000. Picked 'em up at that joke shop I told you about, the one on Fifty-Seventh Street. Whole place must smell like an egg left too long in a dirty sock."

Even from a block away, Thomas could hear continued sounds of coughing and gagging.

"Er, nicely done?" Thomas thought that was what Chubby expected to hear.

Chubby beamed. "Thanks, Tom." He held out his hand, like he expected to shake. "Always good to see you."

Thomas, remembering the shock he'd received the last time he made the mistake of shaking Chubby's hand, quickly tucked his hands in his pocket. "You too, Chubby," he said. "See you soon."

"And try not to learn anything, Len," Pippa said as they parted ways.

"Don't worry, Pip," Chubby said cheerfully. "I won't."

Sheepshead Bay was as far out in Brooklyn as it was possible to go without plunging straight into the Atlantic. Though just down the road from the kaleidoscope clutter of the Coney Island boardwalk and Luna Park, Sheepshead Bay was a quiet place of shingle-sided houses. Beach grass grew between slatted picket fences and seagulls wheeled low in the sky.

It was, Thomas thought, not the kind of place you expected to find a murderer.

Then again, he knew all too well that murderers hid behind perfectly ordinary faces. How convenient it would be, he thought, if everyone's intentions showed plainly on the outside. Instead, people like Monsieur Cabillaud were judged as being freaks while monsters paraded freely in the streets, wearing normal smiles.

Benny Mallett's warehouse was at the end of a short industrial strip. The building, a brick warehouse of modest size, was painted a surprisingly cheerful yellow. There were even flower boxes in the windows.

Yet there was no smoke coming from any of the several chimneys stacked along the roof, and no lights in any of the windows, no machinery grinding or humming. The whole place had a curiously abandoned feel. Thomas began to feel uneasy.

"You think he's gone on the run?" Pippa asked, lowering her voice and echoing Thomas's thoughts exactly. He glanced at her suspiciously to see whether she was actually reading his thoughts, but she was gnawing on her lower lip, squinting up at the darkened windows.

"If he has, I guess we know who killed Erskine," Thomas said. He took a step toward the door and lifted a hand to test the knob. But a sound from within stopped him and he froze.

"What?" Sam said. "What's the matter?"

"Shhh." Thomas pressed his ear to the door. The sound repeated itself: it was a low moan, as if somebody was in pain. Pippa must have heard it, too. Her eyes went wide.

"Stay here," he whispered to the others. If Mallett was dangerous, he might have someone with him inside—a hostage, another victim, someone who needed help. Maybe Mallett had simply snapped. Either way, it would be stupid to waltz through the front door without knowing what was waiting for them on the other side.

He stepped back, scanning the building facade. His

first move was easy: he sprang onto one of the stone ledges beneath the first-floor windows, skirting the flower boxes carefully, trying to get a look inside. But these windows were covered in a fine metal mesh that completely obscured the view. He'd have to go higher.

Climbing, stretching, bending, squeezing, slithering, and wiggling: Thomas was an expert in all of them. In less than a minute, he'd scaled the facade, finding foot- and handholds in the brick, and reached the second line of windows.

"Be careful," Pippa hissed from the ground.

Thomas waved to show he was okay. Then, crouching on one of the narrow stone ledges, he cupped his hands to his eyes and pressed his face against the dirty glass.

From his position, he had a clear view of a large open space and various vats, compressors, and furnaces that Mallett must use to manufacture huge quantities of Fleas-B-Gone. But, as he'd suspected, no gears were turning, no pipes were hissing steam, no chemicals boiled in great copper tubs, no workers scurried around, white-gloved, wearing masks to protect them from the fumes.

Instead, there was a single person in Mallett's otherwise-empty factory: a man with a bald shiny cap of a head and tufts of dark hair sprouting above each ear. He was slumped over a desk in one corner, resting his forehead on one hand and gripping a tall glass of brown liquid with the other. Even as Thomas watched, he sat up with a sudden lurch, swaying a little in his chair, and threw back the last of his drink. When he tipped his head back, Thomas caught a glimpse of a red and swollen face, and a network of burst capillaries stretching across his cheeks and nose.

He climbed down the way he'd come, wedging his fingers and toes against the brick and shinnying, spiderlike, to the street.

"It's all right," he said when he rejoined the group. Down here, the sound of Mallett's moaning was louder, and Pippa looked anxious. "It's Mallett," he said. "He's not hurt. He's just—"

"DRUNK!" The sudden roar of Mallett's voice made Pippa shriek. Thomas jumped, spinning around to face Mallett, who'd flung open the door and now stood, clutching a bottle, lurching in the door. Thomas was shocked to see that Mallett, standing, was tiny—hardly bigger than Danny the dwarf, and at least two inches shorter than Thomas.

He was wearing a slim pinstriped suit with a matching vest, and had a flashy red handkerchief in his pocket. But now his suit was rumpled and covered with old stains. "Drunk as a thief on Sunday. Drunk as a boiled owl!" He lifted a finger at Thomas, his eyes temporarily crossing and uncrossing. "But who're you?" he slurred. "If you came to be paid, you can scram. I don't have any money. It's gone—all gone! So be gone, fleas! Fleas-B-Gone! Get it?" He took a long swig straight from the bottle and then started to cough, leaning heavily against the doorframe to keep from pitching forward into the street.

Thomas waited until the coughing fit had subsided. "We didn't come for money." He was trying to figure out whether Mallett was crazy or dangerous or just hopeless. Maybe all of the above. He improvised quickly. "We just came to hear your side of the story."

It was the perfect thing to say—a remark so general that nobody could find fault with it. Mallett straightened up as though he'd been shocked. "*My* side of the story," he said, nodding very fast. "Nobody ever wants to hear my side of the story. Nobody cares. Come in, come in." He turned away from the street, waving for the children to follow him into the warehouse.

Inside, it smelled like ancient chemicals and, unmistakably, like whiskey. Mallett trundled clumsily back to his desk and sat down. He was so short that his shoulders barely cleared the blotter, and had he leaned forward he might easily have rested his nose on the stack of paperwork centered there.

"Nice place you have here," Sam said, obviously doing his best to sound cheerful.

"Yeah," Max said, with trademark bluntness. "So what happened to it?"

"What happened?" Mallett's eyes were bloodshot and unfocused. It took him several seconds of blinking and squinting before he could focus on Max. "What *happened* is that someone set out to ruin me."

A shiver moved down Thomas's neck. Was Mallett a killer after all? Was he about to confess? Neither of his hands was visible behind the desk. He could easily have a weapon trained on them.

"Who?" Thomas asked. He waited for Mallett to say Erskine.

To his surprise, Mallett just shook his head. "I don't know," he said sadly. "Wish I did. But I guess it doesn't matter anymore. I'm over and done for. *Ruined*'s what they wanted, and ruined's what they got."

"Talk to us," Pippa said firmly, placing both hands on the desk. "Tell us what happened."

Mallett looked sheepish as Pippa removed the bottle when he tried to reach for it, but he made no objection.

"I've been working this business since I was twelve years old," he said. "Started out with a Bunsen burner and a dream, fiddling around with different formulas. I made my first bottle of Fleas-B-Gone when I was twelve years old. Two or three spritzes of the stuff, bam. Whole colonies of fleas just keeled over. Built the whole place up myself. King of the Flea Killers. That's what everyone called me." His chest, momentarily swelled with pride, now collapsed again. "Then a few months ago some Staten Island kingpin starts buying up all of the primary ingredient on the whole East Coast."

"Ethyl parathion," Thomas said.

Mallett's fuzzy eyes swung to Thomas in surprise. "That's right," he said. "Amazing stuff, ethyl parathion. On its own, it's harmless as milk. But mix it with a little hydrogen and you've got one of the deadliest poisons on earth. Even the military won't use it anymore. Killed too many men—on both sides—during the war. They used to call it the reaper gas, you know."

Thomas decided it was time to go for a direct approach. "Do you know Ernie Erskine?"

Mallett frowned. "Erskine." He slumped back in his chair. "Erskine. Sounds familiar . . ."

"He sent you threatening letters," Pippa prompted him.

181 ☞

Mallett just shrugged. "I get dozens of them every day," he said, waving to the stack of mail on his desk. "Had to stop shipments and couldn't afford to pay anyone back. Well, what can I do? I'm bankrupt."

Suddenly, Thomas had an uncomfortable sensation of something *pushing* directly between his eyeballs. It was a little like getting nudged with an elbow, but directly in the brain. And then Pippa's voice was there, speaking softly to him, as clearly as if she'd whispered in his ear.

Ask about Rattigan, the Pippa-in-Thomas's-head said.

Get out of my head, Thomas thought back, simultaneously shooting Pippa a death stare.

The real Pippa only shrugged as if to say, *What?*

The Pippa-in-Thomas's-head said, *Just do it*. He was about to ask—or *think* to ask—why, when he remembered that Rosie had mentioned that a man with a straggly mustache had been seen coming out of Erskine's place on the night of his murder, a similar description to the man who'd held them up at the bank.

I'll ask, Thomas thought, *if you get out of my head*.

There was a temporary pressure behind his eyelids— and then the weight withdrew, and Pippa was gone. He felt a rush of tremendous relief, followed by irritation. It had been much better, he thought, when Pippa could only read the contents of people's pockets and purses.

182 🖙

Mallett's connection to Rattigan seemed like a big stretch. Still, Thomas kept his end of the bargain—if only because he feared Pippa might otherwise slip herself uninvited into his mind and start humming a particularly annoying song. "What about Nicholas Rattigan?" he said. "Have you ever heard of him?"

Mallett frowned. His eyes crossed and uncrossed. "Rattigan . . . ," he said thoughtfully. "You mean that crazy bat who escaped from prison?"

Thomas nodded.

Mallett shook his head. "Bad news. Read about him in the paper. Heard he used to run tests on living humans, treating them like lab rats."

So that was a dead end. It seemed they had run out of questions—and leads.

"Thanks very much for your time, Mr. Mallett," Pippa said as brightly as she could.

"Yeah. You've been a big help," Thomas lied.

"We're sure things will turn around for you soon," Sam added.

Mallett shook his head. "It's no use pretending. Fleas-B-Gone is finished. Dead."

And then, to Thomas's horror, he leaned forward, thumping his forehead directly on the desk, and began to cry.

After a moment, Sam shuffled forward awkwardly. He lifted a hand as though to place it on Mallett's shoulder—then, obviously remembering how much damage he could do to Mallett's spinal cord if he wasn't careful, merely dropped the hand by his side.

"Don't cry, Mr. Mallett," he said. "It can't be that bad. There's gotta be something else you can do."

"Yeah," Max said. "Maybe you can go into rat poison."

Mallett looked up with a look of such pathetic misery, Thomas couldn't help but feel sorry for him.

"Fleas," he said. "Fleas have been my entire life."

There was, Thomas felt, nothing more to say.

17

Even before it came into view, you knew you were close to Coney Island. As you headed down Surf Avenue toward the great glittering amusement park, you could feel the vibrations of the Cyclone roller coaster as it rumbled along its tracks and hear the excited clamor filling the air: the shrieks of children on the thrill rides; the whistle and pop of the booth games; the roar of the operators as they called to the crowds, trying to tempt them into spending their nickels and dimes.

It was late in the season but crowded nevertheless. In the warmth of the early evening, couples strolled together on the boardwalk while children ran laughing across the white sand beach. In the distance, the lights of Luna Park—250,000 of them, according to Thomas—were just flickering on, though it wasn't yet totally dark. The air was thick with smells of roasting hot dogs and buttered popcorn, all intermingling with salt air and perfume.

For a moment, Sam could forget about poor ruined Mallett and poor dead Erskine and poor General Farnum, still languishing in a jail cell. He could forget about deadly chemicals and bank robberies and monsters like Rattigan, who used people the way people used handkerchiefs. He could forget about everything he'd seen and, instead, enjoy the feel of the late-day sun on his face and the swoops and curls of the great Steeplechase Park rides, like a whole city built in midair.

"Look," Thomas said. "See that Ferris wheel?" As usual, when Thomas got excited, he didn't wait for an answer. "It was the very first Ferris wheel on the East Coast, and named after—"

"Where's Max?" Sam interrupted him. Max had been, as usual, wandering slightly behind the group, as if she didn't want to be associated with them. Every so often Sam sneaked a glance over his shoulder to make sure she was okay—casually, very carefully, so she wouldn't see and plunge a dagger between his eyes. But she'd disappeared somewhere along the boardwalk.

Thomas turned around, scanning the crowd. He frowned. "Weird," he said. "She was right behind us. . . ."

The boardwalk was packed with people—women in dresses and men strolling with their shirtsleeves rolled up and a thousand children carrying balloons or prizes or cotton candy. Where could she have gone?

Rattigan. The name was there, like a blade slicing through all of Sam's earlier pleasure. He tried to push the idea away. Why would Rattigan have snatched Max alone? Besides, Max would never let herself get caught so easily. Still, he couldn't shake a bad feeling. He would never fully be able to shake it, not until Rattigan was dead.

"Should we split up to look for her?" Even Thomas sounded uncertain.

"No need," Pippa said.

Sam and Thomas turned to look at her. She was standing with her arms crossed with the weirdest expression on her face—like she'd just swallowed a whole peppercorn. She jutted her chin in the direction of the park. "What do you want to bet I know *just* where to find her?"

Sam turned in the direction Pippa indicated. Extending above the ticket booths that dominated the entrance to Steeplechase was an enormous structure that looked as if it had been assembled entirely from paper signs, cloth banners, and electric lights: a massive, asymmetrical, misshapen monster. Perched at the top of the slanted roof was a huge sign burning with rose-and-white lights: *Coney Island Curiosity Show*, it read.

Beneath that was another sign, this one hand-painted on heavy tarp and hastily tacked to the eaves: *Featuring New York City's Only GENUINE Human Wonders! Don't Be Fooled by Cheap Imitations!*

The creeping heat on the back of Sam's neck turned into a full-blown itch. The Coney Island Curiosity Show, Tom and Pippa had told him, was where Howie had gone to work.

"She wouldn't," he said halfheartedly.

"She did." Thomas pointed, and Sam caught a glimpse of Max's wild tangle of dark hair among the crowd of people flowing through the entrance to the park.

"I should have known," Pippa said, shaking her head. She started moving toward the Steeplechase gates. Thomas followed her.

"Where are you going?" Sam called after them. His concern for Max had turned quickly to irritation. No way was he following her into that mismatched dump of a place so he could watch her ogle her *ex-boyfriend*. Or whatever Howie was.

Pippa turned around, shooting him an exasperated look. "Come on, Sam," she said. "Aren't you just a little bit curious?"

He was—but only a teeny, tiny little bit. Still, faced with the alternative of standing on his own or following his friends, he crossed his arms and shuffled after them, muttering so they'd know he wasn't happy about it.

As they approached the entrance, Sam noted that the cost of admission had been increased to a quarter. He didn't have a penny on him—and neither, he knew, did Thomas or Pippa. He had no idea how Max had slipped in—then again, Max had a way of blending into a crowd. It's what made her such a good pick-pocket.

Thomas had obviously had the same realization. He'd stopped a few feet away from one of the ticket vendors, rooting in his pockets for money.

"Don't bother," Pippa said. "You've got nothing on you but a safety pin and a navy blue button."

Thomas fumbled in his left pocket, extracting the button with a triumphant cry. "I've been looking for this everywhere."

Pippa rolled her eyes. "Follow my lead," she said.

Then, in less than two seconds, she transformed: gone was Pippa-the-mentalist, Pippa-the-mind-reader, Pippa-the-maybe-just-a-little-too-bossy-at-times. In her place was a scared-looking girl with a severe sweep of glossy black bangs, almond-shaped eyes, and a trembling lower lip.

"A quarter a ticket," said the man behind one of the ticket stalls when they made their approach.

Pippa let out a noise so unexpected that Sam jumped and turned to look at her. It sounded as if she had a bullfrog caught in her throat. Then he realized she was pretending to cry.

"Please," she said. "We've lost our parents. They're still inside."

Thomas immediately picked up on the game. "I told you," he said. "We were supposed to meet them outside the Steeplechase *ride*."

The ticket collector looked over each of them appraisingly. They couldn't look less like brothers and sisters. Thomas and Pippa were roughly the same height, but Thomas was pale and blond and so freckled it looked as if an accumulation of dust had become permanently stuck to his cheeks and nose. Pippa, on the other hand, was dark and angular, with creamy skin and glossy, straight black hair cut to her chin. And Sam had at least seven inches on both of them, with a too-large nose and protruding ears and floppy brown hair.

Pippa let out another fake sob. "I don't want to be an orphan!" she wailed. Several people swiveled to look at them and the ticket collector waved them through.

"All right, all right," he said. "Quick, now. Before my manager sees."

Once inside the gates, Sam paused, momentarily overwhelmed by the sheer quantity of people strolling the avenue and lining up for the rides and waiting to take their turns at the shoot-'em-up booths. There were monstrous roller coasters arranged in ribbon-like formations, built on high wooden scaffolding that reminded Sam of an arrangement of bones. Above it all, the Ferris wheel turned majestically in the sky, casting them in its shadow.

But they headed straight for the Coney Island Curiosity Show, which up close was even larger and uglier than it had first appeared from the other side of the ticket booths. Flanking the entrance were hand-painted banners showing a variety of performers—dwarfs, fat ladies, dog-men, Alicia the Armless Knife-Throwing Wonder, a lasso-thrower named Tiny Tex, and, Sam was furious to see, a full rendition of Howie's simpering smile and slicked-back hair, with his head rotated 180 degrees.

"You've got to be kidding me," Pippa said. She pointed to a neatly lettered sign by the door, which announced the Coney Island Curiosity Show as the official home of S.U.P.E.R.I.O.R—the initials of Howie's pompous organization, Stop Unnatural Phony Entertainers from Ruining and/or Impairing Our Reputation.

"I swear," Thomas said, his face flushing so dark his freckles momentarily disappeared, "if I ever see that kid alone in a dark alley, he better know how to run."

At the entrance to the freak show, a carnival barker who might have moonlighted as one of the show's giants was perched on a sturdy three-legged stool, working the crowd, talking so quickly all of his words formed one continuous wave of sound. Sam wondered how he even breathed. Maybe he had gills and doubled as one of the performers.

"Step right up, ladies and gentlemen! Don't be shy! You'll be amazed! You'll be astounded! You'll see

marvels and wonders that you will remember for the rest of your living days! This is a one-of-a-kind show, ladies and gentlemen, the only exhibit of gen-u-wine human curiosities in all of New York City—"

"Now what?" Sam said crossly. He couldn't stop staring at that dumb poster of Howie.

This time, it was Thomas who took the lead. "Follow me," he said.

The barker never stopped shouting, even as they approached. "Just twenty-five cents, ladies and gentlemen! You'll see Derrick the Dog-Face Boy, a perfectly normal lad in every regard except for his uncanny resemblance to a Saint Bernard! There's Alicia the Armless Wonder, who can perform the most intricate acts of manual dexterity using only her feet—"

"Sorry we're late," Thomas said breathlessly, cutting off his speech. "Should we head straight to the theater?"

The barker spluttered, as if he had to physically swallow back his words. "Late?" he said. "What do you mean?"

"What I mean is we got lost, and if we don't get changed in a hurry we'll get roasted alive," Thomas said. The barker was staring at him, openmouthed. "So should we head straight through to the theater? Or is there a faster way?"

The barker shut his mouth with a little click. "You're saying you belong to the show?" he said. His eyes narrowed suspiciously. "Then how come I never seen you?"

Instead of answering the question directly, Thomas just turned to Sam.

"Go on," he said, still feigning impatience. "Show him."

"Me?" Sam squawked.

Thomas nodded, staring at Sam with a look that said *don't mess this up.*

Sam had no idea what Thomas expected of him—clearly, some kind of demonstration of strength. After staring helplessly at Thomas for another half second, Sam pivoted, bent down, and grabbed one leg of the stool with his right hand. Then, with the barker still seated on it, he hoisted the stool into the air.

The barker let out a gasp, pinwheeling his arms to keep his balance. "Put me down," he said. All the color had gone out of his face. "Right now! This very instant!"

Sam did as he was told. As soon as the stool touched down, the barker staggered to the ground.

Pippa smiled up at him. "So," she said brightly. "Can we go in?"

"Go," he said. His face was beaded with sweat. "But be quick about it. The show's about to start."

"That was genius," Pippa whispered to Thomas as they passed into the vestibule.

He shrugged, smiling. "I learn from the best."

The vestibule was long, narrow, and dark and lined on both sides with glass cases like the kind Mr. Dumfrey used to display his curiosities. Sam was shocked to see that all of the one-of-a-kind items that belonged to their museum weren't, in fact, one of a kind. Because here, too, was the coonskin cap worn by Davy Crockett and the goosequill pen used by Thomas Jefferson to sign the Declaration of Independence.

Sam had always known, deep down, that Mr. Dumfrey fudged the truth about his various curiosities. But he had at least believed that Mr. Dumfrey's lies were entirely original. Now it seemed that every unique, priceless, historical relic had its duplicate here. Except that everything at the Coney Island show seemed a little bit—well, actually, quite a bit—*better.*

At the end of the long vestibule a sign pointed them through a set of heavy curtains toward the theater. This, too, made the Odditorium at Dumfrey's Dime Museum look sad and small. The ceiling was gilded with gold leaf and painted on every square inch to depict the fantastical scenes that would, presumably, soon play out on the stage: a strongman bending an iron pipe in two; a contortionist arching her back so far she could peer through her legs; an alligator man with a long snout and sharp, vicious teeth. The chairs were covered in actual velvet—not just brushed felt, repeatedly patched and covered over with shoe polish, like the chairs at Dumfrey's. The stage dazzled with footlights and headlights and spotlights and sidelights. And it was *packed*. All the seats were taken, and a good portion of the crowd was standing, craning to get a better view of the stage.

It didn't take long to find Max. She was standing just behind the last row of chairs, arms crossed, glowering at the stage. When Thomas, Pippa, and Sam finally pushed their way over to her, she barely glanced in their direction. As if she'd known, all along, they would follow.

Sam's annoyance came rushing back all at once. "Couldn't miss the chance to see your boyfriend?" he whispered sarcastically, squeezing in next to her.

Max turned, narrowing her eyes. "You know," she said, raising an eyebrow, "if you're jealous, you might as well say so."

The word—*jealous*—hit Sam like a two-ton ice block to the chest. "*Jealous?*" he repeated. His voice rose to a squeak. "You think I'm . . . I'm not *jealous*. No way. Of

Howie? Why would I ever be—?"

But at that moment the lights dimmed and several people hushed him. Sam was glad, at least, that in the darkness, no one would be able to tell that he was blushing furiously.

The show began. Another barker—not the one who'd nearly stopped them outside—strolled onto the stage, dressed like a circus ringmaster, in striped pants and a top hat. He had large protruding front teeth and a black mustache, slicked and curled to perfection, which gave him the look of a particularly well-groomed rat.

"Welcome, ladies and gentlemen"—even his voice was somehow ratlike: silken and hoarse at the same time—"to New York City's only *true* sideshow." Several people whooped and called and stamped their feet. "Don't be fooled, ladies and gentlemen, by imitators and pretenders. Don't be taken by *impostors*." His eyes swept over the crowd and landed on Sam, and Sam had the brief, paralyzing fear that he'd been recognized. "Ours are the only true curiosities in New York. One hundred percent authentic, natural-born *monsters*." More people were clapping and stamping their feet, laughing, calling for the monsters.

Sam now felt as if the ice were in his body, in his *blood*.

They came one by one to the stage: Derrick the Dog-Face Boy, whose entire chin and brow were covered in stiff, bristly hair; a pair of dark-haired conjoined twins who must have been only eight or nine years old; a humongous twelve-year-old wearing a cowboy outfit, advertised as Tiny Tex, the Texas Fatboy, who with several flicks of a wrist lassoed first the hat off an audience member's head and then the lipstick out of his wife's hand.

The strongman was named Trogg, and roughly the dimensions of a water buffalo. However, although Trogg did indeed bend iron pipes onstage, eliciting applause from the crowd, Sam was pleased to see that he did not bend them into any animal shapes, which was Sam's particular specialty. (Iron rabbits were his favorite.)

Trogg lumbered offstage to various cries of "Bravo!"

Then Howie the Human Owl was announced.

Sam's stomach tightened. He hadn't seen Owl-Boy since late summer, when Howie had been thrown out of the museum in disgrace after the discovery that he'd been attempting to drive the place out of business for a month. But Howie hadn't changed. He had the same black hair, practically lacquered in place, the same cold blue eyes, the same jaw that looked as if it had

199 ☞

been chiseled by a sculptor attempting to render perfect human proportions. Most of all, he had the same smile, halfway between a sneer and a smirk, that made Sam want to drive his fist straight through the roof of Howie's mouth.

As a hush once again fell on the crowd, Howie positioned himself with his back toward the audience. Then, with no warning, he pivoted his head around completely so his chin was positioned directly between his shoulder blades and he was once again grinning into the spotlight. The crowd burst into appreciative applause. He repeated the trick, this time swiveling his head in the other direction, and then held up a hand for quiet.

"Ladies and gentlemen, boys and girls, and"—his eyes landed on Sam then, and Howie's expression changed slightly, becoming narrower and meaner, so he looked not like an owl, but a hunting falcon—"*old friends*." He half snarled the word, and Sam knew they'd been spotted. "Allow me to introduce New York's *premier* knife-thrower." This time, Howie was staring at Max, and Max made a low growling noise and started to move for her pocket, before Thomas held her back.

"It isn't worth it," Thomas whispered to her.

"A tragic story turned to one of triumph," Howie said, "Alicia was orphaned at a young age after losing both arms to the same factory accident that killed her parents." The audience murmured their shock and sympathy. One woman actually dabbed her eyes with a handkerchief. Max rolled her eyes. "Cruelly abandoned to the streets, Alicia survived only by learning to feed herself with her feet. The day she learned to twirl spaghetti with her feet was the proudest of her life."

"What a bunch of baloncy," Max muttered.

"A brutal and senseless accident may have cruelly taken her arms, but by virtue of her talent and grit, she has become one of New York City's star performers. Please give a warm welcome," Howie continued, "to the incomparable, the unrivaled, the exquisite Alicia the Armless Wonder!"

Sam could practically feel waves of fury radiating from Max's skin when Alicia took the stage. She was dressed in a trim red jacket with the loose sleeves tied neatly behind her back, dark tights rolled up so her feet were visible, and a pleated skirt. She was as different from Max as could be imagined: all sugary smiles, blond ringlet hair, and pink cheeks. And she was good—there was no denying that. Before starting in on the knives, she shuffled a deck of cards, buttered a slice of toast, and tied a ribbon in her hair. All with her feet.

Next to Sam, Pippa was white-faced, squinting with concentration. Sam recognized now what she was doing: she was trying to read Alicia. But he couldn't imagine why.

Suddenly, even as Alicia prepared to throw her knives and the crowd once again fell silent, Pippa let out a loud snort. Sam stared at her.

"What is it?" he whispered.

Pippa's expression cleared. She slumped backward. "She's a fraud."

"Shhhh." Several people pivoted around to hush them. Howie—who was now serving as assistant to Alicia's act by balancing an apple on top of his head so that Alicia could knock it off with a knife—scowled in their direction.

"What do you mean?" Sam whispered. This time, several more people said *shhh* and glared. She shook her head.

Onstage, Alicia gripped a long-handled knife with her toes, balancing expertly on one leg. Pippa leaned across Sam, cupped a hand to Max's ear, and whispered something. For the first time since entering the Coney Island Curiosity Show, Max smiled.

"Ladies and gentlemen," Howie was saying as Alicia raised the knife, one knee hooked like that of a crane, "please watch carefully. For her grand finale, Alicia will—"

Suddenly there was a sharp whistling sound. For a split second Sam saw two blades crisscross in the air, metal glinting under the stage lights, and he thought, confusedly, that Alicia had must have thrown her knives. But no—the knives had been thrown from the audience.

From *Max*. He hadn't even seen her move. But sure enough, the knives had sailed directly over the heads of the seated crowd, slicing off the feather from a woman's hat in the process, and, like skimming a surface of mold from a block of cheese, perfectly shaved the jacket right off Alicia's shoulders. The jacket, now nothing but rags, plopped to the stage.

The whole audience gasped.

And Sam burst out laughing.

Alicia's upper body was wrapped like a mummy's in what looked like a single long strip of cloth bandage.

And beneath that bandage, held tight to her torso and concealed by her jacket, were two perfectly functional arms.

Howie's face went completely white. Alicia stood

blinking under the spotlight, mouthing soundlessly, even as the audience's protest grew to a roar.

"It's a scam!" someone shouted.

"There's nothing wrong with her."

"We paid to see *freaks*, not frauds!"

The rat-faced barker—whom Sam now assumed to be the owner—hurtled onstage, trying to calm the outraged crowd. And still Alicia stood there, stuttering apologies, with her arms strapped around her waist and Howie staring at her as if she were a three-week-old turkey sandwich.

"Nicely done, Max," Thomas said. The crowd surged around them, rushing the stage, so they were comfortably engulfed in a wave of sound.

Max shrugged. But she couldn't conceal her look of pleasure. "I had help," she said. For a moment, she and Pippa shared a smile. Around them, the audience was still shouting.

"I want my money back!"

"And *my* money!"

"And *mine*!"

"All right," Pippa said. "I think that's our cue."

They began moving toward the exit, fighting the surge of people still flowing toward the stage. Alicia had at last fled into the wings, although Howie was still standing under the spotlight with that stupid apple on the middle of his head, as rigid as a statue. Only his eyes moved: darting back and forth over the crowd, scanning the individual faces. And for a split second, just before Sam reached the exit, Howie's eyes found his in the crowd. His lips were curled back like an animal's, and Sam had a flicker of misgiving.

Howie, he knew, was not the type to forgive and forget.

18

Max barely registered the long subway ride back to the museum. She kept imagining the look on Howie's face when Alicia's jacket had thudded to the stage, revealing both arms wrapped up tightly like meat in a sausage casing. Good old Pippa. Max couldn't remember why she was so often annoyed with her—at this moment, it seemed to Max that Pippa had never once done anything wrong, not even when she corrected Max's grammar or lectured Max on the correct way to make a bed or made a disgusted noise when Max licked her plate.

The sun was just setting when they reached Times Square, and to Max the sky had never looked more beautiful, striped with pinks and yellows and blues like the layered cookies in one of the Italian bakeries on Mulberry Street. As they approached the museum and saw a small crowd gathered on the steps, necks craned toward the sky, Max thought for a second that the other residents of the museum were simply admiring the colors. Then she saw Mr. Dumfrey pointing to something in the air, while Miss Fitch wore her usual expression of faint disapproval.

"What?" Thomas said. "What is it?"

"Just wait and see, my boy," Mr. Dumfrey said, keeping his eyes glued to the sky. "Any second now . . ."

Max looked up. Above them, a prop plane appeared, silhouetted against the blue—and as everyone watched, made a sudden dip and twist in the sky, leaving behind a puff of wispy white cloud that slowly began to resolve itself into a letter. The plane kept going, looping and curling, leaving a trail of puffy white letters in its wake, even as a cheer went up from the assembled crowd. Soon an entire sentence was etched across the sky, and several of the performers read it out loud in unison.

"'Dumfrey's Dim Museum. Home of Emily the Tattooed Wonder.'"

"Magnificent," Mr. Dumfrey said with a happy sigh.

Gil Kestrel grunted. "Looks shaky to me." Max

remembered what Sam had told her: that Gil, too, had once been a pilot.

"Dim Museum," Pippa read out loud. She frowned. "Shouldn't it say *Dime* Museum?"

"Dim Museum, Dime Museum!" Mr. Dumfrey waved a hand. "It's Emily that counts."

Lash chuckled. "Ace O'Toole was never big on spelling," he said. "Good pilot, though. Best crop duster in Oklahoma."

"Crop duster?" Max had never heard the words. "What's that?"

Lash smiled at her. When he did, his eyes crinkled so much they nearly disappeared. "You're a born city slicker, ain't you? A crop duster's a pilot hired to fly low over the fields, spray 'em down with 'secticide to keep the pests away. O'Toole had one of the best reps in the biz."

Max squinted again at the words in the sky, which were even now breaking apart on a faint breeze.

"What about the big orange turkey?" she said. "You going to advertise that?"

"I assume," sniffed Mr. Dumfrey, "that you are referring to my rare Ethiopian Firebird. And about that . . ." His expression cleared. "Ah, here he is now. Sir Roger Barrensworth! Thank you for coming, sir!"

Max turned and saw a man moving deliberately down the street, punctuating every step with a silver-tipped umbrella, despite the fact that it had been sunny all day. He had a sharp, narrow, sunburned face, with an eager expression made all the more pronounced by his large front teeth. His hair was long, dark, and curled at his collar, and he was well dressed in a slim-fitting jacket, highly polished shoes, and a bowler hat. Max disliked him immediately.

"Mr. Dumfrey, a pleasure to see you again," he said, offering Mr. Dumfrey his hand limply, as if he expected it to be kissed, not shaken. His words were tinged with an accent that didn't sound *quite* Italian.

"Sir Barrensworth." Mr. Dumfrey pumped the man's hand vigorously—so much so that Sir Barrensworth winced. "Thank you for coming so promptly, sir. You see," he said, turning back to Max, "I contacted Sir Barrensworth to complain about certain, er, features of the bird."

Pippa crossed her arms. "Like the fact that it can't keep its mouth shut?" she said.

Mr. Dumfrey inclined his head. "Sir Barrensworth kindly agreed to come right over and give the bird a talking to."

"The bird can be trained, on my honor," Sir

Barrensworth said. "We sailed back together from Africa, you know, all around the tip of Cape Home and across the Strait of Gibberish."

Thomas frowned. "You mean the tip of Cape Horn?" he said. "And the Strait of Gibraltar?"

Sir Barrensworth gave Thomas a weasely smile, revealing a wad of gum stuck in the corner of his mouth. "That's what I said, isn't it? The sailors swore up a storm, and the bird picked up the habit. Show him to me and I'll soon set him straight."

"Thank you, sir," Mr. Dumfrey said. He looked as if he might be inclined to shake Sir Barrensworth's hand again. Sir Barrensworth wisely crossed his arms as they started up the museum steps. "I can't tell you how much I appreciate it. I know a man like you . . . with your busy schedule . . ." And together, they disappeared into the museum.

Thomas raised an eyebrow. "What do you think of Sir Barrensworth?" he asked.

"Looks like a cheat to me," Max said.

Pippa sniffed. "Filthy pockets," she said. "It's an absolute *mess* in there. Gum wrappers and pen caps and ferry tickets and tissues." She shivered. "Awful."

Max, Pippa, Thomas, and Sam followed Mr. Dumfrey and Sir Barrensworth into the museum. As soon as they entered the lobby, the phone on the ticket desk began to ring. It was rare for anyone to call the museum. Max was struck by a terrible thought: her little performance at the Coney Island Curiosity Show must somehow have been reported to the police.

"I'll get it!" she shouted, skidding around Lash, who'd already started in the direction of the desk. She practically threw herself on the telephone.

"Dumfrey's Dime Museum," she said breathlessly.

"I have Rosie Bickers," came a nervous squeak from the other end of the phone, "for Mr. Dumfrey, please."

Instantly relieved, Max cupped her palm over the receiver. "Mr. Dumfrey," she called, before Mr. Dumfrey could get halfway up the stairs. "For you."

"You go ahead, Sir Barrensworth," Mr. Dumfrey called unnecessarily, since Sir Barrensworth showed no signs of being inclined to wait. Mr. Dumfrey came trotting back down the stairs. *Rosie Bickers*, Max mouthed, in response to his questioning look. Mr. Dumfrey straightened his bow tie and took the receiver from Max's hand.

"Rosie!" he said with a beaming smile. "To what do I owe the—?" He fell abruptly silent. "Mmm-hmmm," he said, and his smile dimmed and then faded altogether. "Mmmm-hmmm."

211 ☞

Pippa, Thomas, and Sam had all been hanging back, waiting for Max. Now they drew closer to the ticket desk. "What is it, Mr. Dumfrey?" asked Pippa.

Mr. Dumfrey shook his head, holding up a finger. "Yes, I'm still here. Yes, I can hear you. You were saying something about Mallett . . . ?"

A zip of fear raced up Max's spine. Thomas stiffened as if he'd been shocked. And Sam and Pippa exchanged a worried look.

"What about Mallett?" Pippa tried again, this time in an urgent whisper.

But Mr. Dumfrey didn't seem to hear her. Now his mouth had settled into a hard line. "Yes," he said. "Yes, extremely. I understand." And without another word, he hung up. Instantly, his shoulders sagged, as if instead of a telephone he'd been carrying a fifty-pound weight.

The children waited in nervous silence for him to speak, until finally Max couldn't bear it anymore. "What did Rosie have to say about Mallett?" she asked.

Mr. Dumfrey exhaled—a faint, whistling sound that reminded Max of steam leaving the kettle. "Rosie's just heard from one of her friends in the police department," he said. At last, he raised his eyes. "Mallett's dead," he said. "He killed himself this afternoon."

19

"'Benny Mallett, aged forty-seven, was discovered by Sergeant Schroeder and Officer Gilhooley at five thirty p.m. yesterday afternoon,'" Thomas read. He was huddled over *The Daily Screamer*, sitting shoulder to shoulder with Pippa. "'The officers would not disclose the reason for their visit to Mallett's remote warehouse . . .'" He paused to flip a page and resumed, "'seven hundred feet above the ground, to moor directly atop the Empire State Building.'"

"What?" Max wrinkled her nose. "That doesn't make any sense."

Thomas scanned a finger over the line of type.

"Sorry. Wrong column. That one's about the dirigible launch. Here we go. 'The officers would not disclose the reason for their visit to Mallett's remote warehouse in Sheepshead Bay, Brooklyn, but sources say that it was in connection with new evidence that has surfaced in the ongoing investigation into the murder of exterminator Ernest Erskine, a crime for which General Archibald Farnum is currently awaiting trial.'"

Pippa straightened up. "Rosie must have bugged the police about Mallett after all," she said. "They never would have made the connection on their own."

"Fat lot of good it did," Sam said, stretching his arms above his head and yawning.

It was seven thirty in the morning, and the children were the first and only ones in the kitchen. Max had barely slept at all last night, and her eyes were gritty with exhaustion.

Her dreams were a strange collision of past and present: Mallett's face, bloated and red, displayed behind a glass case like the ones in the Hall of Worldwide Wonders next to a placard that read *Murder Suspect, Wrongly Convicted*; a turbulent sea in which she struggled helplessly, her arms tied behind her back, while high above her on the boardwalk a crowd had gathered to point at her and laugh; planes that turned and wrote eerie messages in the sky. *Watch out. I'm coming for you.*

Finally, shortly after four, she'd given up trying to sleep. Still, she couldn't shake the pathetic image of Mallett alone at his desk. According to the paper, they'd seen him only a few hours before he'd ended his life. Could they have stopped him? Could they have helped?

Thomas cleared his throat and continued reading. "'But the police were too late. When they arrived, they found Benny Mallett dead, the victim of an apparent suicide. A preliminary medical examination has concluded that he died instantly of a shot to the chest. The gun that was used to kill him was still in his hand.'" Thomas pushed the paper toward the center of the table. "Look. There's even a picture."

"Ugh. No thank you," Pippa said, making a face. "I've seen enough dead bodies for one lifetime, thank you very much."

"Don't be a baby," Thomas said serenely. "You can't even see any blood."

"Thanks. That's very reassuring. Corpses turn my stomach. *Pass.*"

Max dunked four tea bags into her mug of hot water at once, waiting until the liquid turned mud-black. She took her mug to the table, ignoring Pippa's look of disgust when she dumped five teaspoons of sugar into her tea. Whatever good feeling had existed yesterday between them was now gone. Had ended precisely at four thirty, actually, when Pippa had suddenly thrown off her covers, sat up, and hissed, "If you're going to be tossing and turning every two minutes, can you at *least* have the grace to do it elsewhere? Some of us actually enjoy *quiet* when we sleep."

Max bent over the newspaper, taking a long slurp of her tea. Immediately, she felt more alert.

Thomas was right: you couldn't see any blood. The picture was grainy and showed Benny Mallett, head slumped forward on his desk beside a tower of correspondence. His right hand, still clutching the gun, was visible next to it.

"Poor Benny," Sam said. He had physically recoiled from the newspaper, as if the phantom of Mallett might float off the page. "He really loved those fleas."

"Loved killing them," Max corrected him.

Sam sighed. "Maybe if we'd stayed with him . . ."

"We couldn't have done anything," Thomas said firmly, taking hold of the paper again and bending forward to study it.

"We could have talked to him," Pippa said, snatching away the peanut butter before Thomas could go in for another dip. "He was *depressed*."

When Thomas glanced up, he looked grimly

satisfied, as if he'd successfully answered a question he wished had never been asked. "Maybe," he said. "But it wasn't suicide."

There was a moment of silence. This was the kind of statement that Thomas sometimes made, out of the blue. It made Max want to take his shoulders and shake him until that remarkable brain came out through his nose.

"But," Sam spluttered, "but the paper said—"

Before he could finish speaking, Danny and Smalls came thumping down the stairs, side by side—or as side by side as they could get, given that Danny only reached Smalls's kneecap—and arguing about who had been snoring the loudest the night before.

"Since when has the paper ever gotten anything right?" Thomas adjusted his glasses and stood up. "Hold on. I'll show you. Danny, can you come here for a second?"

Danny's only reply was a grunt. Max had been living at the museum for long enough to know that he required at least four cups of coffee before you could get a single word from him that wasn't an insult or a complaint—five if you wanted more than one syllable. But he begrudgingly came over to the table.

"Sit down, Danny," Thomas said.

"Do I look like your trained monkey?" Danny growled.

"Please," Thomas said. "Just do it."

Grumbling, Danny took a seat on the bench. This required him to clamber up on his hands and knees before sliding into a seated position. He didn't, Max realized, look all that much shorter than Mallett. Danny was insecure about his size, which was a source of tension between him and his other dwarf friends, who felt he was too tall.

Thomas took a step back, squinting, and then grabbed a telephone book that was being used to correct an extremely wobbly table in the corner. He set it down on the bench and had Danny perch on top of it. Now Danny's head and shoulders were visible above the table, just as Mallett's had been. "Much better," Thomas said. "Now pretend to shoot yourself in the chest."

Danny made a gun with his pointer finger and thumb and held it to his chest—or at least Max thought he did, since even sitting on the phone book, most of Danny's chest was invisible and she could see only the very tip of his thumb.

"Bang," Thomas said, and then nudged Danny's shoulder with a hand, indicating that he should slump forward onto the table—just as Mallett had done, so that his forehead was resting on the wood. His gun hand fell unseen on his lap, below the tabletop.

"Alas, poor Danny! Untimely death hath closed

thine gentle eyes!" Smalls recited, clutching a massive fist to his chest.

Max felt a prickling sensation that began in her hands and then spread, as she always did when an idea was dancing just out of range—an itch to reach out and simply grab hold of it. Something was wrong with the picture, but she couldn't make the thing, the wrongness, come to light.

Danny turned his head, still pressed to the tabletop. "Can I sit up now?"

"One more second," Thomas said. He turned to the others triumphantly. "You see?"

Sam frowned. "Not really," he said.

Thomas smiled. "The police report says that Mallett died instantly," he said, and pointed to the grainy picture of Mallett, his forehead resting atop his cluttered desk, with his hand, still clutching the gun, a few inches away. And suddenly the itchy feeling turned, for Max, into a full-on burst of understanding.

"I don't get it," Pippa said crossly.

"Gravity," Thomas said. "Mallett's hand would have dropped onto his lap after he shot himself. But in the picture, his hand is lying on his desk. Which means he would have had to raise his hand—*after* he was dead."

"Murder," Smalls whispered. "Murder most foul."

20

"Murder," Pippa repeated in a whisper. Then she snatched the newspaper, as if she would find evidence in it that Thomas was wrong.

Sam's expression was grim. "Mallett and Erskine's murders *have* to be connected. And there's no way Farnum could have done it—he's been locked up this whole time." He looked around at the others. "We've got to talk to Rosie Bickers. We've got to tell her."

Max made a face. "What's *she* going to do? She's been exactly *no* help so far."

Sam rolled his eyes. "You just don't like her."

"So?" Max fired back.

"So?" He threw up his hands. "You don't like *anyone*."

Thomas expected Max to snap back. Instead, she just turned and made a strange face, as if she'd accidentally taken a gulp of sour milk. "That's not true," she said shortly.

"Oh, sorry." Sam rolled his eyes. "You don't like anyone except for *Howie*."

"If you say his name one more time," Max said in her normal tone of voice, which was somewhere between a grunt and a snarl, "I'll take your tongue out through your nostrils."

"Technically speaking, that's not physically possible," Thomas felt compelled to say, and then quickly shut his mouth when Max glared at him.

Pippa was doubled over the article about Mallett's death, her long black bangs hanging down over her eyes, her nose skimming only an inch above the ink.

"What happened to your sensitive stomach?" Thomas asked.

But Pippa ignored him. Suddenly, she let out a short cry and sprang up from her seat. "A magnifying glass," she said. "I need a magnifying glass!"

By this time, most of the residents of the museum had come down to breakfast, and Pippa's sudden demand provoked a babble of responses. Smalls offered to lend his reading glasses, which proved totally useless. Danny suggested that she use a juice glass, tipped upside down, which proved even more so. Betty said that Pippa would ruin her eyes, and the twins gloatingly implied that she was already getting frown marks just from squinting so long at the newspaper. Nobody had a magnifying glass, in any case, although the children were temporarily encouraged by Goldini's appearance, since he always had a bunch of odds and ends concealed in his vest and waist pockets. But after a thorough search, he produced nothing but some trick coins, five aces of spades, a long multicolored handkerchief, and, in a hidden pocket he had entirely forgotten about, an Easter egg, dyed a mottled red color.

At last Thomas had the idea to look in the chamber of horrors portion of the Hall of Wax and discovered a magnifying glass clutched in the wax fist of the famous surgeon Joseph Bell, on whom the character Sherlock Holmes had supposedly been modeled.

Immediately, Pippa dropped to her knees and flattened the newspaper on the floor, once again peering at the photograph showing poor Benny Mallett's body. They were all alone in the Hall of Wax, which on the busiest days was one of the museum's most popular exhibits. Now, however, in the early morning, it was dark, full of shadows and echoes. All of the dozens of wax figures, many of them created by Siegfried "Freck-les" Eckleberger, stared out from their displays with blank, unseeing eyes. Though he knew it was stupid, Thomas couldn't shake the feeling that they really could see him—that they were watching.

"I knew it." Pippa leaned back on her heels. Her face was flushed. "I wasn't sure before, but now it's clear as anything."

"What's clear?" Max said, shouldering Pippa out of the way and snatching the magnifying glass.

But just then there was a loud commotion from upstairs, and they were temporarily distracted by the colorful string of curses coming from the attic. There they found Lash Langtry trying to wrangle the Fire-bird back into its cage.

"What happened?" Thomas asked.

Lash was sweating as he strained to force the fran-tically flapping bird to pass through the narrow cage entrance. "Mr. Dumfrey left the cage open after a feeding," he said, grunting with exertion as the bird squawked and protested. "The filthy varmint tried to make a break for it."

"And you brought it *back*?" Max asked in a tone of disbelief. Thomas had to agree with her: so far, the Firebird had proven to be nothing but a pain. Even

Cornelius, Mr. Dumfrey's pet cockatoo, was so angry about the new arrival that he would do nothing but chirp the same song over and over again, an awful dirge called "Why the Caged Bird Weeps."

They got back to reading the newspaper. Max, who still had the magnifying glass, spread the photo on the floor of the attic and kneeled over it. "What am I supposed to be looking at?"

"You're not supposed to be looking at anything," Pippa said, snatching back the glass. "What you *are* looking at are gum wrappers. Five of them, Tendermint brand, sitting right on top of the wastepaper basket."

They took turns with the magnifying glass. Pippa was right. Crumpled at the very top of the collection of old envelopes and unpaid invoices were the same wrappers that Sir Barrensworth had left in Mr. Dumfrey's wastebasket.

"It could be a coincidence," Sam said. "Ten thousand people might chew Tendermint gum. Maybe Mallett liked it."

"I've never heard of it," Pippa said. "Besides"—she wrinkled her nose—"I got the feeling Mallett hadn't gone near a mint—or a toothbrush—in days."

"It doesn't make any sense." Max crossed her arms, blowing her tangled bangs out of her face. "What's in it for Sir Barrenswott or whatever his name is if he bumps off Mallett?"

"I don't know," Pippa admitted. Her chin was inching incrementally into the air. When she was extremely angry, you could see all the way up her nostrils. "Didn't he just get back from Africa?"

"So he claims," Thomas said. Something was bugging him: he could feel a corner, an angle of the picture that wasn't aligning right. Or maybe *he* was the one who wasn't aligning things correctly. He was missing something important.

What had started as a simple enough problem—to prove that Farnum didn't kill Ernie Erskine—had taken so many sharp pinwheel turns to the left, Thomas now felt almost totally lost. And Rattigan was still out there, plotting something, free from police interference. Thomas was sure of it. They should be spending their time trying to find him. But now that they'd started down this road, they couldn't just turn back—no matter how twisty and difficult the road had become.

Pippa shrugged. "Maybe Barrensworth was settling an old score."

"So Mallett and Erskine's deaths aren't related?" Sam said, scratching his head.

Even Pippa had to admit that seemed unlikely. What had felt like an electrifying breakthrough now seemed to be another dead end. Still, Thomas kept having the poky sense that he was missing some fact or connection—but every time he reached and stretched for it, it was like bending backward too far and coming face-to-face with nothing but floor.

He closed his eyes. Sir Barrensworth . . . the Firebird . . . the mess of papers on Mallett's desk . . . mess . . . messy pockets . . .

Bing. Just like that, a small alarm went off in his head.

He opened his eyes. "Pippa," he said excitedly, "remember when you read Sir Barrensworth's pockets?"

"Unfortunately," she said, shuddering.

"Can you remember everything he had in them?"

She narrowed her eyes suspiciously. "More of that gum, for starters," she said. "And—I don't know—the usual stuff. Loose coins. Pen caps. Subway tokens and ferry stubs—"

"*Which* ferry?" Thomas asked. Now Sam and Max were staring at him, too.

"Don't be a pill," Pippa said. "You know very well which ferry. There's only one, and it goes to Staten Island. So just tell us what you're thinking."

Thomas felt a warm rush all the way to his fingers, as he did whenever he was closing in on the solution to a complicated math problem, or when he had just managed to free himself from a particularly small and airless space. "Mallett told us he couldn't get any supply of the poison he needed," he said. "He told us some kingpin on Staten Island was buying it up by the truckloads. Well, Sir Barrensworth has been going back and forth to Staten Island."

"You think Sir *Barrensworth* was Mallett's big competition?" Max said.

"Maybe," Thomas said. "Or maybe he works for the competition." He'd only met Sir Barrensworth the day before, and then only briefly, but he hadn't gotten the impression of any great intelligence. The Firebird hadn't shown any signs of improving its attitude, either, despite Sir Barrensworth's offer to help. The bird had spent half the night letting off a stream of words, most of them curses.

Sam shook his head. "But why kill him, then? The poor guy was already deep in the hole. You heard what Mallett said. He was done for."

"I don't know," Thomas said firmly, even as he was making his way to the stairs. "But we need to talk to Bickers. Maybe she can find out." When Max opened her mouth to protest, Thomas quickly cut her off. "I don't care if you like her or not," he said. "It's the only way."

"Who're you calling filthy, you stinking hunk of beef jerky?" the bird shrieked.

"Beef jerky, huh?" Finally, Lash managed to force the bird onto its perch and shut and latched the cage door, but not without accidentally detaching one of the Firebird's extraordinary rainbow-colored feathers. The bird, however, hardly seemed to notice. Puffed up with outrage, it continued insulting Lash in its large and colorful vocabulary, sticking to a theme of Lash's poor personal hygiene and general stupidity.

Lash stood up wearily, dusting off his knees. "Should have let the darned thing fly off, as far as I'm concerned," he said. "Been nothing but trouble since it came through those doors."

"Look on the bright side," Thomas said. "Thanksgiving's not that far away. And I bet Firebird tastes great with cranberry sauce."

"Mmm, I'm not so sure," Pippa said, raising an eyebrow, as the bird continued to huff and swear. "I think it might leave a *very* bad taste in the mouth."

They hadn't taken two steps out the door when Sam stopped short, causing Thomas to run directly into him—which felt a little bit like running straight into a cement wall.

"Ow," Thomas said, rubbing his elbow, which had made impact with Sam's lower back. "What's the matter with you?"

Sam didn't take his eyes off the street. "I don't believe it," he murmured.

Thomas followed the direction of his gaze and saw nothing out of the ordinary. Emily was leaning against the gate—wearing not her typical long-sleeved, ankle-length coat but a simple day dress whose sleeves reached only to the elbow, leaving many of her vibrantly colored tattoos on display—talking and laughing with an unfamiliar man wearing a dusty hat. Every so often, a passerby would swivel around to stare at the coils of color looping around her wrists and ankles—as, in fact, Mr. Dumfrey had hoped they would. He had actually suggested that Emily should start spending part of her lunch breaks outside, as a form of free advertisement for the museum.

"What?" Thomas's elbow ached and he was annoyed about it. "I don't see what's so special about . . ." But then the man in the hat turned slightly, so that the shadows fell across his face differently, and the words died in Thomas's throat. He stood there gaping next to his friends.

The man was none other than Gil Kestrel, the

perpetually foul-tempered janitor. He had been momentarily unrecognizable for the simple but absolutely astounding fact that he was *smiling*.

Never once since Kestrel had joined up with the museum had Thomas ever seen Kestrel crack a smile—not when the twins had fumbled a step during a complicated *pas de deux* and ended up flat on their backs with their legs, still in unison, kicking in the air; not when Smalls and Danny, for a joke, had posed as mannequins in the Hall of Wax and spent the morning jumping out at people; not even when one of Goldini's doves had swooped off the stage and snatched the toupee off of a man in the front row who had been complaining loudly about the poor quality of the acts. So bizarre, so totally unexpected, was this change that it made Kestrel look like a stranger.

Even weirder was the fact that, just after spotting the kids, he immediately waved them over. At least he still had a toothpick wedged in the corner of his mouth. Had he removed this permanent accessory, Sam might have fainted.

"Come here," Kestrel said, still smiling widely, as if all along they'd been the best of friends. "You've gotta see this! Go on, Emily. Show them," he urged her, turning back to Emily and nudging her with an elbow.

Pippa and Max exchanged a smirking, knowing glance.

"Oh, they don't care," Emily said, blushing. "It's just an old story."

"It's better than any story I ever heard," Kestrel said. "Come on, tell them."

"I was telling Gil about Icarus," Emily said. Even the way she said *Gil* was surprising—everybody else called Gil *Kestrel*, except for Mr. Dumfrey, who called him, for reasons related to an old joke on which he had never elaborated, Butter Boy or Bean Shooter. "You know the story of Icarus, don't you?"

"I do," Pippa said importantly, before Thomas could say that he did, too. "He wanted to fly so he made wings of wax. But he went too close to the sun and the wings melted."

Emily turned over her arm so that the soft skin of her inner wrist was revealed. Painted there were vivid blue waves reaching up to swallow a pair of kicking ankles, and a set of enormous, gold-tinged wings.

"How about that?" Kestrel's voice was now lower and more melancholy. "He was a fly-boy, just like me. Crashed and burned, just like me, too."

"Oh, but there's another lesson to be learned, Gil. Here. I'll show you one of my favorites." She hitched her left sleeve even higher. On her bicep, just above her elbow, was a beautiful tattooed illustration of a bird, with flame-colored feathers and a look of pure, soaring joy on its face. It was rising up from what looked like a campfire.

"What is that?" Kestrel asked, making a face. "Another Firebird?"

She laughed and shook her head. "It's a phoenix," she said. "Legend has it that phoenixes live and die in flame. They crash and burn, too. But they always rise again. That's why it's my favorite tattoo. It reminds me that no matter how dark things get, there's always a chance to be reborn."

Kestrel didn't speak right away. When he did, his voice was thick with feeling. "Emily . . . ," he said, and then stopped, as if the force of his emotions was strangling him.

It was time to make an exit. Thomas coughed awkwardly. "Okay. Well, then. I guess we'll see you later," he said as loudly as possible, since he was afraid that Emily and Kestrel might simply start kissing in front of him. But Emily and Kestrel, now gazing deep into each other's eyes, obviously didn't hear.

21

The air had a bite to it. Despite the early hour, the sun was lagging behind the buildings, striping the streets in shadow, and the wind had the sharp blow of autumn. Soon the weather would turn, and the rain would arrive to tumble the leaves from the streets and turn them to mulch in the gutters, to send the city, shivering, inside.

It was amazing to think that at this time last year, Max had been a perfect stranger. Thomas, Pippa, and Sam had in some ways been strangers to one another—coexisting without being friends, maybe afraid to admit to the similarities among them, afraid to acknowledge what they all suspected: that of all the other residents of the museum, they were the real and true freaks.

That was before Max had arrived on the doorstep, fierce and proud and perfect—there was no point in trying to deny it anymore; Sam *did* think she was perfect, except perhaps for her tendency to look at him as if he was a squashed bug on the sole of her shoe—before Rattigan had escaped from prison and revealed their awful pasts and ripped a hole in their world. Ever since then, it seemed that trouble followed them everywhere. It was as if Rattigan was a kind of evil eye in reverse. Once he had turned his gaze on them, they'd learned to see as he did and found evidence of evil everywhere.

Could Sam ever forget what Rattigan had done to them? Could he forgive? And would things ever return to normal?

But even as Sam thought the question, he knew that there had never been a normal—not for him, not for anyone at the museum, maybe not for anyone in the world. And he thought again about what Mr. Dumfrey had said: that change always came, that it was bound to come. That Thomas, Max, Sam, and Pippa would someday have to look out for one another.

And maybe, just maybe, they were ready.

As soon as they entered Rosie's office, Sam knew it was a mistake to have come—especially when they almost immediately had to dodge an enormous blizzard of papers that came flying at their heads.

"I told you to *stay* out!" Rosie was bellowing from an unseen portion of her office—a sentence presumably uttered at the young man they'd once again seen fleeing down the stairs—while her harried assistant once again did her best to melt into her desk. A moment later, Rosie's head appeared around the corner and Sam accidentally let out a cry of alarm. Her hair was an enormous frizzled mass around her head, kind of like a giant sea anemone that had become stuck to her forehead and was frantically waving to be let off.

"Oh, it's the kid wonders," she said. She didn't sound exactly upset to see them, but she didn't sound exactly happy, either. She patted down her hair, which had the effect of doing absolutely nothing. "Come in, come in. Sorry for the mess. Busy week. Had a little tiff with the opposing counsel on one of my cases. You might have seen him on his way out. Last time he'll expect *me* to settle."

Sam had not thought that Rosie's office could have grown messier since the last time they'd seen it. But the piles had definitely multiplied. It looked as if someone were making a miniature of the Manhattan skyline in paper.

"How do you find anything in here?" Pippa said, wrinkling her nose. Sam knew how much Pippa hated disorder—she color-coded all her clothing and often sneaked into the exhibits late at night to reorder any objects that had been slightly disarranged.

"Oh, I have a system." Rosie waved a hand vaguely and took a seat on top of the radiator, which was one of the only clear surfaces in the place. "To what do I owe the pleasure?"

Thomas, Sam, and Pippa exchanged a look. Max was staring resolutely at the floor, scowling.

"Well," Thomas said. "It's kind of a long story." He took a deep breath and started in. He reminded Rosie about how they'd gone to Erskine's workshop and found the letter to Benny Mallett. He told her about the visit to Mallett, and about the photograph in the newspaper, and that it proved Mallett couldn't have killed himself. He even told her about the mysterious Sir Barrensworth and his habit of leaving gum wrappers everywhere.

"So you see," Thomas finished, "General Farnum couldn't have done it—couldn't have done any of it."

For a long moment, Rosie said nothing. Then she stood up. "I see," she said. "I see holes. More holes than in a grandmother's pincushion."

236 ☞

"But—" Thomas started to protest. Rosie held up a hand to silence him.

"Listen to me." She shook her head. "I'm on your side. Farnum didn't do it—I know that. But I've got to be realistic. I've got to look at it the way a jury's going to look at it. The connection between Erskine and Mallett? Could be a coincidence. And if the police are saying suicide, that's what most people are going to believe. As for Sir Barrensworth . . ." She shook her head. "A gum wrapper isn't exactly a smoking gun."

"But—" This time, Pippa tried to speak.

"I said *listen*," Rosie said. But then, for at least a minute, she didn't say anything. She turned her back on them and instead stared out the window, where Sam could see cranes and construction, buildings half-finished, stretching for the sky. When she finally spoke again, it was in a totally different voice—hesitating, soft. "You kids are special," she said. "I get that. But what *you* don't get is how lucky you are." She turned back to face them. "Dumfrey's done his best to keep you protected. Maybe he went about it differently than most people would have, but there you have it. So you're smart and you're different and you're strong, and you think you can take on the whole world." She looked at each of them in turn—even Max, who'd finally unglued her gaze from the floor. When her eyes landed on Sam he understood why she could win hopeless cases, why she was one of the most famous lawyers in New York City. He *believed* her. He knew that everything she said would be the truth. "You grew up a little and you learned about evil. Well, now you're going to grow up a little bit more. Evil isn't always obvious. It's not always the people who make headlines. Evil is sometimes in the failure of people to do the right thing. The brave thing. Evil sometimes just looks like going along with the crowd. And you know what? In that way, we're all a little bit evil."

And Sam knew then that somehow she had *seen*. Not like Pippa could see, but with a kind of understanding that was almost like magic. She understood them, and she understood that the world would never consider them normal. And she also understood that their difference was a strength and not a weakness or an excuse.

As always, Sam felt the strength running through him like a current. But for the first time in his life, he wasn't ashamed.

"That's why I like the hopeless cases, you know." For a split second Rosie Bickers, in her fuchsia suit, with her hair sticking out straight from her head, looked beautiful. "I like to go against the crowd. Somebody's got to. And it's a reminder that we can."

For a moment, there was silence. Even Max was staring at Rosie with newfound respect. Then Rosie cleared her throat. Suddenly, she was all business again.

"I want to help you," she said in her usual brisk tone, turning her attention to a stack of papers on her desk. "I do. So I'm going to do my best for General Farnum. As for the rest of it—the theories and the this-and-that . . ." She shook her head. "Sorry, kiddos. You're on your own."

22

"I knew it." They'd barely reached the street when Max allowed her rage to bubble up. "I *told* you seeing that old crow was a waste of our time."

"Come on, Max," Sam said, toeing the sidewalk with a scuffed-up shoe. "Rosie's not that bad, is she? She's just trying to be realistic. She's right. No jury's going to believe us."

Max opened her mouth, then shut it again. It was *so like* Sam to disagree with her. Every time she turned around, he was still needling her about Howie, or telling her to *calm down, be reasonable, don't be so angry.* What on earth, she wondered, was his problem?

So now she didn't bother answering. She just spun

around and plunged back into the crowd heading south.

"Wait!" Thomas quickly caught up to her, and the others hurried behind him. "Where do you think you're going?"

"You said Sir Bottomsworth, or whatever his name is, might be wrapped up in this mess, didn't you?" Max said, tossing her hair. For once, it was her turn to take the lead. "Well, I'm going to ask him."

What she couldn't admit, of course, was that she had no idea what she would actually *say*. She guessed that Sir Butterswhat wasn't very likely to roll and 'fess up to murdering two people, just as a *by the way*—especially not a soggy toast like that, with a *Sir* at the front of a name that sounded like something you'd cough out when you had the flu. He probably thought he was smarter than everybody else. Still, no one objected to the plan—not even Sam, Max was pleased to see.

They hadn't gone half a block when a tall, skinny man with the look of a frightened jackrabbit burst out of the post office, nearly colliding with Max and forcing her to take a quick step backward.

"There you are," he said, and it took Max a second to realize he was deliberately addressing her. "Been waiting for the past forty-five minutes for you lot. Began to think someone was pulling my leg, on account of my being new." He was wearing the uniform of a postal worker. His nose twitched agitatedly as he spoke. "Had my face practically squashed to the window, worried I would miss you."

"Worried you would miss *us*?" Pippa stared up at him.

He seemed not to have heard her. He rummaged in his pockets and produced a small folded slip of paper that Max recognized as a telegram. She'd never received a telegram before and for a moment after she unfolded the slip of paper she stood there blinking, trying to unpuzzle the message, which was written entirely in capital letters and totally without punctuation. Next to her, Pippa gasped and Thomas let out a little strangled sound.

"What is it?" Sam's voice was a low and urgent whisper. "What does it say?"

Max blinked, forcing the words to come into focus.

HELLO DEAR CHILDREN STOP HAVE YOU MISSED ME STOP I'VE MISSED YOU STOP DON'T WORRY I WILL SOON RISE LIKE A PHOENIX FROM THE ASHES AND MAKE BEAUTIFUL FIRE

Chop-chop-chop. Her brain churned slowly across the lines of text, chopping the message into phrases that made sense. *Hello, dear children. Have you missed me? I've missed you. Don't worry, I will soon rise like a phoenix from the ashes and make beautiful fire.*

"No." Sam was reading over Max's shoulder. "No, it's impossible."

"Where did you get this?" Max demanded. Suddenly she felt exposed, as if she'd been turned inside out. *Hiding in plain sight.* The phrase came to her abruptly— she didn't know where she had heard it. But that's what Rattigan was doing, and had been doing all along. He wasn't skulking around in the shadows or living under subway tunnels or abandoned apartment buildings, as the police imagined. He was strolling around in the sunshine, smiling, tipping his hat to passing ladies, blending in, doing what was least expected of him.

The man sniffed, as if he was offended by her attitude and had instead been expecting thanks. "Telegram came through direct to me about an hour ago. Short message—just said for me to give the very next telegram to four kids who would be coming out of that building." And he pointed to Rosie's office. The hairs on the back of Max's neck stood up. "A minute later, another telegram came through, so I waited and

243

watched and delivered it like I was told. Just doing my job." And he turned around with another injured sniff and retreated into the post office.

Max crumpled the telegram in her hand, filled with a sudden fury, and took aim at a corner trash bin. Thomas grabbed her wrist before she could throw.

"Don't," he said, gently removing the balled-up paper from her hand.

"He's watching us," Max said. "He's *following* us."

"It's more than that," Thomas said. He unfolded the telegram and read it over, frowning. Even his freckles had gone white. "See this part—about the phoenix? Emily mentioned a phoenix only this morning. Lash was squawking about it to anyone who would listen. It can't be coincidence. Rattigan doesn't do coincidences."

"What are you saying?" Pippa crossed her arms, shivering.

Thomas took a deep breath. "I'm saying he's got a spy," he said. "He's got a spy in the museum."

"No," Pippa said quickly. Sam stared at Thomas, openmouthed.

"Think about it," he said, and began ticking off evidence on his fingers. "He knew we were going to Rosie's office before we even showed up—that's how he knew to call in a telegram across the street. He's been listening in to our conversations—he knows what we're planning just as soon as we do." The more agitated he became, the more quickly he talked. "Haven't you all felt it? As if he's there, breathing on our necks, looking over our shoulders, just laughing at us?"

Max shoved her hands into her coat pockets, comforted by the feel of her knives there. She didn't want to believe it. But Thomas was right. She *had* felt it.

"Emily must be reporting back to him," Thomas finished.

"Emily?" Sam shoved a hand through his hair, which immediately swung back over his eyes, curtain-like. "You think Emily's the spy?"

"Who else would it be?" Thomas frowned. "She popped up out of nowhere the moment this trouble started. She's the one who told us the story of the phoenix. She could have easily overheard us talking about going to see Rosie."

Max had to admit it made sense. But she liked Emily—liked her far better than those drippy twins who were always squabbling about a borrowed hairpin or lost eyeliner.

"Poor Kestrel," Pippa said, sighing. "I feel so bad for him."

Max frowned. "What's Kestrel got to do with it?"

Pippa stared at her. "Really?" She threw up her hands. "Really? Am I the only one who sees anything?" And then, turning away, she muttered something under her breath that sounded suspiciously like *blind* and *idiots* and *wouldn't know love if it smacked them in the face with a baseball bat.*

"All right." Sam sighed. Max could tell that he, too, was struggling with the idea of Emily as a spy. "What do you want to do about it?"

Thomas gnawed on his lower lip. "Let's stick to Max's plan," he said finally. "We'll sort out Sir Barrensworth first, and see if he has any connection to Mallett and Erskine. We can deal with Emily later."

They set out again, entering the subway at Thirty-Third Street and heading uptown, a portion of the city Max rarely visited. As soon as they exited at Ninety-Sixth Street, she remembered why.

This wasn't the New York she loved, the New York of trolleys and taxis blasting their horns and the rattle of subways beneath the grates; of crowds and tourists and pretzel vendors and shopkeepers shouting out to one another across the street; of everything crammed together, a mishmash of people and accents and buildings standing stiff-shouldered and narrow next to their neighbors, as if doing their best to take up as little space as possible.

Here, the buildings were enormous, with fancy scrolled stonework and white-gloved doormen standing at every entrance. They were the kind of buildings that didn't say *please come in* or *thanks for noticing me* but instead *wipe your feet and mind your manners*. Instead of the usual clamor of voices and traffic, it was strangely quiet, as if the whole neighborhood were holding its breath, worried about offending. And everyone they passed gave them a dirty look, as if they were something rotten that had accidentally been carried uptown on the sole of a shoe.

Thomas remembered that Sir Barrensworth's card had listed his address as 1270 Park Avenue. But when they arrived at the correct block, they found that number 1270 didn't exist. There were only two apartment buildings on the street, both of them enormous, with identical green awnings and identically snooty-looking doormen.

"Are you sure you didn't make a mistake?" Pippa asked, staring up doubtfully at the ornate iron numbers, which jumped straight from 1260 to 1280.

"I'm positive," Thomas said firmly. "His card said 1270 Park Avenue. I'd swear to it."

"Maybe we should double-check," Sam suggested gently. "Just to be sure."

"You go, Pippa," Max said cheerfully. "You look like the kind of priss who'd live up here."

Pippa scowled. In Max's opinion, this only completed the effect. "Fine," she said. "Wait here. I don't want you ruining anything." With a toss of her dark hair, she disappeared into the first building, her white shoes slapping loudly on the pavement. She reappeared a minute later, shaking her head.

"No Sir Barrensworth," she said. She tried next at number 1280, with the same result. No Sir Barrensworth had lived at any time at either address. Just to be safe, they crossed the street and tried the apartment buildings there. But no one, it seemed, had ever heard of a Sir Barrensworth.

"What now?" Pippa was growing so impatient she was practically dancing in place.

Thomas's mood had also plummeted. "*Nothing* now," he said, shaking his head in disgust. "That's it. No more. It's a dead end."

"What about the Staten Island connection?" Sam said.

"Do you know how big Staten Island is?" Thomas shook his head. "Forget it. Let's go home. Sir Barrensworth's bound to turn up sometime. He's supposed to be training that stupid Firebird, isn't he?"

"I still don't understand what's in it for Barley-horn," Max said as they started back toward the subway. "Why'd he do it? Why'd he do *any* of it?"

Thomas shoved his hands in his pocket. "Barrensworth, Erskine, and Mallett. Emily and Rattigan." He fell into a moody silence. Max tried to put herself in Thomas's shoes, to see what he was seeing. She wished, in that moment, she had Pippa's ability to slip into another person's mind at will. All she saw was a series of disconnected images: Mallett, red-eyed and miserable, complaining that he was ruined; Emily tracing the outlines of her phoenix tattoo; poor Farnum siphoning his dead fleas into a matchbox.

"And don't forget about the bank robberies," Pippa said. "Rattigan's got to be wrapped up in that, too."

Still, Thomas said nothing. Max held her breath, waiting for the moment that he would figure it all out, when he would give a cry of "I know!" and make sense of everything that had happened, when he would complete the whole puzzle.

But Thomas just sighed and shook his head. "Missing piece," was all he said.

ippa felt as if she'd just been forced to eat one of Goldini's awful dinners: there was a hard knot at the bottom of her stomach that simply wouldn't go away. Rattigan-Emily-Erskine-Mallett-Barrensworth. Erskine-Rattigan-Barrensworth-Mallett-Emily. The names chased themselves around and around in her head, like bees circling endlessly around the same flower. Was Sir Barrensworth in fact responsible for killing Mallett and Erskine? If so, why? And why had Rattigan sent Emily to spy on them? Was it just for fun, to make them feel unsafe? Or was he trying to keep them from discovering some truth, from stumbling onto the connection that, even now, was floating just out of reach?

Thinking this way made her feel as if her brain were tangled up into one of the complex knots from which Thomas freed himself during his acts, and she soon gave up. The fact was that they were no closer to freeing General Farnum than they had ever been. They would have to count on Rosie to do her job, or else . . .

Well. She didn't want to think about the *or else* part.

The others were obviously just as worried and unhappy as she was. She didn't need to be a mind reader to know that. Thomas was unusually silent, and instead of babbling on about the way to mine steel or the chemical characteristics of charcoal or how a dual-compressor engine was manufactured or any of the other billions of facts he'd read in a book, he stared moodily at the ground, biting his lip. Max cleaned her nails with one of her knives, struggling to appear unconcerned—but her hands were trembling, and she nicked herself twice. And poor Sam gripped the subway pole so tightly, he made a hand-shaped indentation in the steel, causing several people to swivel around and stare as the children hurriedly exited, a full two stops early.

"Sorry." Sam blushed deeply. "I was distracted."

"I feel like a walk anyway," Pippa said quickly, so Sam wouldn't feel bad. "It's too claustrophobic down

251 ☞

here." The subway did feel close and small after the telegram they'd received. Pippa had the sense of many minds reaching for hers like so many clammy hands. She couldn't relax.

But even the late afternoon sunshine couldn't break up the shadow that had fallen over them. They walked together as a group, but might as well have been alone. They said not a single word to one another. Occasionally Thomas stopped and looked up, and Pippa's heart soared, thinking he'd had a breakthrough. But every time he only shook his head disgustedly and continued on, head bent, kicking at the occasional stray candy wrapper or empty tin can.

They passed the old movie theater where earlier in the summer they'd met with Ned Spode—who had proved, ultimately, to be an agent for Rattigan. Sometimes Pippa still had nightmares about what had happened in that factory, of Rattigan's face illumined by twisted shadows, and Spode's mangled leg, a horrible construction of metal and muscle and skin, remodeled by Rattigan in a laboratory, just as they had been built—remade differently, stronger, *stranger*.

She shook her head, as though she might physically clear her mind of the idea. Just then she spotted a cheerful-looking store across the street. A small crowd had gathered to point at various items—whoopee cushions, trick decks, exploding gum, squirting flowers—arranged in the tiered window display.

"Hey, Thomas." She stopped. The big red sign above the door announced: *McNulty's Novelty Shoppe*. "Isn't that the store Chubby's always going on about?"

Thomas looked up. For the first time in an hour, his expression cleared.

"Come on," she said. "Let's go in." When he hesitated, she nudged him with an elbow. She hated to see Thomas so upset. "You're curious, aren't you? Besides"—she lowered her voice—"you said yourself there's nothing more we can do right now."

"Think they got any more of those stink bombs?" Max said thoughtfully.

Pippa knew enough about Max to be deeply suspicious. "Why?"

Max shrugged. "Was thinking maybe we'd give Emily a reason to want to leave the museum, that's all."

At this, Thomas broke into a smile. "Sometimes, Max," he said, clapping her on the back, "I think you might be the genius of the group."

McNulty's Novelty Shoppe looked, on the inside, like the deranged imaginings of a mischievous twelve-year-old.

253 🐾

Mr. McNulty also gave off the impression of youth, despite the single tuft of gray hair that stuck straight from the top his otherwise bald head, the withered flower he wore in his lapel, and the fact that he walked with a cane.

"Welcome, welcome!" He thumped out from behind the counter to greet them. "What can I tempt you with? A nice rubber chicken? Itching powder? Exploding bubble gum? X-ray glasses? A few trick candles? Or maybe a good old-fashioned slingshot?" And he pointed at each object in question with the tip of his cane.

"We're just looking for now," Pippa said. "Thanks, though."

Mr. McNulty leaned heavily on his cane, which was painted a bright yellow. "Look away, look away," he cried, reaching one hand into his jacket pocket. "Just be careful. It's all fun and games until somebody gets— *Squirt*." The hand inside his pocket twitched and, all at once, a stream of water shot out from his lapel flower— straight into Pippa's eyes.

Pippa shrieked and stumbled backward while Max exploded into laughter.

"That was *not* funny," Pippa said, glaring fiercely at Mr. McNulty, even as she attempted to wipe the water from her cheeks.

"Oh, come on, Pippa." Thomas slung an arm around

her shoulder. All traces of his earlier bad mood were gone. "You have to admit it was a *little* funny."

"A very little," she said. But she still scowled when Mr. McNulty began to laugh.

They circled the shop, stopping every so often to admire one of Mr. McNulty's gags: a jar of peanut butter that released a spring-loaded snake when the top was unscrewed, a fake ice cube containing a cockroach. To Max's infinite disappointment, Mr. McNulty had recently sold the last of his stink bombs and was waiting for a new order.

"But I got something even better." Mr. McNulty picked up a tin from a display beside the register. "Sergeant Schnorner's Superior Sneezing Powder! One hundred percent guaranteed to get the best, the biggest, the tickliest sneezes. Want to hear a neat trick?" He didn't wait for an answer. "Put a little powder into a balloon—just a tablespoon or two will do the trick—and blow the whole thing up nice and full. When you let go, the balloon goes shooting around the room like an airplane, giving everybody a dusting of the stuff. You should hear the sneezes! Like a lion's roar. Like a plane engine!"

"Thanks," Pippa said. "But we were really looking for—" She stopped speaking when she saw Thomas's face, which had gone paper-white. "What?" she said. "What is it?"

Thomas ignored her. He was still staring at Mr. McNulty, transfixed and terrified, as if he'd just seen a ghost. "Airplane," he croaked. "What did you say about an airplane?"

"Sneezes like a lion's roar," Mr. McNulty said. "Like a plane engine!"

"No," Thomas said. "No, before that. About the balloon."

Mr. McNulty picked up at last on the oddness of Thomas's expression. He frowned. "I said it zooms around like an airplane," he said. "Like one of those crop-duster planes, letting off a spray."

"A spray . . ." Thomas closed his eyes and swayed on his feet, as if he was about to fall over.

"What is it?" Pippa hissed. "Are you sick or something?"

For a second, he didn't respond. Then he opened his eyes again, and color flooded back into his face all at once. "The dirigible." He turned to Pippa, grabbing her arms. "Where will the dirigible launch?"

"The dirigible?" This was such a sudden change of topic, Pippa thought she must have misheard.

"Yes, the dirigible," Thomas snapped. "Where does it launch tomorrow?"

"I don't know." Pippa was flustered. She had a sense

of his mind moving quickly—she could feel it, whirling and whirling, like a carousel spinning so quickly all the individual horses became a blur. "I can't remember what the radio said. Some big factory on Staten Island—" She broke off, inhaling sharply.

"That's where all the poison's been going," he said. "That's why Mallett couldn't get any of the ingredients to make Fleas-B-Gone. And that's why he and Erskine were killed—because they were asking too many questions."

"I don't understand," Sam said, even as Pippa did understand. Finally—she knew, she saw it, the missing piece, and a pit yawned open in her stomach.

Thomas dropped Pippa's arms. He turned to Sam, looking suddenly exhausted. "The dirigible," he said, lowering his voice so that Mr. McNulty wouldn't overhear. "He's going to load up the dirigible with reaper gas and let it loose over the city. He'll kill thousands—tens of thousands. Maybe more."

"He . . . ?" Sam's eyes went wide. "You don't mean . . . ?"

"Who else?" Thomas said grimly. "Rattigan."

"He must have been planning this for months," Thomas said. They were on their way back to the museum. Pippa had to jog to keep pace with the rest of the group: Sam's legs were nearly double the length of hers, Thomas was naturally quick, and Max was used to dodging and weaving through a crowd. "It must have cost a fortune to get all the materials together. That's why he's been robbing banks. And calling in favors, too. Whoever's sponsoring the dirigible flight—"

"Woodhull Enterprises," Pippa interjected.

"Woodhull Enterprises, yeah. They must be in Rattigan's pocket. Maybe they owe Rattigan a favor from long ago, before the war. Of course, they don't know what he's planning to do."

"So that rat-faced guy who nearly kidnapped you at the bank—?" Pippa said.

"Working for Rattigan," he said. "Just like you thought. And he was spotted outside Erskine's apartment, too, the night Erskine was killed."

"It wasn't a coincidence," Pippa said.

"But how do we stop him?" Sam said, dodging a man's hot dog cart, hands up so he wouldn't accidentally overturn it. "If Rosie wouldn't listen about Barrensworth—"

"Forget Rosie," Thomas said. "There's no time to try and persuade her. Dumfrey will have to go to the police. I know," he added, when Max made another face. "But we have no choice. The dirigible launches tomorrow. And you heard what Chubby said. Half the city is planning to turn out."

Pippa had a sudden image of the vast dirigible whirring above the city, casting the streets in shadow, and all the people clustered on rooftops and sidewalks to see it—kids, families, babies, grandmothers—as the poison went hissing through the air . . . unseen . . . unnoticed . . .

Her stomach rolled into her throat.

New York would turn into a graveyard.

24

Sam was the first through the front door, shoving
so hard it smacked against the interior wall and
dislodged a large portion of plaster. But he was
so consumed with thoughts of Rattigan and his terrible
plan, he didn't even feel guilty.

Uncharacteristically, the twins were sitting behind
the ticket desk, enjoying a rare moment of peace and
painting each other's nails an awful shade of crim-
son that, against their alabaster skin, looked just like
blood.

"Where's Dumfrey?" Sam burst out. "We need to
talk to Dumfrey."

Caroline barely flicked her eyes in their direction.

"Gone," she said simply.

"Gone?" Thomas parroted. "What do you mean, *gone*?"

Caroline rolled her eyes. "You don't expect me to define the word, do you? Hasn't Monsieur Cabillaud taught you *anything*?"

Max made a growling noise and took a step forward. "Listen, you overcooked piece of—"

"Max." Pippa put a hand on Max's shoulder, presumably to keep her from jumping over the ticket desk and clocking Caroline directly in the nose. She turned back to the twins.

"Where did he go? Please. It's important."

Caroline rolled her eyes. "If you must know," she said, "he's gone to visit Farnum in jail. Afterward, he's going to—ahem—*talk strategy* with Rosie over dinner."

Quinn giggled. "I'll bet he is, the salty dog."

Caroline smirked at her sister. "He told us specifically not to expect him until *very* late."

Max said a curse word that cannot be reprinted on the page. Thomas spun around and aimed a kick at nothing. Pippa stood very still, her lips pinched so tightly together they looked as if they'd been sewn to her face. And Sam's heart dropped, stonelike, to the bottom of his stomach. The cops would never listen to them. They were running out of time—and options.

"We'll have to go to the police ourselves," Pippa said, voicing his thoughts aloud. Sam wasn't sure whether it was related to Pippa's powers, but she seemed always to know what other people were thinking, even when she wasn't reading minds.

"But—" Max began to protest.

"I know what you're going to say," Pippa said, even before Max could finish. "They'll probably just laugh at us. But we have no choice, do we? We can't exactly expect to track down Mr. Dumfrey on his *date*. He could be anywhere in Manhattan!"

"I say we go straight for Staten Island," Thomas said in a low voice. "Woodhull Enterprises owns half of Bay Street. And we *have* to destroy that airship."

"But how?" Pippa cried. "You said yourself, Woodhull Enterprises is in Rattigan's pocket. He has friends everywhere. How are *we* going to stop him?"

"We've stopped him before," Thomas said. His eyes were very dark. "Besides, what other choice do we have?"

For a second, Sam almost hoped that Pippa would continue to argue. The idea of going up against Rattigan was bad. The idea of what would happen if they failed was far, far worse.

But Pippa just gave a small nod, and Sam knew, too, that Thomas was right. They had run out of options. Soon, they would be out of time. It was up to them.

Even as Thomas was reaching for the door handle, however, the door flew open, forcing him to spring backward with a yelp. A glowering Monsieur Cabillaud stood in the doorway, hands on his hips, his tiny bald head mottled with color.

"Aha! *Zer* you are!" he cried. "I have been looking for you everywhere! Naughty, naughty students." He waggled a finger. "You think you can just forget about ze studies, is zat it? You think you can make Monsieur *Cabillaud* forget. But you are in error, *mes amis*! Upstairs, now, and quickly. Zer is still an hour for a lesson before ze bedtime."

"A lesson? *Now?*" Sam cried. Frustration squeezed like a fist in his chest. "But, you don't understand. We can't possibly study now."

"And why is zat?" Monsieur Cabillaud crossed his arms.

"Okay, look." Thomas stepped forward. He took a deep breath. "The truth is going to sound crazy. We're trusting you with a secret. A big secret, okay?" He looked at the others for support, and Sam nodded. "It has to do with Nicholas Rattigan."

Monsieur Cabillaud's neatly plucked eyebrows shot upward. "Ze scientist?"

Thomas nodded. "We know where he is. And we know he's planning something—something big."

"I see," Monsieur Cabillaud murmured. "And I suppose zat you are ze only people who can stop him?"

"Exactly," Thomas said, nodding so vigorously his glasses jogged on his nose. "That's just it."

"Mmm. And I also suppose zer is no time to lose?"

Sam felt a heady rush of relief. Cabillaud understood. "No time at all," he said.

"I see, I see. Zen what I say to you, *mes amis*, is"— Monsieur Cabillaud leaned forward, as though to tell them a great secret, and they all leaned forward with him—"NICE TRY!"

He screeched the last words so loudly that all four children jumped.

"Despicable lies," Monsieur Cabillaud cried. "Unspeakable fictions. Upstairs, all of you, now, or I will see to it zat you are locked into the museum for ze rest of ze month!" He herded them toward the stairs, still shrieking, his chest puffed up in outrage. "*Allez!* Ze dates, please, of ze French Revolution . . ." Monsieur Cabillaud kept them at it all through dinnertime. Soon after, Miss Fitch directed them straight to bed, and they had no choice but to go through the ritual of changing into their pajamas and brushing their teeth and pretending to fall asleep. Sam lay with his blankets pulled all the way up to his chin, as if that might stifle the sound of his heart—which was going so hard he worried the noise might prevent the other residents from sleeping.

And, in fact, it seemed to take everyone far longer than usual to settle down. Sam felt time passing like the crawl of an insect on his skin. But at last, the final light was extinguished and the attic room was filled with gentle snoring and the occasional rustle of sheets as someone turned over.

Sam glanced over at Thomas. Even in the darkness, he could see Thomas's eyes were wide open. Thomas nodded to him, and together they slipped carefully out of bed. Sam peeked over the top of the bookshelves that kept their sleeping area separate from Max and Pippa's and found the two girls already standing in street clothes. Sam had stored his shoes and clothing beneath his bed and changed quickly, hardly paying attention to what he was doing. His thoughts were already outside, flying down the streets, leaping over the water to Staten Island. Would they be in time?

They took the performers' staircase, which carried

the risk of bringing them directly past Mr. Dumfrey's office on the second floor and Miss Fitch's quarters below it, but it was much quieter than the vast, echoey marble staircase used by the general public. Outside Mr. Dumfrey's office, Sam paused, pressing an ear to the door, which was open a crack. Mr. Dumfrey's office was silent. He still had not returned to the museum, though it must have been close to midnight.

They really were alone.

"Come on." Max stood on tiptoe to whisper to him, and for a brief second—a second so quick it might just have been his imagination—he thought she took his hand.

The Hall of Worldwide Wonders was cool, dark, and so quiet Sam could hear Max's breathing behind him. Sam felt as if he were moving through an enchanted tomb. The glass display cases winked in the faint light coming through the windows from the street, and the dark treasures nestled inside of them seemed like buried hearts, pulsing with an invisible energy. On the ceiling above them, the reconstruction of a prehistoric pterodactyl, enormous wings spread midflight, creaked lightly on its suspension wire.

They were about to pass into the lobby when Sam heard something, a muffled cough or a footstep, behind him. He froze.

"Did anyone else—?" he started to say.

Before he could finish his sentence, someone seized him from behind and squeezed. All of the breath went out of him in a whoosh. It was no ordinary someone, either: the arms felt like ten-ton steel belts cabled around his chest. He couldn't breathe. He couldn't get his arms up to fight.

Suddenly, everyone was shouting. Sam saw a figure moving in the shadows. Before he could cry out, a lasso spun through the air and yoked his three friends together.

Then the overhead lights snapped on.

Just inside the doorway, one hand on the light switch, stood Howie.

"Well, well, well," he said. "Looks like you're all in a bit of a *bind*, aren't you?"

"Very funny," Thomas spat. "How'd you snake your way in here?"

Howie raised an eyebrow but addressed his words to Tiny Tex, the Texas Fatboy, who was struggling to keep a grip on one end of the rope restraining Thomas, Pippa, and Max. "You'll want to keep an eye on *that* one in particular," he said, jerking his chin in Thomas's direction. "He's a wiggly one."

"You're going to pay for this." Sam at last managed to draw a breath. But try as he might, he couldn't break free of the hairy arms that encircled him. He realized, to his shock, that he was immobilized.

A foul breath blasted his ear.

"You strong for a boy," said a voice in a low growl, even as the grip tightened around him, so Sam felt as if even his organs were being squeezed. "But Trogg stronger."

It was the strongman they'd seen at the Coney Island show, the beast who was nearly seven feet tall. And Sam knew, with a welling sense of hopelessness, that Trogg was right—Trogg *was* stronger.

"Let us go, you creep," Max cried.

"Oh, I'll let you go," Howie said, making a show of examining his fingernails, which were buffed and newly clipped. "We're just going to take a little stroll first. The Bowery is lovely this time of night, as long as you steer clear of the muggers. And of course, it's the perfect place for a makeover. I'm thinking matching crew cuts. Might as well burn those rags you're wearing, too. Mr. Dumfrey always wants publicity, doesn't he? Let's see what kind of publicity he gets when his prize freaks are parading home in their birthday suits."

"You're out of your mind." Sam was practically

shouting. They didn't have time for this. They didn't have time, period. If they didn't get to Staten Island to stop Rattigan, thousands of people would die. "Let us go, or—"

"Or what?" Howie came forward suddenly, his face contorted with fury and triumph. "You'll call for your precious Mr. Dumfrey to save you?" He barked a laugh. Sam had, in fact, been about to cry out—then he remembered, with a sinking feeling, that Mr. Dumfrey hadn't even returned to the museum. And really, what would Mr. Dumfrey do? "I'm not scared of you, Samson," Howie said. "And I'm not letting you go, either. Not until you pay for making me look like an idiot."

"Please, you don't need our help for that," Pippa said, tossing her hair and doing her best to look dignified despite being trussed up like a turkey. "You do a great job of looking like an idiot all on your own."

"And you deserved it." Max's eyes were narrowed to slits. Sam couldn't believe he'd ever been jealous, believing that Max still liked Howie. She *hated* him. "You and all your Mr. Superior stuff. All along you've been the biggest fraud of all."

"I didn't know about Alicia," Howie snarled. "But better a fraud"—he reached out as if to touch Max's cheek—"than a monster."

Max lunged for him. Pippa and Thomas, lashed together, stumbled forward with her before Tiny Tex managed to rein them in, jerking the rope backward so Max was left wheezing.

Sam's vision went red. Fury pulsed through his body, thrumming in his head. He took a deep breath and, as he felt Trogg relax his grip, flexed and threw his right elbow toward Trogg's face. Trogg, startled, lost his grip on Sam's arm. Howie backpedaled quickly with a small, startled yelp as Sam swung for him. But before Sam could make contact, Trogg had wrestled his arm behind his back again and Sam doubled over.

"Nice try." Howie bent forward. His face hovered only inches from Sam's. "The truth is painful, isn't it?"

Sam was so angry it felt like being inside a stew—something roiling and hot was eating him up. Rattigan would win. Rattigan would *kill*—all because of Howie and his hatefulness. "The only monster in this room is you," he snapped.

"We'll see about that." Howie straightened up. "You know, you should all be grateful to me. Did you ever think about what would happen if everyone in New York found out about Rattigan's little science experiments? You'd be thrown in a cage. You'd be zoo animals. That's if the mob didn't get to you first." His smile was cruel. And worse, Sam knew he was right. "So I suggest you play along, if you want your little secret to stay safe."

They had no choice but to do as Howie said. Tex took the lead, hauling a struggling Max, Pippa, and Thomas forward. Trogg moved Sam forward next, keeping Sam's arms wrenched so far behind his back Sam thought they might tear out of their sockets.

"A fine little parade." Howie wore the same gloating expression that made Sam want to peel off his face. "Just think. If you hadn't—"

He broke off suddenly, holding up a hand for silence, as a noise sounded from the shadows. Sam heard it, too—a faint mechanical click. Trogg froze. Only Tex was still moving forward, straining on the rope, his face red from exertion, huffing loudly.

"Shut up, you idiot," Howie whispered. Above him, the pterodactyl creak-creaked on its thin wire, swaying faintly back and forth, as if it were really flying. Tex at last stopped moving. "Did anyone hear—?"

Crack.

A rifle shot echoed through the room. Tex cried out and dove for cover, as with a clean hiss the thin metal wire keeping the pterodactyl tethered to the ceiling snapped neatly in two—and sent the monstrous, winged creature crashing toward the ground. Howie dove to avoid getting buried, throwing Sam and Trogg off their feet. In the confusion, Trogg loosened his hold on Sam, and Sam shoved him off. With one quick wrestling move, Sam took hold of Trogg's wrists and rammed a knee in his lower back, so Trogg's cheek was squashed flat to the floor.

"You're pretty strong," Sam panted. He was still dizzy from pain and the chaos of shouting and dust. Who on earth had fired the rifle? "But looks like I'm stronger."

Thomas had already freed himself from the lasso. Now, as Howie struggled to climb to his feet, Thomas dove and pinned him to the floor again.

"Let go of me," Howie snarled.

"I don't think so." It was Thomas's turn to smile. The sound of the shot must have woken the other residents, and already Sam could hear footsteps pounding on the stairs, and Miss Fitch crying out, "What is it? For heaven's sake, what's happened now?"

The air was still cloudy with dust from the pterodactyl's spectacular fall. The once-magnificent model lay scattered in splinters, bones jutting from within the wings of heavy canvas, beak pointed to the ceiling as though crying out for help.

A moment later, Miss Fitch appeared on the landing in her nightgown, her hair neatly slicked into its usual bun. Lash was close behind her, scrubbing his bleary eyes.

Then Mr. Dumfrey, dressed in a neat black suit and carrying a vintage Winchester rifle over his shoulder, emerged from between exhibits. "It's all right, Miss Fitch," he said cheerfully, surveying the scene with detached curiosity—as if Tex, Howie, the broken pterodactyl, and Pippa and Max, still struggling to disentangle themselves from the rope, were all part of a tableau he was considering adding to the museum's Hall of Wax. "Just some unwelcome intruders. It's under control."

Sam stared from Mr. Dumfrey to the rifle on his shoulder to the fine wire, hardly wider than a pencil line, that the bullet had severed.

"But . . ." He found he could barely speak. "That shot . . . it's impossible . . . how did you ever manage . . . ?"

On the stairs, Lash snorted a laugh. "Good to see you still got it, Horatio."

Mr. Dumfrey waved a hand. "Oh, well. Some things stay with you, I suppose."

Lash came down into the lobby and made quick

work of disentangling Max and Pippa. "Back in the day, Dumfrey was known from coast to coast as a crack shot," he explained as he curled the rope in his hand. "Could thread a bullet through the eye of a needle at fifty yards. Oh, no you don't." This last bit was directed at Tiny Tex, who'd begun crawling for the door. With a quick flick of his wrist, Lash lassoed him backward. "Just like tying up a steer," he said.

"So *that's* your big secret," Pippa said wonderingly. "You're a sharpshooter."

Mr. Dumfrey actually looked embarrassed. He clucked his tongue. "*Was* a sharpshooter. Now I run a museum. Speaking of which"—his eyes fell on Howie— "can someone explain to me what on earth is going on?"

Sam and Thomas exchanged a look. Sam knew that they couldn't explain why they'd been out of bed—not here, anyway, in front of everybody. More and more of the museum's residents had gathered in the lobby and on the staircase, straining to get a view of the action. And they were in a bigger rush than ever.

"We heard a noise downstairs," Pippa said quickly. "We came down to make sure everything was okay. And then . . ."

"We got ambushed," Max finished, still glaring at

Howie. "They must have broken in."

"We didn't break in," Howie said. Despite the fact that Thomas was keeping him pinned, he still managed to look superior. "The kitchen door was unlocked. Some idiot must have left it open."

"That *idiot* was me," Mr. Dumfrey said calmly. "I knew I'd be returning late and wanted to make sure I didn't disturb anyone. Either way, you're trespassing on private property. Lash, please stay with our new friends while I ring up the police from my office." He handed over the rifle, which Sam now recognized as the one typically on display in the Hall of Worldwide Wonders and having supposedly belonged to Buffalo Bill. "Take this, just in case anyone is stupid enough to attempt a quick getaway."

"Sure thing, Mr. D," Lash said, grinning as he took up the rifle. "Course, I'm not such a crack shot as you. Might blow off a knee or an elbow without meaning to."

"You'll pay for this," Howie hissed, sitting up as Thomas climbed to his feet and then quickly rearing back when Lash took a step toward him. "This isn't over."

"Hmm. Perhaps you should aim instead for his mouth," Mr. Dumfrey said to Lash, raising an eyebrow. "Max, Pippa, Thomas, Sam. In my office, please."

"But Mr. Dumfrey—" Sam began to protest.

"In my office," Mr. Dumfrey said, in a tone that clearly meant *no arguments*. "Now."

Sam's stomach turned heavy again. They would never get out of the museum now. He stood up, leaving Trogg still groaning on the floor. He sidestepped the giant and deliberately avoided so much as glancing at Howie. But Max stopped directly in front of Howie, with a strange expression on her face that reminded Sam somewhat of a cat trying to cough up a hair ball.

Howie's cold eyes glittered. "What do *you* want?"

Max said nothing. Instead, she wound up and clocked Howie straight in the face—so hard that his head spun *completely* around and then, like a watch mechanism unwinding, ticked slowly back around to its correct orientation.

"That," she said with an angelic smile. And Sam had to stop himself from dancing.

25

The knuckles of Max's right hand still stung from where they had connected with Howie's jaw as she and the others made their way upstairs. But it was the most glorious pain she'd ever known.

"Close the door," Mr. Dumfrey said as soon as they were all crowded inside his office. He didn't even bother to sit. Instead, he pivoted to face them, with a look as stern as any Max had never seen. "As you've just witnessed," he said, and though his voice was steady, it held a fine edge of warning, "although I may be getting older, my eyesight is as good as it ever was. And what I see just at this minute is that you haven't told me the truth. Out with it."

So Thomas told him, and Max, Pippa, and Sam filled in the gaps where they had to: about the relationship of Mallett and Erskine's deaths to Rattigan, and about the dirigible filled with poisonous gas and Rattigan's terrible plan for the city. As they spoke, all the light and color drained from Mr. Dumfrey's face, until he looked almost like one of the wax figurines in the chamber of horrors: pale and hard and terrible.

"So you see," Pippa finished, "it's up to us. We have to stop him."

"Absolutely not," Mr. Dumfrey said immediately.

Max gaped at him. "But Rattigan—"

"It's far too dangerous," he said, raising a hand to cut her off. "My half brother—as much as it pains me to say—has demonstrated again and again that he will stop at nothing and spare no one to achieve what he wants. I hope you're wrong," he added. "I pray that you are. But we can't take any chances. This is a matter for the police. I won't risk your involvement."

"What if the police won't listen?" Sam said.

"They'll have to," Mr. Dumfrey said. But he sounded unconvinced. "Now to bed. All of you."

"You said that we were growing up," Thomas argued. "You said we had to look after one another."

Mr. Dumfrey removed his glasses and stared at them

each in turn. "I said there would come a time when I wouldn't be there to protect you," he said. "Fortunately, that time is not today. You heard me. Upstairs and into bed and no arguments. I'll handle the police." And with that, he pushed the kids out of his office and slammed the door closed behind him. It felt as if he took all of the air with him, too. Max was left with a breathless, frightened feeling.

She shook the hair away from her face. "What do you want to bet the cops take the whole thing as a joke?" she said. "No way are they going to believe Rattigan's going to pull a stunt this big. Not when half the force has been looking for him for months."

"They'll have to do *something*, won't they?" Pippa turned to Thomas.

"I don't know." He put a hand through his hair, making it stand like a head full of exclamation points. "I hope so."

Sam shook his head. "We can't risk it," he said in a fierce whisper. "What if they don't? What if they just laugh?"

"Sam's right," Max said. "There's too much at stake."

"All right, then." Thomas nodded. "We'll stick to the plan and head to Staten Island ourselves."

They couldn't sneak out the front. The doors were

280 ☛

no doubt locked for the night, and only Gil Kestrel had the keys. Besides, Lash was still standing guard over Howie and his band of creeps in the lobby. Instead, they retreated as quietly as they could down the performers' staircase, glided through the hall, ducked into the special exhibits room, and made their way down the set of old wooden stairs that led down into the basement. In the kitchen, faint moonlight came through the narrow windows, illuminating corners and edges, drawing the familiar furniture in broad painted strokes. They moved in a line toward the door that led out to the sunken courtyard where the garbage cans were kept and Farnum's fleas had been buried. Max couldn't believe that had been three days ago: so much had happened.

Pippa reached the door, released the dead bolt, and yanked on the handle. Nothing happened.

"Oh no." She turned, her eyes wide in the dark. "Mr. Dumfrey must have locked up after he came in." There was a second lock, rarely used, that required a key. Mr. Dumfrey kept a copy in his desk.

"Anyone know how to pick a lock?" Thomas asked hopefully.

Max realized that both Pippa and Thomas were looking at her. She sighed. "You got a bobby pin?"

"I have a better idea." Sam stepped forward. He placed a hand on the door and leaned. There was a small groan, and the door popped off its hinges neatly, like a cube of ice out of a metal tray.

"After you," he said, and Pippa giggled.

"Now that's what I call breaking and entering," Thomas said.

"Breaking and *exiting*, you mean," Max said. They passed out into the night, pausing only so that Sam could pop the door back in place.

They reached the ferry dock at a little after two o'clock, and found the ticket office closed. A little sign announced that the next ferry departed at exactly 5:30 a.m.

Max kicked the closed door, ignoring the pain that shot through her foot. "Five thirty? That's too late."

"Maybe we don't have to wait." Thomas pointed to a series of weather-beaten fishing boats bobbing in the shallows.

Max nearly choked. "You want to *steal* a *boat*?"

"Please," Pippa said, already scrabbling down the gangplank toward the rocky beach. "Now isn't the time to sprout a conscience. Didn't you used to pick pockets for a living?"

Max scowled. "Only in the case of emergencies."

"Well, I think this counts as an emergency, don't you?" Pippa hopped into one of the boats and began to untie it from the moorings. "Besides, we'll bring it back. Now come on."

Max had never before been out on the water and found herself gripping her seat as Thomas piloted the boat away from the shore.

"You're sure you know how to drive this thing?" she cried as the boat hit a wave and nearly threw her overboard.

"Sure!" Thomas called back. "Read a book about it once!"

Sam groaned and closed his eyes.

The air stung Max's cheeks and she clutched her seat. Her stomach rolled with every wave and she felt a little like a popcorn kernel in danger of popping right into the water. But after a minute she grew less terrified and began to enjoy the up-and-down motion of the waves and the look of lights reflecting off the inky surface of the bay as they drew closer to Staten Island. Thomas maneuvered them successfully into the harbor, and they climbed onto the dock, securing the boat to a moss-coated piling.

"See?" Pippa turned to Max, smiling. "That was easy, wasn't it?"

"You know what I think, Pippa?" Max slung an arm around Pippa's shoulders. Despite the seriousness of what they had come to do, in that moment, with the silhouette of Manhattan etched against the starry sky, and the waves lapping quietly on the shore, and her three best friends standing beside her, she felt a sense of joy and well-being. "We're going to make a criminal of you yet."

"I suppose, coming from you, that's supposed to be a compliment," Pippa said. But she didn't turn away fast enough to conceal the fact that she was smiling.

Max's happiness was snuffed out as quickly as it had come, replaced by a creeping sense of anxiety. The streets of Staten Island were still, silent, and dark. Max had the uncomfortable feeling of trespassing in an abandoned house. Even the area around Borough Hall, bustling with activity during the day, looked ominous in the dark, everything shuttered and locked, and a lone dog barking somewhere in the distance.

They found Bay Street easily. As the name suggested, the street ran parallel to the water and took them away from the municipal district and into an area of looming industrial buildings, boat repair shops, truck lots, and canneries.

Soon the pavement petered out and was replaced by loose gravel and then, finally, by hard-packed dirt, rutted with deep tire marks and wagon wheels. The trees grew thicker on either side of them, tall pines that crowded out the moonlight, and owls hooted from the branches.

Fear tightened in Max's stomach. She was never afraid in any other section of New York, even in the worst, the dingiest, most dangerous areas. She was at home among the clamor and the filth, the guttersnipes and the street urchins, the hobos and the hustlers. It was here, in this wide-open space, with nothing but the sound of wind through the trees and the crunch of their feet on the road, that she felt truly afraid.

Finally, she couldn't take it anymore. "Are you sure this is the right way?" she blurted, hoping her voice wouldn't squeak.

At that instant, Thomas stopped, sucking in a quick breath. "I'm sure," he said, and pointed.

Just down the road was a break in the trees and a tall chain-link fence that ran parallel to the road. Beyond, the dark silhouette of a group of buildings was just visible, and a large sign, barely illumined by the moonlight, read: *WOODHULL ENTERPRISES. PRIVATE. NO TRESPASSING.*

They advanced more quietly now, sticking close to the shadows, expecting guards to be patrolling. The chain-link fence was at least eighteen feet high and topped by thick strands of spiked barbed wire. The single metal gate, which when opened would have been broad enough to admit two trucks side by side, was locked from the inside. Beyond the fence was an expanse of bare dirt the size of four football fields laid end to end, a small brick building, and a vast airplane hangar that gleamed a pale pearl-white.

"That's where Rattigan must be housing the dirigible," Thomas said, indicating the hangar.

"Okay." Max eyed the fence in frustration. "But how do we get in?"

"I'll do it," Sam said, stepping forward to rip a hole in the fence.

"No," Thomas said, laying a hand on his arm. "If anyone's patrolling, they'll see that someone's inside who doesn't belong. We can't risk an alarm. *I'll* do it." Before anyone could stop him, he sprang onto the fence and began climbing, moving soundlessly, like a spider up a wall.

"Thomas, *no*," Pippa whispered. She turned to the others, wide-eyed. "He'll get hurt."

Max moved to the fence and grabbed hold of it,

trying to shake Thomas off. But the fence was thick and sturdy, and Thomas was already nearly at the top of it. He hesitated, scanning the complex arrangement of barbed wire, searching for a way around it. It looked, to Max, impossible: like a thorny metal hedge sprouting from the top of the fence.

But all at once, Thomas flipped. Max's breath caught in her throat. Pippa gasped. Thomas kicked his legs upward, above his head, so for a second he was balancing in a perfect handstand.

Then he arched his back and his body formed a U-curve as he carefully bridged the first curl of barbed wire. Releasing his grip, he shinnied carefully under the second. Almost immediately, he swept sideways, under a third curl of wire, and somersaulted down onto the opposite side of the fence, so that he was temporarily frozen there, catlike, sweat glistening on his forehead. Then he clambered down the fence and reached the ground safely.

"You did it!" Max burst out, and Pippa hushed her sharply.

Sam, Max, and Pippa hurried to the gate while Thomas worked the lock open from the inside. A moment later, they were all slipping into the Woodhull Enterprises compound. Still, no one had appeared.

Everything was perfectly silent. But Thomas replaced the lock on the gate, just in case.

They started across the yard toward the airplane hangar, bent nearly double and trying to stick to the shadows just in case some unseen guards were watching. Max's instincts were going crazy, firing off warning signals, blazing sirens in her head. Where was everybody? What if the dirigible wasn't even here?

But as they circled the vast hangar they at last heard voices and the muffled sound of heavy equipment being moved. Half a dozen trucks were parked in front of the loading dock. The doors were open to reveal the dirigible, bullet-shaped and enormous, gleaming in the murk. Thomas gestured for them to hang back, ducking underneath a truck bed and concealing himself in the wheel well. Max flattened herself against one of the truck's enormous tires next to the others, trying to calm her frantically beating heart, inhaling the smell of rubber and, beneath that, soft ground. When she was no longer shaking, she risked a glance toward the loading dock.

From one of the trucks, workers in gas masks were unloading crate after crate and disappearing with them into the hangar. As one of the men passed beneath a circle of light, Max saw a skull and crossbones emblazoned on the load he was carrying and the words *Danger! Hazard!* painted in huge black letters beneath that. In their masks, the men looked like enormous insects.

"Are you okay?" Sam whispered to her.

She wanted to say something clever and confident, so he would know she wasn't afraid, but in the end she only nodded.

"There it is." Thomas was nearly invisible, concealed as he was in the dark. "What do you want to bet that's all the gas?"

"What are we going to do?" Pippa whispered.

"We have to get onto that dirigible," Thomas said. "We have to make sure it never gets airborne."

"Now's our chance," Sam said. "Look—the coast's clear."

Sam was right: the workers had all vanished, and the night had once again gone still. *Wrong,* Max's inner alarm was still shrieking. *Wrong, wrong.* It was all this silence: so much of it she felt like she was going to be swallowed.

"Follow me," Thomas said. Before Max could protest, he was on his feet, and Pippa was hurrying after him, staying low to the ground, and Sam slid out from underneath the truck bed. Max tried to stand and found that although she could hear her brain screaming the command at her legs, her legs had decided to ignore her. She would be left alone—she wouldn't be able to move, and the others would leave her here, huddled in a shadow, just waiting for Rattigan to find her.

"You're sure you're okay?"

Max looked up. Sam was still next to her, ducking low to meet her eyes. He hadn't abandoned her after all. All of her confidence came rushing back at once. She reached out, seized the hand he offered her, and wiggled free of the underside of the truck. She checked to make sure that her knives were in her pockets. They were.

"Ask me again," she whispered back, "and you'll be picking your teeth with a pocketknife."

"There's the Max I know," he said, and even managed to smile.

"Pssst." Pippa and Thomas had already crossed to the loading dock, carefully avoiding the light cast by the giant flood lamp on the roof. Pippa waved them forward and they hurried across the yard, Max's heart going like a fist trying to punch through a wall. But she wasn't afraid, not like before. She was focused.

She was angry.

The hangar was cool, dark, and smelled like dust.

Max had the feeling of passing into an ancient tomb, as if the dirigible were a prehistoric creature that had been sealed up forever in darkness, turning white from lack of sun. The dirigible itself was larger, and more strangely beautiful, than she could have ever imagined, like a building turned on its side. For a moment, though they should have been hurrying, Pippa, Sam, Max, and Thomas were all struck dumb with wonder.

There was one problem with the dirigible's design: Max saw no obvious way of getting onto it.

Sam had obviously realized the same thing. "So how, exactly, are we supposed to keep it from taking off?"

"Oh, I don't think you'll want to do that. You'd miss out on the show."

The voice behind them made Max's whole body go to ice, as if she'd been thrown headfirst into a snowbank. They whirled around.

Rattigan. Silhouetted in the light, his face was a dark mask, completely unreadable. But Max knew he was smiling.

"Hello, my children," he said with a happy sigh. "You're late."

26

"You know what I love most about New York City?" Rattigan sighed as a view of the Upper Bay, glittering in the morning light, unfolded beneath the airship's windows. "How *enormous* it is. All of that energy. All of those people! Millions of people. And yet from here, it might as well be a toy city. Like something that might be crushed with a simple footstep."

His voice was light, teasing, but Thomas's stomach coiled up in a knot. He knew what Rattigan was implying: the streets of New York City would be filled by now with all the people who'd come to watch the dirigible float over the skyline of Manhattan. And yet in a single instant, Rattigan could wipe out every one of them.

"You won't get away with this," Thomas said, wishing he sounded more confident. He, Pippa, Sam, and Max were huddled together across from Rattigan and two of his henchmen. One of them, a reedy man with a straggly mustache, named Clyde Straw, Thomas recognized as the same guy who'd shoved a gun against his neck during the holdup at the bank. The other man, Mickey McClure, had been previously known to the children as Sir Barrensworth. He'd dropped his fake accent and let his real voice—gruff, Brooklyn-inflected—come through.

Both men had very large guns pointed precisely in their direction.

"Oh, I already am," Rattigan said airily, with a wave of his hand. "In less than fifteen minutes, we'll reach Manhattan. Thank goodness for all the windows. The view is bound to be spectacular." His mouth twisted into a cruel smile.

"What's the point?" Pippa said, struggling against her bindings. She and Max had had their hands bound in front of them by Clyde Straw, just before they'd been marched onto the airship. Thomas and Sam had been left free—"there's no point with these two," Rattigan had said, smiling pleasantly, "but I think both will have a hard time finding their way around a bullet"—and instead, for the hours they'd sat on the dirigible while the final preparations were made and the sun crept higher in the sky, they'd been watched by a constant procession of armed guards to make sure they had no possibility of escape.

"You're going to gas all those innocent people for nothing," Pippa continued. "You'll be shot out of the sky. Even if you're not killed, everyone in the world will go on the hunt for you."

"I don't think so," Rattigan said, settling back in his seat—a chair made of soft leather, like something that belonged in a cushy office. "Have you ever played chess, my dear?"

Pippa narrowed her eyes. "Of course I have," she said. "What's that got to do with anything?"

"Chess has *everything* to do with it," he said. "In chess, as in life, you have to take out a few pawns before the kings and queens will come into the game." He folded his pale hands, which had always reminded Thomas of things that were dead and fished out of the water, across his stomach. "You see, my dear, I realized I'd been going about everything the wrong way. For example, I'd been hoping that you would see that your proper place is with me. I'd been, perhaps, counting on it. But then I remembered that the people who *get* in this world are the people who *take*. So I changed tactics. I decided simply to take you. And here you are."

"You didn't take us," Max said. "We came looking for you, remember?"

"As I knew you would," Rattigan said smoothly. "How could you miss the opportunity to play the hero? I'm the only true family you have. How could you miss the chance to prove that you belong, that you matter, that you aren't the monsters everyone surely thinks that you are? How could you fail to rush out to save all of those poor, innocent people, all of those boys and girls, fathers and mothers, whose lives will end today? You see," he said, spreading his hands, "I understand you. I'm the *only* one who truly understands. Haven't you ever wondered why I chose you to be my soldiers?"

"You *chose* us because you're crazy," Max spat. "There was no reason for it at all. Mr. Dumfrey told us so."

"And you believed him, I suppose?" For a second, Rattigan's face transformed: all of his twisted hatred for his half brother was revealed. "I don't blame him for lying. If you knew the whole truth, you might not be so fond of your dear old Mr. Dumfrey after all."

"Liar," Thomas said. He felt a black hatred so thick and deep he thought he might suffocate in it. This was Rattigan's effect, his ultimate power. It wasn't only that he was evil. It was that he made you forget that anything in the world was good.

Rattigan's lips curled back to reveal his long gray teeth. "You poor, strange, broken creatures—unloved and unwanted. Unnatural. You deny the truth even when the truth is undeniable. You deny me—the man who made you, who knows you better than you know yourselves. I do," he said, cutting Thomas off before he could object. "I see what you will do before you do it—before you even think it. I know what you dream, and think, and wish, and fear." Rattigan shook his head. "That's another thing about chess, Pippa. To win, you must always be four steps ahead. To be honest, Thomas"—Rattigan turned to Thomas—"I would have expected you to know this. I would have expected *more*."

Rattigan's eyes were strangely inhuman, flat and at the same time calculating, like the eyes of a snake. But Thomas refused to look away.

"Tell us," he said, knowing that Rattigan would never miss the opportunity to boast. Thomas had to delay Rattigan long enough to figure a way out of this mess—to figure out how to turn the airship around or crash it or do *something*. "Tell us how you stayed so far ahead of us."

"You flatter me," Rattigan said, but he looked

pleased. "Most of it, you know. After our last little encounter, I realized I needed a new approach. All of the hiding and lurking, sneaking through the sewers like a common rat . . ." He shivered. Thomas and Pippa exchanged a look. So that explained how Rattigan had managed to escape the old trolley factory. He'd followed a path down into the sewers through the hidden trapdoor in the floor. "But don't worry, I don't hold that against you," he added, as though they'd asked for his forgiveness. "You helped me, you see. You inspired me to attempt more—a single act of greatness, an act of power, that would make the knights and rooks, the kings and crooks, bow to my command."

"Robbing banks?" Max said sarcastically. "That was your big act of greatness?"

"That was a regrettable but necessary part of the plan," Rattigan snapped, looking, for the first time, irritated. Thomas shot Max a warning glance. "Airships don't come cheap, my dear. Neither, unfortunately, do the ingredients to manufacture two tons of reaper gas. Luckily, I had an old friend to help me out on that front." He indicated Clyde Straw, who smiled his weasely smile.

Sweat beaded on Thomas's upper lip. Manhattan was fast approaching. Through the dirigible windows,

297

he could see the tall buildings rising closer. The network of streets was starting to take shape, and he could even see the glint of cars and buses in the streets and small dark spots that must be all the people gathered to watch the dirigible's approach. Among them, Thomas knew, were Chubby and Andrea von Stikk. He pictured all of them with their hands up to their eyes, squinting against the sun, smiling excitedly, totally unaware of the danger that was even now bearing down on them. . . .

They were running out of time.

"But then Erskine started asking questions," Thomas said, fishing desperately for a way to keep Rattigan talking.

Rattigan frowned. "And Mallett," he said. "Both of those idiots had to go. Erskine was becoming just a little too curious. He couldn't understand why Mallett couldn't get his hands on any more of his precious chemicals. I couldn't risk that my *chef d'oeuvre* would be revealed too early. I have spies all over the city, you see," Rattigan said, casting an amused glance at the man the children had known as Sir Barrensworth. "I have spies parroting back every word you say, every single move you make."

Thomas felt as if he'd just swallowed one of Max's

knives. His whole body shook with a violent under-standing. They were almost directly over Battery Park. Now, through the windows, Thomas could definitely make out people, little individual splotches of color crowding the streets and waving from balconies and rooftops.

Rattigan stood up. "Here we are. After today, every-thing will be different. The whole *country* will bow to my demands. The president and the army will answer to me. New York is just the first step. There are other cities. There is more gas. More and more people will die." He shrugged, as if he were talking about cleaning mold out of a bathtub.

Thomas finally understood. Rattigan was going to use the dirigible to blackmail the government into giv-ing him whatever he wanted: money, freedom, even an army, so that Rattigan could perform his sick experi-ments, so he could manufacture soldiers, so he could make the perfect world he envisioned, with Rattigan the creator and commander. The plan was disgustingly simple, and Thomas didn't doubt it would be suc-cessful. And even if it wasn't, how many hundreds of thousands of people would die?

Thomas could feel Pippa trembling. Her eyes were closed. She looked the way she did when she was struggling to think her way into a closed space, like a locked steel drawer—or somebody's mind. Thomas couldn't imagine why she was wasting her energy trying to read Rattigan, when he'd just told them everything they wanted to know. Maybe she was hoping to find information that would help them escape.

But it was too late. They'd reached Manhattan. Thomas saw a family cheering on a nearby balcony, waving streamers and homemade signs. Rattigan waved back at them, cooing a little, as if he were Santa Claus on a sled, bearing gifts.

"Well." Rattigan turned away from the window. His face was practically glowing. "I think it's time, don't you? Mickey, release the hatch, please. It's time to show the world what Nicholas Rattigan can do."

"You got it, boss," said the former Sir Barrensworth, shouldering his gun and moving toward the back of the dirigible. Now there was only Clyde Straw covering them.

Just beyond the tank containing the reaper gas, a giant hatch in the floor of the dirigible opened like a jaw, revealing the colorful patchwork of buildings and people and buses and cars beneath them. Wind whistled through the dirigible, sounding almost cheery.

A bead of sweat rolled off Pippa's forehead and

landed on Thomas's arm. Her lips were moving, as if she were murmuring a prayer under her breath.

And Thomas saw that Straw had begun to *twitch*, jerking his head to the left as though to dislodge a pesky fly.

Suddenly he understood: Pippa wasn't reading Rattigan's mind. She was trying to get into *Straw's* head.

She was doing her best to distract him.

Rattigan extracted a cigar from his vest pocket.

"I don't usually indulge," he said, lighting the cigar and gesturing with it, so the smoke whipped around his head. He had to speak loudly to be heard over the thrumming of the wind, which was growing louder by the instant. "But I think in this instance—" All at once he broke off, frowning. "What *is* that?"

As soon as he spoke, Thomas realized that the thrumming wasn't the sound of the wind at all, but of something mechanical, like an engine.

Like a *plane* engine.

Outside the window, a small, two-seater propeller plane floated into view, pulling level with the dirigible. Lash Langtry was riding in the backseat, his face grimly determined. And in the front cockpit, goggles obscuring half his face, was a man hunched over the controls, his jaw working back and forth, back and forth, as though over an invisible piece of gum.

301 ☞

Or a toothpick.

"Is that . . . ?" Sam said.

"It's Kestrel!" Thomas cried. He couldn't believe it.

Rattigan sprang to his feet, his face contorted with rage. "Open the valves!" he snarled. "Release the gas!" He whipped around to Clyde Straw. "And you—take care of our new friend."

But at that instant, Clyde let out a sharp cry of pain and staggered forward, bringing a hand to his head. At the same time, Pippa slumped backward. Thomas didn't have time to see whether she was okay. Tucking his head to his knees, he hurtled forward like a bowling ball, colliding directly with Clyde's ankles. Clyde went flying off his feet, letting out a spray of bullets that dinged off the metal tank and ripped through the airship's thin shell. Thomas was on his feet again in an instant. Sam had lunged for Clyde's gun and, with a simple series of twists, tied the barrel into a useless pretzel shape. Before Clyde could stand again, Sam gave him a nice plunk on the top of the head, and Clyde once again slithered to the floor.

"Nicely done," Thomas panted. "But where's Rattigan?" Rattigan had vanished, leaving only his cigar smoking in a silver ashtray.

"Sam, Tom, look out!" Pippa cried.

They turned to see Mickey McClure sprinting at them, gun drawn. But before he could fire, Max sprang to her feet. Her hands bound in front of her, she snatched up Rattigan's still-smoldering cigar and fired it directly into Mickey McClure's left eye.

"Aaaaaagggh!" McClure let out a howl, collapsing to his knees and simultaneously releasing a volley of gun-fire. Several of the bullets tore through the window directly at Kestrel's plane. Before they could hit, Kestrel sent the plane into a nosedive, then spun skyward, drawing level again with the dirigible

Before McClure could get to his feet, Sam shoved him forward onto his stomach. He removed the rope coiled around Max's wrists and used it to lash McClure to Rattigan's chair.

"Thanks." Max's wrists were bright red and raw from the binding. She winced, massaging them gently, and then bent down to rummage through McClure's pockets. When she straightened up again, she had her knives, the same ones he'd confiscated earlier.

"Rattigan." Pippa staggered to her feet. She could barely stand. She looked exhausted. "We have to stop him from releasing the gas."

"You're too late."

They turned. In that instant, Rattigan looked like a

wild animal: ferocious and desperate, his jacket ripped and his shirt untucked, his ice-blue eyes wild and staring. He reached for the valve on the tank and gave it a quick twist. Thomas's stomach plummeted as he heard the telltale hiss of leaking gas.

"I win," Rattigan said simply. And before anyone could react, he'd thrown on a parachute and hurtled out of the hatch. The dirigible had drifted toward the East River now, and Thomas saw at once that Rattigan intended to land at the seaport, where a crowd of people was cheering him, clearly believing this was all a part of the show.

"No, you don't!" Max leaped, hurling her knives.

For a moment the knives seemed to be suspended, like small metal birds, flashing in the sun.

Then they passed cleanly through the lines holding Rattigan to his parachute. The crowd gasped as Rattigan screamed and began to plummet—straight toward the foaming water of the East River. A second later he disappeared beneath the sparkling water, even as the parachute fluttered, handkerchief-like, down after him.

Sam threw himself at the gas valve and gave it a desperate twist. The knob snapped off uselessly in his hand. He looked up, an expression of pure terror on

his face. The gas was still pouring out of the hatch, a dark gray chemical stream that quickly dissipated in the air. "Oh no . . ."

"And we're heading straight into midtown . . . ," Max said.

She was right. The dirigible, buffeted by the winds, was now veering away from the river and back toward the city.

"How can we stop it?" Pippa cried.

"There must be a way to steer this thing," Thomas said.

They scanned the instrument panel, searching for a way to turn the airship around. But quickly, Thomas saw that the spray of bullets from McClure's gun had blasted the controls into uselessness. The dirigible couldn't be turned. It was going to continue on over Manhattan, spewing deadly poison over everyone who lived there.

And there was no way to stop it.

"Thomas!" Sam shouted. "Look!"

Thomas turned and, through the window, saw Kestrel's plane hovering just below the hatch. Lash—his cowboy bandana tied over his mouth and nose as a makeshift gas mask—had edged out onto one of the wings.

"The mooring rope!" His voice, muffled by the cloth, was just barely audible. "Throw the mooring rope!"

Thomas saw immediately what Lash intended to do. He dove for one of the mooring ropes coiled at the back of the cabin and hurled it down to Lash. Lash snatched it from the air and, edging carefully back along the wing, fixed it to the airplane's tail.

Thomas held his breath as Kestrel leveled out the plane and turned. They were now directly over the east side of the city, so close Tom could make out individual faces turned up to the sky, mouths open, shocked and confused.

"Come on," he muttered. "Come on."

"It's working," Pippa breathed. "Kestrel's turning us around!"

She was right. Slowly, and then faster, the plane was turning. Kestrel was drawing them away from Manhattan, away from all of its people, out over the East River and down toward the open water of the Atlantic Ocean, as the gas continued to hiss and steam, emptying out into the bright blue sky.

27

"I *still* don't understand why Rattigan picked Barrensworth—or McClure, or whatever his real name is—to spy on us," Sam said, rooting around in an enormous box of mixed chocolates for the caramel. He popped one in his mouth and then made a face. Banana. "Remember how he misspelled his own business card?"

"I still don't understand *how* Mickey *was* spying. He only showed once or twice." Max's voice seemed to be coming from an extremely large arrangement of calla lilies—courtesy of Andrea von Stikk—which dominated the silk footstool in Mr. Dumfrey's office. A second later, her head appeared above it, so that she appeared to be growing directly out of its branches. "Aha," she said, brandishing a small paper-wrapped box. "I knew there was a box of toffee somewhere."

"It wasn't Barrensworth," Thomas said. He was perched on Mr. Dumfrey's file cabinet, one of the few surfaces that wasn't completely obscured beneath a layer of gifts, candies, chocolates, notes, flowers, and other thank-you gifts that still, a week after the almost-disaster, flooded the museum on a daily basis. A specialty cutlery designer had even sent Max a set of knives to replace the ones she had lost during their aerial battle with Rattigan.

"Don't tell me you still think Emily had something to do with it." Pippa, who was modeling a red silk kimono gifted to all of the children by a grateful downtown seamstress, had been angling to check out her reflection in one of the dusty windowpanes. Now she turned around to face Thomas, plugging her fists on her hips. "She wouldn't. She *couldn't*."

"Not her, either." Thomas jumped neatly off the file cabinet and dodged the stacks of unopened gifts. "Ladies and gentlemen, I give to you . . . Rattigan's spy!" With a flourish, he swung open the door.

But there was no one there except for Mr. Dumfrey, just barely keeping hold of the enormous cage that

309 ☞

still housed the Firebird. Sam peeked into the hall as Mr. Dumfrey staggered into the office, to see whether someone else was waiting there, but it was perfectly empty. He turned to Thomas, expecting him to look disappointed—maybe he had *intended* for Rattigan's spy to show, but had somehow lost him—but to his surprise saw that Thomas's eyes were practically glowing. And yet the hall was most definitely empty.

"I don't get it," he said. He hated feeling slower than the others and was relieved that, at least, Max and Pippa seemed as confused as he was.

"Is this a joke?" Pippa asked, shaking off the kimono and folding it neatly.

Max stood up, scowling. "Yeah," she said. "What happened to your big theory?"

Thomas opened his mouth to reply, but whatever he said was lost beneath the bird's screams of protest.

"Let go of me, you flabby-fingered frump!" the Firebird screeched. "Let me out, you dwindling dumpling!"

"Quiet," Mr. Dumfrey said, between huffing breaths, "or by tomorrow you'll be feathering my pillow." Elbowing aside another hideous arrangement of flowers—this one, Sam had noticed, addressed specifically to Mr. Dumfrey from *A Secret Admirer*—he set the cage down on his desk with a groan. "You wouldn't think," he said, turning back to the children and mopping his brow with a handkerchief, "that a bird could be so *heavy*."

"Maybe that's because it's not a bird at all." Thomas strutted around the desk, his chest so puffed up that for a second it looked as if *he* might sprout feathers. Then, suddenly, he leaned forward, banging both fists on the desk on either side of the bird's cage. Sam swallowed a yelp. *"It's a rat."*

There was a moment of silence. Thomas glared at the bird. The bird seemed to wither, ever so slightly, under the intensity of his gaze.

"Who you calling names?" the bird squawked, but Sam thought that the bird sounded nervous.

And at last, he understood: Rattigan's spy was, very literally, a bird brain.

Pippa began to giggle. Then she began to snort. Finally, she was laughing so hard, she had to bend over and wrap a hand around her stomach. "I don't believe it," she said finally. "I really don't believe it."

"Think about it," Thomas said. "It was perfect. Someone rung up claiming to have a rare species of bird for sale—Rattigan *knew* Dumfrey would bite."

Mr. Dumfrey looked pained. "My half brother likely

remembers the parakeet I had as a small boy," he said. "Euclid was my very best friend."

"The Firebird was trained to repeat anything it heard. Maybe at first Rattigan just planned to keep an eye on us, make sure he knew what we were up to. But after Farnum was arrested and we began poking around, the Firebird was necessary. Then Barrensworth—or McClure—popped up again, offering to help train the bird for the stage. But instead he's bleeding it for information, so he knew what *we'd* found out about Benny Mallett and Ernie Erskine." Thomas shook his head. "It was lucky that Farnum got pinned for Erskine's murder, actually. Otherwise we would never have known what Rattigan was planning."

Max made a face. "Some luck," she said.

"How did you piece it together?" Sam asked. The Firebird was no longer strutting in its cage or puffed up on its perch. Instead, the bird was huddled by its feeder, looking, to Sam's eyes, extremely nervous and unhappy. In less than ten minutes, it seemed to have shriveled to half its normal size. Sam wondered whether now, knowing its secret was out, it also knew there was nowhere for it to go, no one for it to return home to. After all, the Firebird had known Sir Barrensworth, or Mickey McClure, as its rightful owner.

He felt almost sorry for it.

"Something Rattigan said on the dirigible," Thomas said, and for a second the memory of what had happened high above the city passed over them like the shadow of the airship itself, plunging them all into cold. "He said he had spies parroting information back to him, and he kind of winked at McClure. I knew then."

Pippa sighed. "So Emily . . . ?"

"Is completely innocent," Mr. Dumfrey said firmly.

"I'm glad," Pippa said. "Kestrel will be so happy."

Now Thomas looked puzzled. "What's he got to do with anything?"

"Not *you*, too." Pippa threw up her hands. "How can you be so smart and so dumb at the same time?"

Thomas grinned at her. "Natural talent."

"But what are we going to do about the bird?" Sam asked.

Max was fiddling with one of her new knives and didn't glance up. "Maybe we can let Freckles have a turn with it," she said. "He's had the right idea all along."

The Firebird had, by now, begun to tremble. Sam definitely felt sorry for it.

"Oh, I don't think that will be necessary," he said. He reached out and gave the cage a tentative pat. "I imagine that now Rattigan and his friends are gone, we'll find that with the right training and just a little luck, the Firebird's attitude turns around."

"Go train yourself, you ball of blubber," the Firebird replied, but without any real conviction. It even settled onto its perch and preened in silence as Mr. Dumfrey began to sort the gifts that had arrived since that morning, without once criticizing the way Thomas smelled or calling Pippa an animal.

The Firebird even, Sam thought, looked ever so slightly relieved.

Later that afternoon, Pippa, Thomas, Sam, and Max gathered with the other residents outside the museum to await the triumphant return of General Farnum, who'd recently been cleared of all charges related to the murder of Ernie Erskine. It was perhaps the last perfect day of autumn. Tomorrow, the papers were predicting a dramatic temperature drop and rains that would strip the trees of their singed-gold leaves. But today was perfect: brilliant sunny, sharp and cool, the air just edged with the faint smell of wood smoke.

"What do you think?" Gil Kestrel wobbled a little on the ladder as he gave one end of the museum's newest banner a tug. "Look about right?"

Lash shoved his cowboy hat farther back on his head,

squinting against the sun. "I don't know," he said. "I reckon it's slanted a mite too far to the right."

Kestrel made several adjustments. "How about now?"

Lash gave a noise of appreciation. "Straight as a preacher's sermon."

"It's perfect," Emily agreed, taking Kestrel's hand and giving it a squeeze as he came down the ladder. "General Farnum will love it."

Thomas and Pippa had spent the morning painting a large banner announcing his return, which Mr. Dumfrey proudly proclaimed would hang above the entrance of the museum at least until Christmastime.

Welcome Home, General Farnum*! it read in bold red letters, with a special star next to Farnum's name. Mr. Dumfrey had insisted they add in a secondary bit: *Cleared of all charges related to the notorious and fantastic murder of Ernie Erskine, victim of the murderous Nicholas Rattigan and his plot to take down Manhattan!* This had resulted in a banner rather larger than usual, especially after a third addition became necessary when General Farnum, through Rosie Bickers, had communicated that during his time in prison he'd come up with an idea for a new act.

"Listen to this." Thomas had for days been obsessed

with reading all the newspaper coverage about their role in saving the city from certain disaster. Now he had at least several different editions, including *The Journal-American*, *The Daily Screamer*, and *The New York Herald-Examiner*, spread out on the stoop. He snatched up *The Screamer*:

"'There is no doubt that the police department's grossly incompetent search for Rattigan, and failure to tie Rattigan's reappearance to the string of bank robberies that paralyzed the city, nearly resulted in a catastrophe of unknown proportions,'" he read. "'The police'—*blah blah blah*, hang on, we can skip how Rattigan was able to get an airship all to himself. Wait, here's the good part." He cleared his throat. "'"If it weren't for the *extrapotential* children of Mr. Dumfrey's Dime Museum, who knows what would have happened?" said Miss Andrea von Stikk, of the recently renamed Von Stikk Home for Extrapotential Children. "It's obvious that Mr. Dumfrey's educational methods should be commended for their untraditional approach—an approach, I might add, I've long admired. As for the *police*—"'" Thomas broke off, grinning. "From there it goes on for four columns."

"Von Stikk's singing a different tune nowadays, isn't she?" Max said.

"Did somebody say my name?" came Andrea von Stikk's sweet, trilling voice. Pippa turned and saw her sailing down the street, dressed in one of her typically ornate outfits, complete with bows and ruffles and lace, so that she looked more like a parade float than a person. Behind her came Chubby, his hands in his pockets, still wearing a badly fitting school uniform, smiling sheepishly.

"There you are, my darlings." Von Stikk squeezed Pippa into a hug so tight, Pippa felt as if she might suffocate in the older woman's layers of clothing. "And *you*." She repeated the performance with Thomas and Sam and nearly went for Max but thought better of it, especially when Max bared her teeth and growled. She obviously hadn't forgotten that Max had once jabbed a fork into her left hand. "And—er—Mackenzie. And *you*." She turned to Mr. Dumfrey and seized his hand. "Our hero! Our savior! Our *saint*."

"A servant, madame," Mr. Dumfrey said gallantly, bending forward to kiss Von Stikk's hand, as if all of the tension between them had never existed. "As always and ever at your service."

"Oh, Mr. Dumfrey." Miss von Stikk whipped a paper fan from the folds of her enormous dress and vigorously fanned herself with it. "You are too, too much."

"And you, my dear, are never enough!"

Max pretended to gag. Pippa had to turn away, clapping her mouth to stifle the laugh that was rising like soda bubbles in her chest, threatening to burst. She couldn't ever remember a time when she'd been quite so happy and when the museum had felt so deeply and totally at peace.

She didn't know what, exactly, had happened between Gil Kestrel and Lash—only that when Mr. Dumfrey realized that the children were missing from the museum, he had immediately guessed that they were heading to stop Rattigan at all costs and had set Gil and Lash in immediate pursuit. Somewhere along the way—or perhaps even midair in Manhattan—Gil and Lash had come to an understanding about what had happened in the past. All Kestrel would say about it now was that Lash was a good man, a fine friend. And Lash, usually so talkative, would say only that Kestrel was a mighty tall hog at the trough—an expression Pippa didn't entirely understand but knew to be a compliment.

But it was more than that. Rattigan was well and truly gone. Even now, the police were combing the river for his remains. The whole museum had, for the past three days, been in a near-constant state of celebration. Max had graciously congratulated Pippa on what she had done in the dirigible and even suggested that mind manipulation become a new part of Pippa's performance—although Pippa had quickly declined, since the effort had left her exhausted and weak for two days.

Gil Kestrel and Emily had quietly announced their engagement, and Lash had expressed his excitement by tossing the sour-faced Miss Fitch in the air and planting a kiss directly on her lips. Although this had of course made the twins unhappy, even they couldn't be sore for long, especially now that Miss Fitch, shockingly, had begun appearing in the morning with her hair loosened in long waves, seemingly too distracted to notice or care if the performers were late to their curtain calls.

Good luck, it appeared, was contagious. Smalls had just received a letter that his poem "How Sweetly Doth the Pigeons Coo" had been accepted into the *Poets of Our Period*. (Smalls was so thrilled, he didn't even care that the magazine's acronym was POOP.)

"What's the matter, Chubby?" Sam nudged Chubby with an elbow, and Chubby took a quick step sideways to avoid being knocked over. "I thought you were done with school."

"Oh, er, yeah." Chubby coughed and rubbed the back of his neck with a hand, feigning an air of casualness. "Turns out Von Stikk's not so bad. I think I might hang out a little longer. I been working on my vocabulary. And reading's not so bad, once you get the gist of it. Plus the free grub and all," he added quickly. Red splotches had appeared in both of his cheeks.

"Good for you," Pippa said. "That's great."

"Thanks, Pippa," he said, smiling at her. It was the first time he'd ever called her Pippa, not Pip or Philippa, and it occurred to her then that he was not so very, not so *absolutely*, silly-looking after all. In fact, the way he blushed was actually kind of . . . cute. As if tomatoes had been crushed beneath his skin. And his nose was sort of fantastic. . . .

All down Forty-Third Street, she recognized neighbors and friends, all of them lingering outside, hoping to catch a glimpse of the four children who'd saved New York City, or to cheer on General Farnum when he made his triumphant return home. There was Henry from the St. Edna Hotel, for once awake on the job; Barney Bamberg, standing outside his delicatessen; Miss Groenovelt, with one of her many cats encircling her ankles; Sol from the sweet shop on the corner; and there was Gus, from the barber shop below Eli

Sadowski's apartment, still holding a bottle of shaving cream. Even Mr. Sadowski himself could be seen at his window—which was amazing, considering that his window was usually entirely concealed behind stacks of things—and Pippa gave him a little wave before turning her eyes back to the street.

And there, just rounding the corner of Forty-Third Street . . .

"Look!" she cried. "It's Rosie! And General Farnum!"

Rosie Bickers and General Farnum didn't make it halfway down the street before they were absolutely swarmed. Goldini was pumping Farnum's hand and Smalls was reciting bits of *The Iliad* and Andrea von Stikk and Rosie were embracing and in the chaos Mr. Dumfrey kissed Rosie right on the mouth not once but *twice*. They moved back toward the museum as a babbling, many-headed creature, everyone talking at once, and Pippa was carried along on a wave of sound and a crush of her friends all around her.

". . . can't believe it . . ."

"Home at last!"

"Justice prevails . . ."

"Well." Kestrel gestured to the banner hanging proudly above the museum doors. "What do you think?"

General Farnum was momentarily overcome with

emotion. His lips trembled. He seemed to have trouble finding the right words. His mustache vibrated so hard that Pippa thought it might fly right off his face.

"What do I think?" General Farnum's voice cracked, and he coughed to clear his throat. "I think I haven't seen anything so beautiful since the Battle of San Juan Hill. I think that I'm *home*."

"The bit about your new act got kind of squished," Thomas said, eyeing the lettering critically. "Sorry about that."

At the very bottom of the banner was a hasty add-on: *Come See World-Famous Farnum and His Cleverly Cavorting Cockroaches!*

General Farnum's eyes were bright. "It's perfect, sonny."

Then the babble of conversation started up again. Everyone wanted to hear about Farnum's time in jail, and all the performers had news to share of their own. Farnum and Rosie were quickly swept up as the crowd flowed into the museum.

Pippa hung back for a bit, reluctant to leave the sunshine. She had the strangest sensation then, that she was watching a scene that had happened years ago—that all of this, the sunshine and the noise of traffic and happy laughter, was already a memory, long-cherished and often relived. Her heart ached with a feeling so strong she couldn't exactly name it: a sense of time stilled and also rushing by too quickly. It was like Mr. Dumfrey had said. There were, perhaps, other Rattigans in the world, other evils she would someday have to face. They were growing up, and couldn't stay at the museum forever.

But for now, Sam and Max were walking side by side, perfectly in sync. Mr. Dumfrey was directing everyone into the Odditorium for chilled sodas and free sweets. And Thomas stopped with one hand on the door, glancing back to where Pippa still stood, watching it all with a sense of love and rightness and belonging.

"You coming?" Thomas said. Pippa nodded and jogged up the stairs to pass before him into the museum.

It was like General Farnum had said. For now, they were home.